Chasing Carolina Jessamine

Chasing Carolina Jessamine

The Southern Isles

Laurie Beach

Chasing Carolina Jessamine
Copyright© 2025 Laurie Beach
Tule Publishing First Printing, August 2025

The Tule Publishing, Inc.

ALL RIGHTS RESERVED

First Publication by Tule Publishing 2025

Cover design is by Erin Dameron-Hill

No part of this book may be used or reproduced in any manner whatsoever without written permission except in the case of brief quotations embodied in critical articles and reviews.

This is a work of fiction. Names, characters, places, and incidents are products of the author's imagination or are used fictitiously. Any resemblance to actual events, locales, organizations, or persons, living or dead, is entirely coincidental.

AI was not used to create any part of this book and no part of this book may be used for generative training.

ISBN: 978-1-967678-66-2

Chapter One

CAROLINA JESSAMINE BOONE was created to be beautiful. Her mother chose a man for his looks, made a baby, and never told anyone who he was. "A woman's prerogative," she claimed. "What folks don't know won't hurt 'em." Coming from a mother like that, it was a small miracle that Jessa hadn't left a trail of broken hearts in her wake. She could've dated hundreds of men, hidden their existence, and lied to get the things she wanted. Instead, she lived her life simply. She was independent, resourceful, and certainly didn't need a man to swoop in and complicate things.

A father, though. A father would be nice.

On that crisp South Carolina fall day, when the air shifted and the maple leaves began letting go, when the crowds thinned and the employees of the Saltwater Winery enjoyed the lull that came before the harvest, Jessa was caught off guard by a tall man in a fancy suit holding a small leather notebook. He was the first customer of the day, and he seemed more interested in the wines than the blonde female before him. It was odd that he didn't immediately flirt with her. A man of his caliber—gold watch and expensive haircut—tended to give her orders and treat her like his personal servant. He had small eyes, but his straight white teeth and strong chin worked to make him almost classically handsome. Men like him expected a certain amount of attention from people in the service industry, and it was Jessa's job to make sure the customers were happy.

"Do you prefer red or a white?" she asked, placing a large-bellied wineglass in front of him.

"Anything but a blend," he said, barely looking at her. "I like to know which grape I'm drinking and where it was grown."

"Absolutely." She pulled the cork from a single-vineyard Ison Muscadine wine and poured half an ounce more than she normally would for a tasting. His indifference bothered her. "The grapes were grown here on the property."

He put up a hand to stop her from talking. "Spare me the lecture. I know about the grapes." He opened his notebook, a sommelier's journal, and, after swirling and sipping, he set about writing down his opinions. She couldn't help but steal glances. It was no glowing review. As a matter of fact, he used words like *acidic*, *cork taint*, and *mold*.

There were times when she loved her job, and times when she wanted nothing more than to get back to her jungly little bungalow and rummaged antiques. There was something about the man that made her alternately want to curl up in her hand-sewn quilt for a nap or lean in and get to know him. The combination of his sharp jawline and cold arrogance made him mysterious. Maybe even a little dangerous. Since running home for a nap wasn't an option, she opted to get to know him. There was nothing like a challenge on a Thursday morning.

"Do you live nearby?" she asked sweetly.

He paused like it was a bother to answer. "Kiawah."

"It's so pretty there," she said, reaching her hand across the counter. "I'm Jessa Boone."

"Nelson Tucker." The handshake was brief.

He was much more interested in swirling the burgundy liquid in his glass. He smelled it, making sure to put his nose on the far side of the glass instead of up against the rim.

"I don't normally work the tasting room," Jessa said. "I manage this place. One of our employees called in sick. Is there anything in particular you'd like to see?"

His eyes met hers like he was finally seeing her for the first time. "I've seen it all before," he said, leaving her wondering why he bothered coming out to the winery at all. If he'd seen it all, he could just buy the wine at the store. Plus, it was odd that he was alone. Most people came with friends or on a date. He didn't seem to mind awkward silences either and appeared fine with pretending like Jessa wasn't there. But Jessa was the anxiety girl who kept conversations going. If she sensed the slightest hesitation, she felt compelled to start talking. It was one of the many downsides to being a people pleaser. She'd become the Supergirl of conversational lulls, regularly saving folks from the horror of awkward silences.

With a squeak and a slam, the door to the gift shop and tasting room flew open. "Carolina Jessamine! I need help!" It was Dottie Boone in all her glory—blue knit cap and mom jeans.

Jessa was glad to see her. "What's wrong, Mama?"

"I've got to get the truck set up for lunch, and some jackass parked in my spot. There is an entire parking lot wide open, and this yay-hoo takes the one space that is clearly marked as RESERVED."

Nelson slurped loudly, sucking in air along with the liquid to best open up the wine. He ignored the commotion, moving the wine around in his mouth with a look of deep concentration.

Dottie practically shook with annoyance. "Sir," she demanded, "is that your black Range Rover parked out front?"

It was a strange thing to watch. He acted like a movie star, deigning to speak with an annoying fan. Yet somehow, this aloof demeanor served to make him more intriguing. This was a new feeling for Jessa, this fascination.

"It was an open spot," he said simply.

"It's a *reserved* spot," Dottie corrected. "Can you read? There's a sign."

His eyes crinkled at the corners, but he didn't smile. "You don't look like the police to me."

Jessa held her breath and counted down, three ... two ... one.

"Do you have a death wish?" Dottie spat, her entire face pinched like a raisin. "I have half a mind to wallop you clear into the marsh!" She dropped her voice as low as a growl. "You better get your fancy high-falutin' vehicle out of my way before I set the sheriff and every gun-toting person on this island after you."

On this occasion, Jessa was fully on her mother's side. "If you're smart," Jessa said carefully, "you'll do what she says."

The man took a lazy swig of the dregs of his wine before softly placing the glass back on the counter. "Relax," he said evenly. "I will move my car." He smirked when he added, "No need to get yourself in a tizzy."

"I am not in a tizzy," Dottie fumed. "I am pissed off."

"You know," he said, turning on his chair to face her. "It usually helps to ask nicely."

If Dottie was a firework, she'd have shot screeching hot into the sky. Yet, despite her red face and clenched fists, she managed to eke out, "Please."

"My pleasure," he said with a smile. "And when I buy this place, I'll make that spot mine." There was not an ounce of meanness in his voice, which made it even more threatening. "How does that sound?"

Dottie and Jessa said nothing as they watched him saunter toward the door.

He tossed the word *excellent* at them like a generous tip before shutting the door behind him.

"Did that just happen?" Jessa said. "He didn't even pay

for his tasting."

"If Duke sells this place to that man, so help me, I will blow every grape on this property into oblivion," Dottie promised. "You hear me? I will douse this building and every last vine with gasoline and curse that man's name while it burns."

Jessa knew full well that Dottie would never do such a thing, but the fact remained—their family was tied to the Saltwater Winery. Dottie needed their customers for her food truck, and Jessa relied on it for her livelihood. They both had bills to pay and food to buy. But not just that. They'd lived on Goose Island their entire lives. They didn't say it, but the shared fear was palpable. If that man bought the winery, their lives might change forever.

"Mama, do you see anything?"

Dottie's ability to divine things about people was somewhere between psychic and fiction. But the fact that she was usually around 75 percent right made everyone who knew her still ask for advice.

"I'm too mad to see clearly right now. But I do sense him coming back. That horrible, horrible man. He doesn't care. He genuinely doesn't care about anyone but himself."

Aside from a few customers and her best friend, Brooke, Jessa had never really been exposed to wealth. She could count on one hand how many times she'd been to a fancy restaurant, and the number of designer anything in her closet was exactly zero. So, it was hard to judge a man like him.

What would it feel like to have the power to take someone's job and ruin a business? If he bought the winery, he could end the cooperative relationship the Saltwater Winery had with the Dogwood Resort across the bay, and that would hurt both Brooke and her business partner and boyfriend, Nate, too. Heck, he could even turn sleepy little Goose Island into something completely different. Buying the winery meant buying the land. He could build whatever he wanted.

The man had to be stopped, and she could think of only one way to get at him. Maybe God and Dottie Boone had made her beautiful for such a time as this.

Chapter Two

Since her teenage years, Jessa's mantra had been *If you're going to make a mistake, err on the side of kindness.* She must've come up with it during a literature class in high school, because it sounded Shakespearean, but it was all hers, and she lived by it. If she offered an older person her seat on the bus and they took offense, at least she'd offered out of kindness. If she gave up her own desires in order to support her best friend's, at least her sacrifice was made out of love. Some days it felt like her sole purpose on Earth was to please others and make their lives better. There were times she truly believed that she didn't matter at all. But she was going to have to set all of that aside if she pursued Nelson Tucker. She was going to have to pretend like she was something she wasn't. She was going to have to lie.

At closing time, the events of the morning still had her off-kilter. All day, she'd had Nelson Tucker on her mind, which meant that all day she'd felt both horrified and warmly, excitedly intrigued. The silkie chickens clucked and scratched as she corralled them back into their swamp-shack coop after locking up the tasting room. Then she tucked in the goats, Skip and June, and left food for the feral cats in the flower garden named after the owner's dead wife—Amelia's Patch of Happiness. She closed the wooden white gate before heading home for the day. There was still so much to do at her house that going home felt overwhelming. The roof had been fixed, the plumbing and electrical were done, and the drywall had gone in. The rest of it was supposed to be fun. And it was, except for the wallpaper. She'd installed faucets and cabinets and flooring by herself, but it was a horrible idea to put up wallpaper alone. Just the thought of the sticky glue and ruined sheets of thick floral paper lying on her bedroom floor made her panicky. It was only a little after five o'clock, and even though the days were getting shorter, she still had time to shirk her housework and take the boat over to the Dogwood Resort. She was dying to tell Brooke about Nelson Tucker.

The trip across the water only took ten minutes. She tied her metal jon boat next to the big blue and white ferry that shuttled guests back and forth from the resort to the winery. The Dogwood's new wooden pier was sturdy and long enough to tie up most of the recreational boats that had started adding the resort to their days of fun on the Atlantic. Jessa walked toward the swimming hole wondering how Brooke was dealing with all of the people who kept discovering the area. As she approached the main building, guests were paddling around the floating dock and a young man played the guitar, his legs dangling from a wide, flat piece of granite that jutted out over the water. They called it the jumping rock. Most of the Adirondack chairs were occupied, as were the picnic tables, but the place still managed to look calm and welcoming. Maybe it was the Disneyland-perfect flowers spilling out of tall black pots near the buildings or the pansies spread evenly in the ground around the edge of the woods. Boxwood hedges stood guard behind yellow and purple mums while verbena crawled across the freshly turned earth at the side of the walkways. Brooke must have just made the switch from summer flowers to fall. Jessa took a deep breath. The smell of the sea and the brisk salt spray on the way over had already helped to center her. Now the beauty before her made her worries feel small and silly. How could there be bad people when the earth was such a beautiful gift?

Brooke waved from the top of the hill by the clubhouse, and Jessa jogged up to meet her.

"Tell your mother to return my calls," Brooke said as Jessa hugged her tightly. "I need some menu advice."

"You know Mama. She'll call you when she's ready."

Brooke exhaled in a way that showed she was stressed about more than just the menu, then smiled. "Do you want to join me and Nate for supper? Nana is doing her famous crowd work tonight. I think the get-to-know-you game is Two Truths and a Lie."

"Anything to keep from going home." Jessa laughed.

Once inside, Jessa scanned the room for Brooke's boyfriend, Nate, to see where they'd be sitting. Her eyes landed on a dark-haired figure sitting alone in the corner—the superior set of his mouth was too familiar. The shock made her wince, and unwanted tingles erupted from the top of her head all the way down to her toes. What was Nelson Tucker doing there? Quickly, she averted her eyes and focused on following Brooke to a large circular table in the middle of the room. Nate sat with a group of guests like it was the captain's dinner and he was the head of the ship. Jessa had never seen him look so happy. He was completely in his element, a natural smile on his face that grew larger when he spotted his girlfriend making her way toward him.

Brooke sat next to him with a little hello kiss, and Jessa took the seat next to her. She passed the bread basket to the seven other guests at the table and made animated small talk, but it was difficult to keep her eyes from straying to Nelson. He was a magnet, and she was suddenly made of iron, cobalt, nickel, and steel.

Grace "Nana" Sharon Beauregard Warter had her pink-outlined lips pressed up against the screen of the microphone as she welcomed guests and introduced herself. She was dressed more for a luau than dinner at a nice South Carolina resort. Above the pocket of her bright floral button-down she wore what had become a part of her daily outfit—her name tag. GRACE, MISS SOUTH CAROLINA 1959. Which was a lie.

"Welcome one and all to the Dogwood Resort," she said, "where historic Southern beauty combines with luxury and adventure. This is the only place where you can truly have it all."

Nana's lilt faded into the background as Jessa watched Gates Lancaster stride into the room and walk directly to the corner where Nelson sat.

She elbowed Brooke. "What is Gates doing here?"

"He's been bringing his clients out here. It's really sweet of him to drum up business for us with the folks who can afford it. He's been here a lot lately."

So, Gates was the reason why Nelson Tucker had gone to the winery that morning. "It's weird that Gates is here, isn't it?" Jessa whispered. "Does it bother Nate that your ex-boyfriend is coming around?"

Brooke asked Nate in a loud whisper, "Does it bother you that Gates is here?"

Nate smiled and shook his head. "Not at all."

Brooke repeated to Jessa, "Not at all."

A man on the other side of the room stood at Nana's behest to give his two truths and a lie. "I live in Paris. I'm allergic to mango. I met my wife in the second grade." By show of hands, the room overwhelmingly voted in favor of Paris as the lie. They were wrong. As it turned out, the man lived in Paris, Texas, and was smugly pleased with himself for being so clever. He had no allergies he was aware of, so the mango answer was the lie. Everybody clapped.

Nana chose Nelson as her next victim. Jessa held her breath, fully expecting him to be rude and refuse to play the game. She was surprised when he scooted out his chair and stood straight and tall with a smile—yes, a *smile*. "I have a parrot who speaks three languages. I am a multimillionaire. I am the youngest of eight siblings."

Most people thought the multimillionaire answer was the lie. They were wrong. Nelson did not own a parrot.

Gates looked proud. Proud that he'd brought a multimillionaire to the Dogwood—like it elevated him and made him look like a really good financial advisor. If a guy with millions trusted Gates with his money, shouldn't everyone else? It was a smart tactic, bringing the man to a resort where wealthy families vacationed. Maybe Gates would snag more clients. But as Jessa sat with the thought, goosebumps spread across her skin and made her shiver. Gates might have just brought a shark into their waters. What if Nelson Tucker was about to shake up everything? She'd known Gates since childhood; she'd spent every summer with him back when the Dogwood was a summer camp. How could he be so thoughtless and callous?

She renewed her plan to stop Nelson no matter what it took.

"That man, Nelson," she whispered to Brooke. "He said he wanted to buy the winery."

"What?" Brooke gasped. "Are you kidding? Duke wouldn't sell it, would he?"

"I didn't think so, but Duke's in his eighties. He's going to have to do something eventually."

Jessa could tell that Brooke's head was spinning. She might have a rich daddy she could count on, but she'd been running the business all on her own. "What if that guy doesn't want a relationship with us? I rely on the winery to share the cost of the ferry. Plus, it's one of my main marketing points—a winery accessible across the water. I need it, Jess. I need this relationship."

"I know. I need to keep my job too." Unlike her best friend, Jessa didn't have a rich daddy to rely on.

Despite a lifetime of prayers and hounding Dottie to tell her who her biological father was, she still had no name, no photo, and no daddy at all. They both stared at Nelson Tucker while he fielded questions from the people at his table like he was the focus of a press conference.

"Don't worry," Jessa said with renewed resolve. "I have a plan."

Chapter Three

JESSA GOT HOME just before dark. Her long blonde hair was knotted from the boat ride back to the winery, and her stomach was worse. Her questions for Gates and her need to be someone she wasn't in order to woo Nelson Tucker had her feeling as out of sorts as a turtle at an alligator farm—like an attack was imminent. Something terrible was about to happen.

She opened her front door, which she never locked, and purposefully didn't think about the wallpaper mess in her bedroom. She could sleep in the guest room or outside on the screened-in porch where she still had the old sofa from when renovations first began. The weather was finally cooling off enough to allow for an open-air stay.

It was habit to go to the kitchen first. She was full from dinner, but a glass of water might be nice. Instead, she bypassed the sink and went to the pantry where she stood staring like a zombie at a box of Hostess Ding Dongs. Her dessert stomach was her enemy. She sighed. She didn't need sugar, she just needed to feel regulated again. Back to the glass of water.

Stepping out of the pantry, she almost tripped over a box on her floor. How had she missed it? It was right next to the old metal milk door she'd been debating nailing closed. She couldn't remember if she'd latched the small door from the inside, so she assumed she hadn't. Anyone could easily push something into her pantry from outside of her house. It had been created that way for delivery of glass milk bottles when the house was built in 1924.

The box was long and rectangular. Without picking it up, she carefully pulled off the lid. Inside was a bouquet of flowers—white anemone, eucalyptus, peach-colored garden roses, and ranunculus, all highlighted by a yellow Carolina Jessamine vine—the state flower of South Carolina, her namesake. They were all beautifully arranged, like a bridal bouquet. She took them into the kitchen and stared at them on her counter. Who gave them to her, and where did they find such beautiful flowers? They were delicate and simple without being flashy or ostentatious—exactly how she tried to live her life. She searched through her up-high cupboard for a vase as she mentally listed everyone who knew where she lived. Even if a person knew her address, it was hard to find her house on the island. She hadn't yet cleared the front of her jungly two acres, and both her mailbox and the street sign had been almost completely overtaken by creeping vines and kudzu.

She found an old cut crystal vase and filled it with water, then took her scissors from the drawer to trim the stems. The only person she could think of who might do something so thoughtful was her uncle Fred. He ran the local gas station—which was really more like a Southern cafe and grocery store inside a building whose outside concrete walls had been boasting about GAS OIL and LUNCH since 1940. Fred used to be a corporate lawyer before he opted to move into a grounded houseboat behind the most dilapidated-looking store on Goose Island. He would certainly know where to get high-quality flowers, and he was probably the only person in her family who could afford them. It had to be Uncle Fred.

On her way to work in the morning, she would stop by his store and thank him in person. Maybe he'd somehow sensed that she'd had a hard day and needed a pick-me-up. Or maybe her mother had told him about their run-in with Nelson Tucker.

FRED'S LAUGH ALWAYS had a little *ho-ho-ho* in it, like his role as Santa every Christmas had become a permanent part of him. She'd finally waited her way to the front of the line where he stood behind a counter filling breakfast orders. She noticed there were no fresh flowers in the store, so maybe she was wrong to suspect him.

"It wasn't me, sweetheart," he said, "but I wish it had been."

Jessa was now officially stumped. She got the largest to-go cup of coffee Fred offered and treated herself to a sausage biscuit, which she ate in the car on the way to work. Unless her little sister, Tootie, was feeling exceptionally benevolent, there was no one else those flowers could have come from. Tootie would be more likely to leave a shark tooth she'd found or an alligator she'd made from felt, maybe even a cap like the blue one she knitted for Dottie years ago. But never flowers. Not unless she grew them herself.

It had been a bad choice to eat the biscuit in the car. Now Jessa had to add vacuuming the front seat to her long list of chores. Not to mention, sleeping on the sofa had left her with a stiff neck. Rather than taking a shower that morning, she'd opted for twenty more minutes of uncomfortable rest and sprayed dry shampoo onto her roots. Her dark gray sweater matched the shadows under her eyes, which also matched the overcast sky. It was going to be a long day.

The familiar sound of her tires on the gravel parking lot usually revved her up to get to work. She had a job to do, and she loved it. But when she realized that the big black car she'd just parked beside did not belong to one of the harvest managers, like she initially thought, but looked exactly like the Range Rover from the food truck's reserved spot yesterday, she nearly spilled her coffee. There was no way Nelson Tucker was back at the winery. No way that he'd show up again. She thought she was going to have to seek him out.

Yet there he was, standing outside the locked front door, waiting for her to open it. And next to him was Gates. If her sigh was made of words, they would be *Dear Lord, help me.*

"Good morning," she said as they stepped out of the way so she could put the key in the lock of the winery's tin-roofed main building. "Hi, Gates."

"Hey, Jess."

She hoped they couldn't see her hand shake. "The tasting room doesn't open for another hour. Is there something I can help y'all with?" If Gates said they were there to talk to Duke about buying the winery, she would keep them locked out.

"We were hoping you, or whoever is available, might be able to give us a little tour," Gates said.

Gates's friendly expression made her blood boil. He knew full well that none of the other forward-facing employees, the ones who dealt with customers, would be here this early. He had to have orchestrated it this way to rope her in. She pasted a smile on her face as she silently reminded herself it was good that he'd brought Nelson there. "Well," she began, "I have to turn on the lights and open the doors, get the chickens and the goats, and about ten other things. There's a lot to set up in the mornings."

"We'll come with you," Nelson said. It was a clear statement, not a question.

Jessa had been told her whole life that she'd been dipped in sugar on the day she was born. She was known for being the sweetest, most accommodating person. But even she had to get past the annoyance of getting help when she didn't need or want it. She enjoyed doing her morning routine alone. But the fact was, she needed the time with Nelson if she was going to get started on her plan. "Thank you. Many hands make light work, right?"

"When's harvest?" Nelson asked as she opened the front door and stepped aside to allow them in.

"Soon. I've already bought a huge assortment of snacks and refilled the coffee pods." She led them through the gift shop and tasting room into the back offices. "I'm just glad I don't have to get up at three A.M. like Allie and Joey, our winemakers. Not to mention the rest of the crew. It gets crazy around here." She put her purse down on her desk, wishing she didn't have two old cups of coffee next to her keyboard and a ratty pink sweater draped over her chair. The only thing in the room that was pretty was her sister's painting of a pathway through the dunes.

Nelson looked around her space like he was judging every speck of dust. "Where'd you go to college?"

She didn't want to say the words, especially in front of Gates. She was the only one from their old Camp Dogwood friend group who didn't go to college. Not that anyone expected her to. Everyone knew that she was the pretty one and her sister, Tootie, was the smart one.

It must've taken her too long to answer, because he figured it out. "So, you took this job straight out of high school."

She nodded, glancing at him to see if he had a smug or disappointed look on his face. She couldn't tell. He looked the same amount of arrogant as always. Gates, however, had his shoulders slumped forward like he felt out of place—or guilty for bringing Nelson Tucker and his inappropriately probing questions into her office. The guilt would be fitting.

"It's a good job, and I need it." She felt a little like she was begging, but if he was going to buy the winery, it was important for him to know that she didn't have many other options when it came to employment—especially since she wanted to stay on the island. "Let's start outside." Anything to get them out of her office. Maybe the distraction of some chickens, cats, and goats would take the attention off of her.

"Jessa's really good at her job," Gates said, like he was standing up for the defenseless.

Jessa wanted to kick him. A guy like Nelson would assume that she wasn't capable from a comment like that, and she needed to appear not only competent, but fully put together and a great choice as a partner.

She led them across the grassy lawn to the chicken coop. "I believe you get what you give," she said. "If you want kindness, give kindness. If you want to be good at your job, then work hard. Simple."

"Mmmm." Nelson seemed to consider her, and for a moment, she thought she'd done something right. Then he said, "Real money doesn't come without making demands and taking risks."

Gates nodded, and Jessa was sad to see it. She and Gates had been good friends once, and when he'd dated Brooke for seven years, she believed he would make a very good husband one day. She wasn't sure anymore. Comparing him side by side to Nelson was a study in similarities with one glaring difference. They were both tall, both exceptionally good-looking, and of similar age, but Gates was still working his way up the corporate ladder while Nelson had already made a fortune. Gates had to be careful because Nelson had the freedom of whim. Nelson had room to be impulsive, and cushion enough to make mistakes.

"I'm sure it takes risk and a degree of ruthlessness to make money," Jessa said sweetly. "But I wasn't referring to that." No, she was talking about life.

She was talking about how a person treated others, what kind of positive impact they had on the world—and if not the world, then each individual they came in contact with. She might be considered *too nice* or *such a sweetheart*, but the truth was, her sweetness protected her. It was a shield against people with a chip on their shoulder or those who instantly disliked her because she was pretty. She proved them wrong. She won them over. The problem was, her niceness didn't seem to be having any effect on Nelson. He still acted like he barely noticed she was there.

Chapter Four

J ESSA WAS SURPRISED that Nelson didn't run for his life when she let the mass of chickens free from their shack. She expected him to be alarmed or disgusted, but he smiled and laughed at the feathers flying as the birds took off with scratches and clucks toward the food scraps she'd just dumped in a pile. He didn't seem the slightest bit worried about his custom suit or fancy brown leather shoes. Several chickens even ran right over his toes, and he didn't kick at them or even try to move away.

Gates was off feeding Skip and June. He'd been around goats enough in his life to know exactly what to do—replenish the alfalfa hay, put out a bowl of sunflower and grain mixture, and make sure they had baking soda in case they ate too much hay and got indigestion. Gassy goats were not what customers found fun and endearing.

When Jessa and Nelson finished with the chickens, they found Gates busy brushing June with a curry comb. The goat stood perfectly still, her head raised toward the heavens like Gates was the answer to her most fervent prayers. Skip stood on top of an old wine barrel watching the whole thing like he was the boss and would allow it—for the moment.

"Where'd you grow up?" Nelson asked Jessa out of the blue. It was the first time he'd shown any real interest in her.

"Down the road," she said. "I've been on Goose Island my whole life."

"Do you like to travel?" he asked.

She shrugged. "I've always wanted to. Haven't done it much. I do like Nashville, though. I've been there."

"Have you ever been on an airplane?"

What was this sudden interest in her travels? She wanted to say *yes*. Surely, he was looking for someone who was an experienced traveler. "No."

He chuckled. "So, you've never experienced the joy of first class."

"Wouldn't know the difference."

"Most people would say Paris is the place to go, or Rome," he went on. "I do like the food and the culture, of course. But I'm more of an adventurer, you know?"

No, she didn't know. And furthermore, she felt like the folks who went to Paris or Rome had to be adventurers too. Those places were far away, with different languages and customs. "What kind of adventures do you like?"

Gates stopped brushing June and joined them, dusting off his hands on his pants. "He likes bungee jumping and skydiving."

"New Zealand is probably my favorite," Nelson agreed. "Jet boat rides, helicopters, all kinds of things. I guess you can say I'm a little bit of an adrenaline junkie."

"Cool," Jessa said. She had nothing to compare it with. The closest she'd come to a physical adventure was fishing.

"Have you ever eaten haggis? I had that in Scotland. And ant's egg soup in Thailand."

"Like, literal ant eggs?" Was that even a thing?

"Oh yeah," he said, clearly proud of himself.

"You're braver than I am."

He put a hand on her shoulder. *A hand on her shoulder.* What was happening? Why was he suddenly interested in talking to and *touching* her? She smiled sweetly at him, acting like it wasn't a surprise at all. Like multimillionaires touched her all the time.

Gates openly watched the two of them. "Have you ever been to an oyster roast?"

Jessa wondered where he was going with that question.

"Can't say that I have," Nelson said. "I've only been on Kiawah a few months now."

"We should put one on," Gates said to Jessa. "We can invite Brooke and Nate and anyone else you want."

Things had now definitely flipped to Bizzaro World. Gates wanted to invite his ex-girlfriend and her boyfriend to an oyster roast? Jessa wasn't sure how to answer. She felt like she should be noncommittal, in case he didn't really mean it. He'd barely been around in the two years since he and Brooke broke up. What was he up to?

She turned to Nelson. "Now's the time. Oysters are safe

only in months that end in the letter *R*. Mid-October is safe. Otherwise, you run the risk of bacteria." Both men had their eyes on her like they were thinking about anything but oysters. "But that's only if you're eating them raw."

"What do you think, Tucker?" Gates calling Nelson by his last name made Jessa wonder if they were more friends than business associates. "You up for a good ol' Southern oyster roast?"

"As long as some of them are raw too." Nelson winked at Jessa. *Winked* at her.

She was as flustered as she was flattered. Her plan might be working, but it was getting more complicated by the second. It was going to be a balancing act to convince Nelson not to buy the winery if Gates was actively doing the opposite.

Should she wink back? No, that would be weird.

She pretended like she hadn't seen it. "We need to put out the beanbags for the cornhole games, and I always like to make sure the cleaning crew put enough toilet paper in the bathrooms. Duke might be in the garden, if you guys want to meet him."

Nelson nodded. "Duke Bradley, huh? The guy's a legend."

"He is?" Jessa only knew him as a widower, her very grumpy boss, and boyfriend to their self-appointed winery greeter and resident entertainer, Grace Warter, otherwise known as Nana.

"He started this place from scratch after retiring, and now they're selling his wines in Costco. The dude knows how to make money."

Apparently, making money was what impressed Nelson the most. Jessa, on other hand, liked Duke despite his gruff exterior because she knew him to be a good man. Duke was someone who genuinely cared about the plants in his dead wife's garden, his array of animals, his employees, his kooky octogenarian girlfriend, and his wines. She hoped and prayed Duke cared enough to refuse to sell his winery to Nelson.

Jessa grabbed the bucket of beanbags from the shed and walked quickly toward the open expanse of land between the winery buildings and the vineyard. She pointed out the cornhole boards, handed Gates the bucket, and excused herself. "I've got paperwork to get done this morning. Make yourselves at home. The tasting room will open in about twenty minutes."

Nelson wasn't having it. "So, oyster roast tonight?"

He looked like a modern version of Cary Grant, suave and confident. She needed to keep a clear mind, but his attention felt good.

"Jess," Gates called after her. "I'll get the oysters. You get the people."

She stopped. "Tonight?" That seemed awfully soon.

"The sun sets around seven thirty, so we'll meet up at five thirty." It wasn't a question.

"I mean," Jessa said, "tomorrow might be better. I have

things to do tonight." She hoped to appear coy and in high demand, but really, she just needed time to adjust to the plan.

"Your house can wait."

How did he know that her *things to do* were whatever was next on the list for fixing up her house? The truth was, if they were having an oyster roast that night, she needed time to wash her hair, apply some makeup, and pick the perfect outfit.

"We'll meet on the beach behind Fred's place," Gates went on. "I'm sure he'll let us use his fire pit."

It was both a blessing and a curse, this philosophy she had of erring on the side of kindness. It often made her say *yes* when she really should say *no*. But she did need to get Nelson alone, and the beach would be a good opportunity. "Okay."

"Let's show Nelson how it's done," Gates said, acting the part of a cheerleader.

It was annoying how overboard he was going for the guy.

Nelson, for his part, looked pleased. She was pretty sure he was accustomed to being the center of attention. He seemed completely comfortable with people moving heaven and earth to make things happen for his entertainment.

"Do you want me to invite some of my single friends?" she added, hiding her smile. "I mean, it might make it so much more fun for y'all." Jessa watched their expressions closely, knowing full well that playing dumb was a superpower.

A woman who was willing to take the hit for asking a dumb question knew that the tone and content of the answer would disclose so much more than the man was aware. Playing dumb was sometimes the quickest way to get to a man's true character, or at least his intentions. Plus, she needed to know if Nelson was taken.

Gates held no expression whatsoever—he was as stoic as a statue.

Nelson, on the other hand, looked irritated. "That won't be necessary," he said like he had thousands of single women just a touch away.

He even looked down at the phone in his hand. But when he looked back up at her, something had changed. She knew in an instant—Nelson Tucker had made a choice. He was intrigued by her. And she had a feeling that the man was used to getting what he wanted.

Chapter Five

JESSA HADN'T PLANNED to spend all morning inviting people to an oyster roast, but that was how it turned out. One phone call led to another, and soon Brooke and Nate were coming. So were Brooke's nana and Duke Bradley. Brooke's entire family might have shown up if it weren't for her parents, Cornelia and Trig, having already committed to a charity event in Charleston. Jessa's mother, Dottie, got word that her brother Fred's beach pit was about to get fired up, so naturally, she invited herself. Most likely, that meant Tootie would tag along as well. How Jessa's family always managed to insert themselves into whatever event was happening on the island shouldn't have been a surprise, yet she still leaned back in her chair and took a dread-filled breath, knowing that drama was about to ensue. Dottie had no filter, Fred would surely bring his dog and a fifth of bourbon, and Tootie had recently turned into a very flirty teenager. Gates and Nelson would certainly be the recipients of too many questions, inappropriate jokes, and weird compliments. There was no heading it off at the pass, no convincing them not to come, no chance of changing their minds. It wasn't worth trying. She texted Gates to bring enough oysters for ten people.

Jessa left work early. Her professional outfit was not suitable for a fifty-something degree evening on the beach, so she changed into a sweatshirt and jeans at home, then loaded every extra blanket and beach chair she could fit into her trunk. It was going to mean tons of sandy laundry when she got back that night, but she didn't want anyone to be uncomfortable. At least the get-together was near Fred's store. If Gates didn't bring anything aside from a bag of oysters, someone would need to buy the cornbread and macaroni salad. He would at least bring cocktail sauce, right? That had to be a given. She probably should've whipped up a mignonette sauce in case Nelson was serious about eating some oysters raw. It was easy enough to do—just shallots, vinegar, sugar, and salt. Now that she thought of it, she'd feel guilty if she didn't do it. She glanced at the clock. If she hurried, she could get it done in ten minutes.

Before she left the house, she grabbed her shucking tools and gloves since Gates was known for forgetting things. Whatever was at the top of the lost-and-found pile back at camp—a jacket, a lunchbox, a backpack, a basketball—it was sure to belong to Gates.

There were already two cars parked in front of Fred's store. She recognized the little white Audi as Brooke's and knew exactly who owned the black Range Rover. Had Nelson let Gates ride in that vehicle with a bag full of mucky oysters? It seemed unlikely. She supposed she'd find out soon enough and set off the jingle bells when she walked in the front door. The first people she saw were Fred and Nelson talking seriously behind the sandwich counter. She scanned the room for Gates but didn't see him.

"Jessa!" Brooke said, rushing over for a hug with Nate right behind her. "Thanks for inviting us."

"I know y'all have oyster roasts for your guests at the Dogwood almost every night, so it's me who should thank you for coming."

Nate gave her a tight side-hug. "You remember the one and only oyster roast we had back at camp? What was it, our freshman year of high school?"

Brooke made a horrified face. "I still have nightmares about it."

"Gates sliced open his hand," Nate said.

"Yeah." Jessa remembered clearly the way his face paled when he realized what he'd done.

Blood dripped from his hand and formed a puddle on the dirt. A camp counselor ran full-out to get the nurse, and the seriousness of the whole thing scared Jessa. She'd wanted so badly to help him as he stood there holding his injured hand at the wrist, but he wouldn't allow anyone near.

"He pushed the knife in at the hinge of the oyster instead of twisting," Nate said. "We all know better. You have to break the seal."

Jessa added, "Then the fire popped a spark, and it hit

that skinny boy straight in the eyeball. I thought we'd all get sent home after that."

"I can feel my insurance premiums go up just thinking about it." Brooke rolled her eyes.

Running a resort had been challenging for Jessa's best friend, but the growth and professionalism that had come from it was astonishing. "We've all come a long way," she said.

"We have." Brooke reached over and took Nate's hand. "We're the lucky ones." They'd been a happy couple for two years now, running the resort while Brooke lived in the lighthouse.

"Save the date for Brooke's birthday party," Nate said. "We're having it at the resort." That was nothing new to Jessa. As far back as she could remember, Brooke's birthday parties were over-the-top and well-attended.

Jessa felt Nelson's presence before he spoke. "Well, hey there, Carolina Jessamine." His energy was like a grizzly bear's—intimidating and potentially dangerous.

She flinched. "How do you know my full name?" Had Dottie said it earlier? She couldn't remember.

Uncle Fred had a sly look on his face. "Looks like you've got yourself an admirer."

Jessa's eyes jerked back to Nelson. He didn't look the least bit upset by Fred's declaration. As a matter of fact, he seemed pleased. Had he really just admitted to liking her? Now that she had his admiration, she wasn't sure she wanted it. She looked up at him with wide eyes, and he didn't seem embarrassed or even worried about whether she would return his feelings. He was just as relaxed and confident as ever with his smug little smile and perfectly gelled hair.

The bells on the door jingled, and Gates walked in carrying two bushels of oysters in large white bags. "Sorry I'm late!"

"Did you get the good ones?" Brooke asked.

"Yep," he said. "They're covered in wet mud, so you know they're fresh. I'll take 'em out back and hose them down. Did anyone start a fire?"

"Done," Fred said. "Dottie and Tootie are down there now."

"I brought some gloves and shucking knives," Jessa said. "Does anyone have lemon? Cocktail sauce?"

"No worries," Gates said. "I've got everything in my car."

He did? "Do you want me to bring it in?"

"I'll get it," Nelson offered. He didn't seem like the type to bring in groceries, and yet there he was in his Rolex watch, pressed slacks, and golf shirt heading out the door to help.

"You okay, Jess?" Gates asked her. "You look a bit pale."

She nodded. "Fine." She didn't want to talk about how nervous she was about Nelson. "Did you bring the saltines?"

"Of course. And cocktail sauce. The only thing I couldn't find was fresh mignonette."

That made her smile. "I made some."

"Of course you did."

"I'm gonna drag the beer cooler down to the beach, if anybody wants to come with me," Fred announced before whistling for his big dog, Whiskey, who waited outside the back door.

Nelson walked in with two full plastic grocery bags hanging from each arm. Jessa rushed up to relieve him from the weight. She took one and headed out the back door. Nelson followed, and soon they were alone on the sandy single-lane trail to the beach. She wished they'd hurried so Fred and Whiskey were close enough to talk to because she had no idea what to say to Nelson. She could feel his presence behind her like he was a roaring wildfire threatening to consume her.

They could still hear the sound of the hose as Gates rinsed off the oysters. She scoured her brain for something clever to say—anything to make her feel less awkward. Was she being rude by not slowing down to wait for him? Maybe he wanted to walk beside her. She should probably reduce her pace and make room, but the pathway was narrow, so one of them would have to walk on the weeds and risk getting poked by prickles and rocks. She kept walking, unsure of what to do. Surely, if she kept ignoring him, he wouldn't like her anymore. He was probably disappointed in her already. A man like Nelson Tucker was used to women throwing themselves at him—women like debutantes and college graduates and frequent flyers. Whatever he thought he saw in her was probably just in his imagination. He would change his mind soon, find someone more appropriate. She turned her head just enough for him to hear, "So, this is your first oyster roast."

"It is," he said.

His voice was smooth and deep, like a smoky cabernet. It was also closer to her than she expected. He stepped up beside her, walking slightly off the trail and allowing her to have the cleared sand.

"And you've never eaten an oyster before?" she asked.

"Only in oyster stew."

She lifted up her grocery bags. "It looks like Gates got us all some other food, so you won't be stuck with just the oysters. Do you like macaroni salad?"

"I do," he said, and she wondered if he was purposefully making her handle the brunt of the conversation.

She glanced inside the plastic bags he carried. "Looks like he got some bread."

"Mm-hmm."

With every short answer, her anxiety skyrocketed. "What's your favorite food?" She prayed his answer would last until they got down to her mother and sister. They could help carry the conversation.

"Don't have a favorite."

"You have to have a favorite."

"Well, I heard there's this beautiful yellow vine, it's the state flower of South Carolina, and if you sprinkle sugar on it and stick it in the oven, it turns into the most delicious candy."

He was talking about the Carolina Jessamine vine, and she fully understood the subtext.

She giggled for his benefit. "You know, the state flower of South Carolina is extremely poisonous. If you ate it, you'd get very sick, and you might even die." It sounded harsher than she intended.

The fact was, she had little experience with men, and he was clearly trying to flirt with her. Just being near him was discombobulating and a little scary too.

"I'm not afraid of a little flower," he said.

Once again, she had no idea how to answer. So, she moved ahead of him with a little skip and jogged the rest of the way to the beach.

Chapter Six

DOTTIE BOONE SAT next to her brother Fred in a low beach chair, wearing a faded pair of cropped pants Jessa recognized as her mother's old *culottes* from about twenty years ago. Jessa squinted to see her better as she approached. Dottie was wearing lipstick.

"Mama!" Jessa ran straight for her. "What is that on your mouth?" Dottie wore lipstick about once every decade.

"Hush."

"What's going on?"

"Carolina Jessamine." Dottie put a finger up to shush her. "I got no time for laundry so I balanced out the pants with the lipstick. Pigs and pearls, you know."

Nelson sauntered up and extended his hand. "Nelson Tucker. You must be Jessa's mother."

Dottie made a face at him and shook, wiping her hand on her pants afterward. "You're lucky I'm talking to you."

He truly was. The last time those two saw each other, he was half a second away from getting his face slapped.

"DeWayne, stand up and meet the space stealer," Dottie demanded. Fred didn't move from his chair, but he did raise his beer bottle as a greeting.

"Nelson, this is my brother DeWayne—he goes by Fred nowadays 'cause of a nametag on a pair of coveralls at that gas station he bought. I'll have you know that he is a Harvard graduate and a former corporate attorney. You see, us Boones are not as backward as you might think."

Never before had Dottie called any of them backward. The men greeted each other politely, but Fred didn't seem interested in engaging further. He took a sip of his beer and looked out over the ocean rather than at the people standing in front of him.

"Where do you hail from?" Dottie asked Nelson.

"I've got a place out on Kiawah, but I am an NYU graduate, and I spend a lot of my time in the city."

"Oh, a city boy," Dottie said as if she knew a hundred of them. She kept cutting her eyes to Jessa as if to make sure she was watching.

Jessa wanted to make *what in the heck* eyes at Fred, but he refused to be part of the scene.

Dottie threw questions at Nelson with Jessa as a trapped audience until Gates finally showed up carrying the bags of oysters and a bucket halfway filled with water and burlap sacks. Fred finally stood. "I've got the griddle over here," he said, moving in his languid way to a big piece of flat black iron. The two men picked it up and placed it carefully on top of a grate over the fire.

"Is it time yet?" Tootie yelled from down the beach. Her

trim little figure made her look more like a child than a fifteen-year-old, which was exactly why she wore short shorts, a padded bra, and a crop top.

"Just now putting them on!" Gates yelled back.

"Holler when they're ready!" she shouted, then continued walking along the waterline, digging down into the wet sand periodically. Jessa knew she was looking for shark teeth, but it was high tide, so her chances of finding any were slim.

"That's Tulip," Jessa said to Nelson. "She goes by Tootie. And this is pretty much all of us right here—the entire Boone family." Nelson smiled at her but said nothing.

She was grateful he didn't mention the lack of a father; the last thing she wanted was for him to feel sorry for her.

Without a doubt, Gates was happily in his element by the fire. She knew immediately what he was feeling by the set of his mouth. Nelson, on the other hand, was a blank slate. But if she had to guess, she would say he was entertained, possibly even drawn in. There was Uncle Fred with his long beard and big dog, and her mother sporting a missing lower tooth and short manly haircut—the Boones were practically a reality show in the making. Jessa wasn't embarrassed of her people—as a matter of fact, she was proud of them. They were a hard-working family, and a close one. They routinely made sacrifices for each other and genuinely liked to be together—mostly. In her peripheral vision she watched Nelson crack open a beer and interact with Gates and Fred as they dumped oysters onto the hot griddle, spread them out, and covered them with wet burlap to steam. Would a guy like Nelson fit in with her family? It was hard to imagine.

Since everyone else was distracted, Jessa knelt in front of her mother's low chair and whispered, "Why are you acting weird? You never ask so many questions."

"I had a vision."

"Mama, no."

"I did," she whispered back. "Well, first I had a feeling. There is someone on this island who has a supernatural connection to you. The air has shifted. Do you feel it?"

Jessa shook her head. "No, Mama. The air is just like it always is."

Dottie went on. "Now, you know I don't want to think it might be that parking asshole, but the air around him matches yours. You're both walking in it. I reckon we might have to accept it." Dottie took her daughter's hand. "Sometimes it's okay to accept before we fully understand."

"Mama, you hate that guy."

"I do. But we're supposed to believe there's something good in everybody, right?"

Jessa stole at glance at Nelson's back—broad shoulders, long legs, hair cut into a perfect slow fade and gelled to a peak in the front. Could a guy like that be meant for her?

"Last night I had a dream," Dottie said. "I felt it in my forehead, and you know what that means."

"It's scary and must be taken seriously."

Dottie looked around to see if anyone was listening.

"Yeah, but not scary, just important." She leaned in and whispered in Jessa's ear, "I saw a list. It was some sort of a manifestation list, and it had to be all about you—blonde hair, pretty, nice to people, likes animals, knows how to cook. Oh gosh, there was so much more—something about loyalty then a load of weird stuff about video games and football. But we'll let that slide. The most important thing was the number eight, I think."

Jessa slumped onto the sand. "Of course, a list about what I can do for them. Is there a man alive who thinks about the other person?" The wind was starting to kick up, so she took a rubber band from her wrist and tied her long hair into a ponytail. "It doesn't matter. You taught me well, Mama." She sighed. "I don't have the first clue what to do with a man."

"Come on, now. Ain't nothing stopping you from having a little romance in your life."

"Like you?" She knew she shouldn't go there.

There had been too much pain over the subject for her whole life, and Dottie refused to take responsibility for it. Rehashing it for the fifteen millionth time wasn't going to make it any better. But sometimes the tongue directly defied the brain.

"Maybe when it's time for me to have kids, I'll just sleep with a man and never tell him I'm pregnant." Her whisper sounded more like a hiss, but she had to be careful to keep Nelson from hearing what they were talking about. She didn't need his judgment.

Dottie shrugged. "If that's what you want to do. At least you'll have your babies."

"That is *not* what I want to do!" Everyone standing around the fire turned. She immediately fake-smiled and pretended like all was well, when the fact was, not knowing her father was the one thing Jessa would never forgive her mother for. Dottie had subjected her to a childhood of being without. She'd had no great protector, no family tree, no daddy dances or cuddles, not even a photo to see if she had his nose or his chin or his eyebrows. She was fully missing half of who she was. Dottie only ever said he was handsome and tall and very successful—which was virtually nothing and probably made up. Jessa managed to control her voice even though the ever-present anger was right at the surface. "I would never purposefully rob my children of a father. I would never make them spend their whole lives wondering."

"What is it that you want, Carolina Jessamine?" Dottie didn't bother to whisper anymore. "You are on both sides of this coin. You don't want a man, but you do want a man. Which one is it?"

Nelson and Gates both watched the exchange with great interest, but Jessa was focused on the fact that Dottie had once again made a counter accusation instead of taking responsibility for her actions. "This isn't about me, Mama. This is about you."

Fred came to Dottie's rescue. Jessa hadn't seen him walk

up, yet there he was with his arm firmly around her shoulders, leading her toward the water.

"Your mother loves you," he said.

"I don't want to hear it, Uncle Fred."

"Kick off your shoes." He squeezed her tightly, his large hand fully covering the top half of her arm. "You need to put your feet in the water."

She did as she was told, leaving her flip flops where they lay. When they were ankle-deep, standing side by side in the cold water, he continued, "You know, part of the reason I moved here was for you and Tootie."

"I thought you moved here because you hated corporate life."

"I did. And I have never tried to be your father, but I have always"—he stopped to think—"wanted to be available for you."

"Thanks, Uncle Fred." Jessa loved him, but he wasn't helping.

"Your mother asked me to come home," he said. "Did you know that? She wanted more family for you and Tootie."

Jessa had never heard that before. "Are you making that up? Mama never asks for help."

"She asked."

Brooke was walking their way from the campsite. When Jessa waved at her, she broke into a jog, splashing her way into the shallow water. Fred stepped aside so Brooke could take Jessa into a tight hug with four pats on the back. It'd been their signature greeting since childhood.

"You okay?" Brooke asked. "Gates said you and your mama had a tiff."

"Yeah. It's nothing new. I should probably apologize to everyone—we made a bit of a scene."

"Jess," Fred began, as the three of them walked back to the gathering. "It doesn't matter how anyone else feels about this. You are entitled to your anger."

"I don't like the word *entitled*," Jessa said. She moved in between Fred and Brooke and linked her arms with both of theirs. "But I'm grateful for y'all." Between the cold water, Fred's tight squeeze, and Brooke's hug, she felt much better.

The group ahead was lounging and chatting. Jessa watched her mother ordering Gates around with a beer in one hand and a bag of chips in the other. She was probably telling him how to roast an oyster, which the man had been doing all his life.

"I'm going to find out who my daddy is," Jessa said more to herself than to Brooke and Fred. "Whether Mama likes it or not." And she meant it.

Chapter Seven

THE GOOD NEWS was Brooke's nana arrived. Nothing was boring, normal, or even sad when Grace "Nana" Warter was around. In her never-to-be-disappointing way, she'd shown up with old Duke in matching Hawaiian button-downs.

"Well, hey, y'all!" she chirped as they walked up, her wrinkly stick legs jutting out from short shorts. "Dottie Boone, I hope you are prepared."

Dottie had never been one to pay much attention to Nana. As a matter of fact, she tended to avoid the entire Warter family except for Brooke. "Grace, what in the hell are you talking about?"

"It's a full moon tonight," Nana sang.

Dottie's eyes immediately went to the easternmost horizon. Sure enough, there was the beginning of a complete circle rising in the distance.

"Oh no," Jessa and Brooke said at the same time.

"Well, Carolina Jessamine," Dottie said. "No wonder you're picking at me like I'm a dadgum pimple on your chin. It's a full moon."

Jessa ignored her. The anger she felt had nothing to do with the moon and everything to do with the fact that Dottie was selfish.

"I was telling my sweetheart here"—Nana took Duke's fleshy hand and kissed it—"that the moon holds power over us."

"It controls us the same as it controls the tides," Dottie agreed.

Nana spotted Jessa's empty chair and told Duke to sit in it. Then she placed her bony behind directly onto his lap. Jessa was afraid the old man's knees might shatter. "I have another chair," she said, jogging over to the spot where she'd dumped her stuff. She quickly unfolded one and put it next to Nana. "Here you go."

"You are a doll," Nana said as she mercifully abandoned Duke's ancient leg bones. "Just so precious." She eased herself onto the canvas chair and leaned back. "Now, after supper when the moon is high, I am of the mind that we should have ourselves some sort of a ceremony."

"What kind of ceremony?" Brooke asked, cuddling up on a blanket and using Nate's torso as her backrest.

"I'm so glad you asked. You see, I checked on the World Wide Web, and it suggested disrobing."

Duke had the slyest little wrinkly smile on his face.

"Like, undressing?" Brooke was appropriately horrified.

Jessa tried not to laugh. Knowing Nana, she would do it too.

"Oh yes," Nana said. "You take off your clothes while you visualize all of the things you want to let go. Then you put on clean clothes like they're your brand-new skin, and this gives you a fresh start. Then depending on how you feel about those clothes you took off, you can either wash them or we could burn them right here in the fire."

"I'm in," Nelson said, looking directly at Jessa.

His words were like liquid nitrogen, freezing her instantly.

"None of us has a change of clothes, Nana." Brooke was the voice of reason, thank God.

"I recall our dear Fred selling T-shirts in his store just up the way. I'm sure he'd give us a discount, too, wouldn't you Fred?"

"Yup, nineteen ninety-nine." Fred chuckled. The shirts usually sold for less.

Nana dismissed him with a wave of her veiny, brown-spotted hand. "Well, if you can't afford a T-shirt, you are exactly the person who should be asking the moon for help."

"I'll buy everybody a T-shirt," Nelson offered.

Jessa shot him a look. Why was he so willing to be naked? Or to see everyone else naked?

"And what am I going to put on my bottom half?" Dottie challenged. "If you're gonna buy something for us folks, buy us some bourbon." Dottie was nearly falling off her beach chair she was leaning so far forward. "As much as I've been dying to see my brother naked after all these years"—

she looked over at Fred and made a face of disgust—"I have a better idea."

Jessa stared directly at her mother, willing her to stop the nonsense and stick to the normal act of having an oyster roast. No weird moon things were necessary. *Please.*

"Here's what we'll do," Dottie announced.

Jessa held her breath.

"The full moon means it is the end of a cycle, right? So, let's start the new one on a positive note. You got that, Carolina Jessamine? We are gonna bring in the good, which means letting go of emotions that no longer serve us—like being mad at our mamas over something they can't change."

Jessa held her breath and made no effort to hide the furrow in her brow. Brooke looked like she was onboard with whatever Dottie was planning, so did Nate and Gates.

"Yes, I read about this too," Nana said. "We'll write on a piece of paper the things we want in our lives, and then we'll throw them in the fire. The ashes will become part of the universe, just like the moon and God himself."

"Mm-hmm," Dottie agreed. "And if you want, you can say it out loud too. I believe there's a word for it."

"Manifestation," Jessa said, even though she'd promised herself she wouldn't talk to Dottie for the rest of the night.

She had to admit that she'd wondered about asking the universe for what she wanted. Manifesting was something people talked about often these days. Really, it was just praying for something and believing you would get it, right?

How could that hurt anything?

Gates checked the oysters underneath the wet burlap. They were just beginning to open. "Perfect," he said. "Who wants to try one?"

Jessa hopped up. There was nothing better than an oyster that was warm in the middle and barely more than raw. She didn't need an oyster knife; she just pulled up the partially opened shell and slid the oyster straight into her mouth.

"You didn't even use cocktail sauce," Nelson said, making a disgusted face.

Jessa didn't know he was standing behind her. "Doesn't need it." She grabbed another oyster, and this time, she turned toward him as she ate it. There was no need to chew, it just slipped down her gullet. "Are you going to have one?"

"I don't think so," he said.

"I brought the mignonette in case you wanted one raw."

He looked sickened, not at all as adventurous with food as he'd made himself out to be.

"I thought you said you've eaten haggis and ant soup."

Something dark came over his face. "Maybe I was joking."

"Here you go," Gates said, handing him an opened oyster on a paper towel. "I kept some raw for you. I swear you're gonna think you've died and gone to heaven."

Nelson took the oyster reluctantly.

"Just shoot it," Gates said, pouring a smidge of Jessa's mignonette sauce onto the slimy, grayish shellfish.

Nelson looked like he was seconds away from gagging.

He handed the whole thing over to Jessa. "You can have it."

So, Nelson Tucker might very well be a big-talking pretender. With one uneaten oyster, he added in a whole heap of doubt about every other thing he'd ever claimed. Was he really a millionaire? If it hadn't been for Gates introducing him as a client, it would be easy to assume that he was just a hot guy in a Range Rover.

She took the oyster with a smile, slurped it into her mouth, and swallowed. "Can I get you something else? I can fix you a plate of all the sides."

"Sure," he said. "I'd like that."

Just as Jessa handed Nelson a plate of food, Tootie showed up with her friends in tow. Gates was spreading the second bushel of oysters over the fire, so it was perfect timing. Jessa was amazed at how far her little sister had come in just a couple of years. She didn't have an awkward bowl haircut anymore; instead, it flowed long down her back. It wasn't light blonde like Jessa's, which was no surprise since they had different biological fathers. Instead, it was dark brown with golden highlights that matched her perpetually tanned skin so well that she looked like a toasty little biscuit. There was a time when Jessa thought Tulip would be alone her whole life. She was so obsessive about the things she liked that it didn't seem like she would ever have room in her life for friends. But here she was, leading the way with two lanky boys and a shy-looking girl following behind her.

"Welcome," Gates said, waving. "We have enough for all of y'all if you're hungry."

Hungry appeared to be a popular word with the teenagers because they didn't slow down to say hello but went straight to the old picnic table set with food, loaded up their plates, and surrounded the grill to wait for the next batch of oysters to steam open.

When they were all settled, Tootie finally said hello to the group—except Nelson Tucker. Her eyes moved over him like she was sizing him up. Then she turned to Jessa, with no apparent concern for who was watching, and shook her head *no*.

Dottie Boone was either truly in touch with the mysteries of the universe, or she had an uncanny understanding of genetics, because her children were exactly the way she'd designed them to be. The whole family knew to listen to Tootie when she made a declaration.

Nelson stiffened, and the same dark look came over his face. Jessa panicked. No matter her doubts, this was Gates's client, a man who seemed to have wealth and power. She had to do something.

"Nelson? Would you like to go for a walk?" she asked. "We have about an hour before the moon is fully up. I can show you where the rocks curve around to make a natural pool. It's our favorite place to swim." She realized that she'd made it sound like they were going swimming. "I mean, we won't swim, of course. But I can show it to you. There are tide pools nearby with all kinds of sea creatures too."

The darkness was gone from his face, and she was relieved. "So, no disrobing?" He winked at her.

"No." She giggled and tried to play it off like the joke he probably meant it to be. But the truth was, his words felt overly forward and made her nervous. She knew her friends' and family's eyes were on them as she led him away. "We'll be back soon!" She tried to sound innocent and peppy.

But she knew for sure that none of them had ever seen her walk away alone with a man, and they had to be wondering what on earth she was doing.

Chapter Eight

IT WAS OUT of nerves or panic or maybe just her normal way of trying too hard to please, but she jabbered at Nelson for the first quarter mile of their walk. She didn't know what was going to come out of her mouth from one sentence to the next. Her jaw didn't stop moving until she realized that Nelson, even though he claimed to live on Kiawah Island, had no idea what half the things on the beach were. He had never even heard of sand fleas—the crab kind, not the biting kind. She showed him how to dig a quick hole right after a wave receded and grab them from underneath the sand. The fact that she was able to teach him something about her favorite place felt so satisfying that she nearly forgot he was the good-looking man she was trying to manipulate for the good of her family and the Saltwater Winery.

They were both holding small oblong digging crabs in their hands when he said, "It's possible that I've been waiting for you my whole life."

She nearly dropped her crab. Instead, she laughed, which was turning out to be her go-to when she didn't know how to respond to him. How had she won him over so quickly? Still holding her crab, she led him toward the tide pools with her heart beating like a hummingbird's wings. It took her a few steps, but she figured out why he would say that. Falling for someone in the span of a few days was an illusion. People fell in love through their imaginations, not their eyes, and certainly not their hearts. He didn't even know her. So, the question was: What was he telling himself about her that he liked so much? Who was she in whatever story was playing out in his mind?

"It's hard to impress a difficult woman," he said. "It takes a lot of effort. But someone who is naturally sweet and grateful will always be appreciative."

He was saying she was sweet and grateful. He was saying she wasn't difficult. This man, who lived in a world so unlike anything she'd ever experienced, liked those things about her. Surely, he meant it in the most positive way. To want someone to be appreciative was a natural desire. She should feel good about his words. She should bask in his compliment and let it warm her like the sun, yet the truth was, it made her feel small and vulnerable. She stopped to release her crab into the surf and Nelson did the same. They rinsed their hands in the water, and she dried hers on her jeans. As soon as she was done, he held out his hand to her. It was an offer, and she took it.

It was like she was looking down at herself from above. A person she didn't know was strolling along the beach holding hands with a handsome millionaire. It couldn't be her. She didn't do things like that. Could he feel her racing pulse through his fingers? Did he know how nervous she was?

They walked past the larger natural rock pools and tiptoed over to the spot where sea creatures clung to rocks and swam small circles in trapped water. She pointed out a sea cucumber and a tiny fiddler crab in the shallows. She even put her finger in the center of a sea anemone so he could watch the tentacles close around it. But he seemed only interested in looking at her.

"It's hard to find girls like you," he said. "Really. I've dated supermodels and I've dated CEOs. But you're special."

Those words worked. They really did make her feel special. She was used to dismissing attention from men, but his regard felt good. Maybe she needed someone who wasn't afraid of confrontation, who wasn't afraid to be rude. Maybe his confidence could balance out her overly nice personality. He knew the world. He could protect her. Maybe her plan for Nelson Tucker would turn out to be more than just a way to save the winery.

"Hey!" A voice called from down the beach. "Jessa! Nelson! It's time for dessert." Gates was out of breath when he reached them.

Had he really just run all that way to tell them about dessert? It wasn't like it was anything special. She was pretty sure it was just a box of cookies from Fred's store. Jessa and Nelson balanced on the rocks back to the beach, where she stepped aside, allowing the men to have their conversation while she stooped to occasionally to pick up a shell as they walked the tide line back to camp. She was always on the lookout for dried-out sand dollars or starfish. The live ones she put back in the water.

"Oh, good," Dottie said when they arrived. "You're back. Y'all've got some catching up to do. We've all got us a piece of paper here, and we're making lists of what we want to burn up in the fire." She handed a sheet of school-lined paper to each of them. "Share the pen."

"Alright, y'all." Nana took control of the situation away from Dottie. "Here's how we're going to do it. Now, Tulip, stand here so that you're facing both the fire and the moon."

"Only my mama calls me Tulip anymore."

"*Toooootie.*" Nana howled the word like a wolf. "Hold up your paper so that it blocks out the moon."

Tootie did as she was told, and Jessa could see through the paper enough to read the block letters written on the page—Tulip's personal list of desires:

FIX MY TOE THUMBS

MAKE PEOPLE STOP CALLING ME BOY CRAZY

KILL ALL OF THE MEAN GIRLS

GIVE ME AN A IN GEOMETRY

Her poor little sister had the cutest stubby thumbs. Tootie hated them.

"Dottie." Nana pointed at her. "What is it that we do now?"

Dottie recoiled. "How am I supposed to know?"

Nana sighed deeply. "Alright, *Tootie*. Say something nice to the moon. Something about starting fresh."

Tootie rolled her eyes. "Mr. Moon, take this stupid piece of paper and give me something better in my life." She crumpled her paper into a ball. "Please extend my curfew and give me lots of money." She threw the wad of paper into the fire and stepped away as the paper turned to ash and floated up with the heat.

Her friends giggled. Each one of them held their paper up and copied her almost exactly. *Mr. Moon, please give me money. Mr. Moon, please give me a car for my birthday. Mr. Moon, please make all the teachers stop giving us homework.*

"Duke, you're next," Nana declared.

"Yes, dear," he said, taking a moment to stand, like his hips and knees were deciding whether to engage with his weight. When his legs finally allowed him to take a step forward, he held his sheet up to the sky, but Jessa couldn't see any words written on it.

"Almighty moon," he said. "I have only a lifetime of gratitude and one small request." He crumpled his paper and tossed it into the flames. "More time, please."

Without saying a word, Nana carefully folded her paper and slid it onto the coals near his. They held hands as they watched their papers burn. "Same for me," she whispered.

Once all of the damp eyes were wiped dry and the elderly couple were seated, Dottie piped up. "My turn. Carolina Jessamine, you and Fred are doing it with me."

Jessa wasn't happy about her mother's demand. She had every intention of doing her own. She'd put a lot of thought into her list. But Dottie already had a hold of her hand and was leading her around the fire when Fred threw his beer into the trash bucket and joined them. "What about our papers, Mama?" Jessa asked, still holding tight to hers. "You're gonna make us all hold hands?"

"You know what? Everybody, come up here with us. If you've got a list, just throw it in the fire now. The moon already knows what they say."

Everyone still holding a list stood and placed them on the flames, quickly creating gray specks of ash that floated in the air around them.

"Now hold hands with the person next to you."

Jessa held hands with both Gates and Nelson and they wound around the fire pit behind her mother.

"Repeat after me," Dottie said. "Out with the old, in with the new."

They did as they were told while moving to the right in a sideways conga line. All except for Nana and Duke, who chanted from their chairs. "Out with the old, in with the new."

"The moon is a friend to me and you."

Oh gawd. Jessa cringed. Her mother was making up a rhyme on the fly. Still, she repeated it along with everyone else as they continued walking around the fire. "The moon is a friend to me and you."

"Oh, moon, dear moon." Dottie spoke the words like she was trying to reach the back of a huge auditorium without a microphone.

Jessa's secondhand embarrassment got worse with each line. "Oh, moon, dear moon," she repeated quietly. Walking in circles was beginning to make her dizzy.

Dottie stopped unexpectedly, causing a miniature pile-up behind her. "What rhymes with moon?"

"Soon, ummm, coon," Gates tried to help.

"Ruin," Dottie said with an accent that made it sound like *roon*. She started the line moving again. "Oh, moon, dear moon, don't bring us all to ruin."

"Mama, I don't think this moon ceremony is an actual thing," Jessa said, wishing it would end.

"Listen." Dottie stopped again. "I have never pretended to be an astrologer or astronomer, or whatever the hell it is. Just because I see into the future sometimes does not mean I know the difference between a Virgo and a hippo. Alright? I'm doing this for y'all. And if you're not happy with it, then do it yourself."

"This is how you do it." Nana declared, folding herself in half in order to get out of the low chair. Once upright, she spun with her arms out wide, and in true Nana fashion, was not the least bit self-conscious. "Come on, y'all," she said. "We're having ourselves a moon dance. Let yourselves go. Be free." She danced to the sound of the crackling fire and the waves, easily filling in the ceremonial gap where Dottie had left off. Tootie grabbed Uncle Fred in a salsa-styled cha-cha. Every time she spun toward her friends, she motioned for them to join in, but none of them moved. Duke stood next to his chair with his feet in one place and his arms making little churning-butter circles in concert with his hips. Nelson Tucker bowed like a Jane Austen gentleman and offered a hand to Jessa. The funny thing was, so did Gates. She looked back and forth between them. The whole thing was ridiculous. There wasn't even any music. Gates gave way to Nelson, which was appropriate, because Nelson was his client and because Gates and Jessa were just friends. She took Nelson's hand, and expecting to be spun and dipped, was pulled tightly against his body. He swayed with her so close that she had no choice but to put her head on his chest. She could hear his breathing, smell his neck, and was completely enveloped in his heat. She felt everyone's eyes on her, so she closed her own to block them out. They could judge all they wanted. She was on a mission. Wasn't she? Or, maybe, possibly, it was finally time she allowed a man into her life.

Chapter Nine

After the moon ceremony, Tootie and her friends took off down the beach again. When it was finally time to go, Dottie found her youngest daughter engaging in a make-out session with one of the lanky boys. Thank goodness Jessa had gone with her or Dottie might have pulled Tootie off the beach by her hair.

"What kind of girl am I raising?" Dottie spat. "You know I don't give a lick about you kissing a boy, but folks around here will start calling you a hussy, and I am slap worn out of all their talk. Don't be like me, alright? If you're gonna mess around, do a better job of hiding it."

"Mama," Jessa said calmly. "She's not murdering somebody. People are gonna talk no matter what."

"Right, Mother Theresa, like you know." Dottie huffed back toward the fire, then turned around. "Tulip Evergreen Boone, I tell you what." She sighed deeply. "You are smarter than this. I expect more out of you. Boys only lead to trouble—especially at your age."

The poor young man looked distressed, which Jessa kind of liked about him. He might not have tried to stand up for

Tulip, but at least he was raised well enough to feel badly about her getting into trouble.

"You should probably head on home," Jessa said to him. "I'll take Tootie."

The other high school couple was just a few yards down the way, most likely engaging in similar activities on the other side of a sand dune. They had the decency to look guilty too.

"It's okay," Jessa said. "Y'all haven't done anything wrong."

She felt like she was saying it to herself. She might not have kissed Nelson Tucker, but they'd danced for a full twenty minutes like they were superglued together. And, yes, she had the decency to be embarrassed about it. That was why she'd ignored him ever since. She'd only said a quick goodbye with a halfhearted side-hug when he and Gates left. Flirting, especially in public, had never come naturally to her.

Tootie practically skipped back to the fire, holding the boy's hand. It was hard to see up ahead in the dark, but as far as Jessa could tell, Dottie wasn't there. That was good, because it would look like she hadn't done her job if Tootie was both happy and still with the boy. The only person still there was Uncle Fred. Of course he was. Fred would never leave without making sure his nieces were safe. He might be a former lawyer and a current gas station owner, but he was also the most solid, caring person they had in their world.

Jessa couldn't imagine what life would be like if Uncle Fred hadn't moved to the island.

They doused the fire with water and sand, then loaded up Fred's wagon with the beach chairs, blankets, leftover beers, and trash. Whiskey led the way along the path back to Fred's store. It was approaching ten o'clock, so the expectation was that the lights would be off and Fred's employee, Ruby, would have it all locked up. But when they arrived, the building was as bright and as wide-open as a concert venue. And Ruby was nowhere to be found.

Fred tried calling and texting her immediately but got no answer. Tootie checked the bathroom, and Fred checked his backyard houseboat. Nothing. Jessa called Dottie to ask if Ruby had been there when she'd hiked up. Dottie said she hadn't gone inside, but she did recall seeing Ruby's car. Sure enough, when they looked out front, there was her little white VW bug. Tootie ran to it, tugging on every door. It was locked, but they could see clearly through the windows. Ruby wasn't in it.

Fred was already on the phone with the police before Jessa could suggest it. Tootie took Whiskey to search around the building, and Jessa called Brooke, who in turn called Nana, and they all said they hadn't seen Ruby when they'd passed by. Jessa called Gates next. He picked up immediately. "Hey," he said with surprise in his voice. "I was hoping you'd call."

"Hey, Gates. Was anybody in Fred's store when y'all left?"

It took him a second to answer. "We didn't go inside. But I didn't notice any customers if that's what you mean. Did something get stolen?"

"No, it's just that nothing was locked up, all the lights were on, and Ruby's car is still here, but we can't find her anywhere."

"Oh, shoot."

"Where are you?" she asked.

Back when he was dating Brooke, Gates would stay on the island with the Warters. Now, he didn't have a place when he came up from Savannah to visit.

"Are you staying on Kiawah with Nelson?"

"No, in a hotel in Charleston. Nelson went home. Do you need me to come out and help look for her?"

"Uncle Fred's on the phone with the police, so I don't think so." She paused. "I have a guest room, you know. You don't have to stay in a hotel when you come to visit."

"I would love that, Jess."

"Okay, then. Tomorrow's my day for making my Grandma Boone's meat sauce, so I should be home whenever you want to come over."

"Just like you do every fall," he said. "The freezer fill-up."

She was tickled that he remembered. "That's right. And if you're lucky, I'll send you home with a jar or two."

Fred was no longer on the phone, and from the look on his face, he was worried.

"Gates, I gotta go. See you tomorrow," she said, and hung up, turning back to Fred. "What'd the police say?"

"I need to find a picture of Ruby for a missing person report." He tugged at his beard. "We have the right to do that in this country, you know—to go missing. And the police can't tell anybody where we are—only that we're safe. So, it's not like she's broken any laws."

Tootie was inspecting the checkout counter like she was searching for fingerprints. "Does Ruby seem like the type to ditch work?"

Jessa added to the thought. "Would she really just leave and not even lock the door?"

"I don't know her all that well, but no, I wouldn't have hired her if I thought that."

Ruby had only been there a couple of weeks. She drove in every day from some little inland town. "She's going through a divorce," Fred added.

"Do you think her ex-husband kidnapped her?"

"I don't know one thing about him, so I can't say. But I'm sure he'll be the first person the cops reach out to."

"I can't believe this is happening," Jessa said. "Tootie and I will stay with you until the police arrive. Do you want me to call Mama to come out?"

Fred shook his head. "There's nothing she can do."

Jessa almost laughed out loud. Considering Dottie was quite positive she was psychic, the woman would be bent out of shape if they didn't consult her on an actual mystery. Fred must have been thinking the same thing.

"Dammit," he said. "Go ahead and call her again."

Jessa didn't have to. She knew that her mother was behind the headlights moving swiftly up the road.

"She's not dead," Dottie said through her rolled-down window as she pulled up beside them. "I can tell you that for sure."

"Dorothea Boone," Fred said. "I will never doubt you again if you can tell me where that woman is."

"If I could tell you something like that, I'd be so rich my clothes would be made out of hundred-dollar bills."

Jessa took a seat on the curb next to Tootie. What a strange night it had been. The whole thing had left her feeling unsettled.

"Go on home, sweet Jessamine and Toots," Fred said. "Y'all look dead dog-tired, and I've got my sister here to help me now."

Normally, Jessa would insist on staying, but she really wasn't needed, and Tootie did look tired. They both hugged Fred, but Jessa purposefully ignored her mother.

"Hey!" Dottie yelled as Jessa walked away. "I don't care if you're mad at me for something I did a quarter of a century ago, but you are not allowed to leave like that."

"I am an adult, Mama. I can do whatever I want. Tootie, get in." She slammed her car door and started the engine. She was about to put the car in gear when guilt pressed into her tighter than her seat belt. What if something happened to her mother? What if there was a murderer on the island and Dottie was his next victim? The last thing Jessa would remember for the rest of her life was refusing to hug her. Jessa got out of the car, walked over to her mother, hugged her, said "I love you," and then got back into her car and left. She was still mad, but the hug was like cream on a burn. She felt a little better. That was how family worked.

Jessa dropped off Tootie and could hardly wait to get back to her own place. There was nothing like the feeling of driving up to her little bungalow. It didn't matter how small or rustic, it was hers. She owned it and all of the land around it—every tree, every bush, every little yellow dandelion pushing its way toward the sun. The first place she went was the kitchen to get some water before bed. She wasn't even thinking about the old milk door or the flowers that had mysteriously shown up the day before. But there, on the floor of her pantry, was something else. A box.

Chapter Ten

The box was made of brass with a golden latch on the front for a tiny missing lock. It was heavy and had spots of tarnish, like an antique. Whoever left it for her had to know how much she loved heirloom items. Something with a history was always better than brand-new. She put the box on the kitchen counter and carefully opened it. Inside were layers of tissue paper holding a small bottle filled with sand and a typed note.

> A single grain of sand takes millions of years to form.
> When it blows in the wind, it sings.
> It filters our groundwater.
> It regulates carbon dioxide in our atmosphere.
> We melt it into mirrors and glass.
> It glows and shimmers and covers the most ancient deserts.
> But all of the sand in the world isn't nearly as important as you.

Important? She was used to being called beautiful. Special, even. But important? The word brought tears to her eyes. Who would have left her such a thoughtful gift? Whoever it was must have taken the sand from a South Carolina beach. It wasn't the white sand of Florida or the golden hued sand of California. It was quintessentially beige. And perfect.

Ever since the day she met Nelson, her little milk door had been put to use. The words sounded like something he would say. He was an NYU graduate, after all. An intellectual type. He probably knew the detailed components of sand, aside from silica, which everybody knew. He could probably pronounce whatever scientific names it included and where they came from. Why would a man like that be interested in her?

Maybe the more important question was: If he really got to know her, would he still like her?

Jessa shoved the ruined dried-out wallpaper from her bed and fell asleep underneath the feather-filled comforter with thoughts of Nelson and Ruby meshed together into a movie she didn't want to watch. She saw redheaded Ruby working behind the counter at Fred's store. The door jingled as Nelson walked in looking for a bottle of fancy wine. He leaned across the counter, talking to her with his chiseled face, white teeth, and smooth words.

Jessa knew that Nelson was sweet-talking Ruby, and she knew it was just a dream, but she was powerless to stop it.

She could only watch.

Nelson wooed Ruby with the promise of riches, he used his arrogance as power to make her feel small—like she needed him if she was going to survive the world. Poor Ruby was getting divorced. She needed financial help and stability, and she would never get a better man than Nelson. She followed him to his car and got in, not bothering to turn off the store lights or lock the front door.

Just a little way down the road, right in front of Jessa's house, Ruby's lifeless body was thrown from the car like trash—discarded without care for how she landed, no interest for the soul of the woman with the ribboned ponytail wearing blue jeans and a dirty work apron. Ruby was dead in a ditch filled with sticker bushes and dirt.

Jessa's own scream woke her up. She threw off her covers, and air hit cold against her sweat-soaked skin. Was this the kind of vision her mother had? Had she just solved the case of Ruby's disappearance?

Jessa grabbed her phone from the bedside table and called Uncle Fred, still frantic. "I think I just saw Ruby in my dream," she said. "She's in a ditch. I'm going out to look."

"Jess! Jess, hold up." She heard him mute the television in the background. "What are you talking about?"

"I had a nightmare. If I'm seeing things like Mama does, I have a duty to go out looking for her."

"It's past midnight, Jess. Let the cops handle it."

"What if she's still alive? I can't just leave her there. And I think he dumped her body near my house."

"He? Who's he?"

"Nelson."

Fred sighed. "Nelson didn't do it, Jess."

"How do you know? He left before we did, and he and Gates drove separately. He could've done it if he worked fast."

"Dottie left when he did, and so did Grace and Duke. None of them saw Ruby in there when they left. You're saying it was a crime of opportunity? Like, he stayed behind or came back to get her because she was alone? He had to know full well that we would be on our way up at any moment." He paused. "No, no. It doesn't make sense."

"But Uncle Fred, the dream was so real."

Fred sighed again and she heard him turn the television completely off. "And you're not going to sleep until you go out looking for her. Am I right?"

"Yessir."

"Whiskey and I are coming over. Give us a minute."

Jessa waited for them in the kitchen. She had every light on in the house and double-checked each door and window to make sure they were locked. Even though she heard Fred's car drive up, she still jumped when he knocked on the door.

Fred had on a bright orange hoodie, and he pulled two flashlights and an orange reflective vest from the big front pocket. "Wear this," he said. "I need to be able to see you in the dark." He and Whiskey walked into the house. "I informed the cops that we were going out looking in the ditches, so we shouldn't run into a problem there." Whiskey, led by his nose, ran into each room of the house while Fred walked around, actively checking the security of her doors and windows. "Looks like you locked up." He made his way into her pantry and, noticing the milk door on ground level, easily opened it. "You should nail this shut."

She knew she should. It was dumb not to, especially since she now suspected Nelson of two things—leaving her gifts and killing Ruby.

Still, she was reluctant. "It's too small to crawl through."

Fred looked at her questioningly. "Yes, but it's still access to your home. At least keep it locked."

Jessa knelt down and pressed the handle toward the word MILK embossed on the metal door. She pulled to check it—it was closed tight.

"Do you know where the ditch is?" Fred asked.

"Somewhere near my house."

"Let's go."

Outside, the moon gave them enough light to walk to the road without flashlights. There weren't many ditches on the island—it was mostly flat, but all they needed was one. *The* one. They walked toward the bridge away from the island, each taking a side of the street. After an hour with no ditches, Jessa began to feel like maybe her dream was just that—a dream—and not one of her mother's visions. She could tell Fred was tired from the way his pace had slowed and his head and shoulders lowered.

"Wanna give up and go home?" she called over to him. "I appreciate so much that you came out here and tried with me."

"I probably should," he called back. "People are already talking, and tomorrow is not going to be pleasant."

"Why?"

He and Whiskey crossed to her side of the street. "You know how it goes. I'm a single man, never been married, no kids. I hired an attractive divorcee to work in my store. If they can't get her ex-husband, they're going to come after me."

"But you were with us. You have witnesses."

"Yes, and they're important. Do you know if anyone took pictures? Did Tootie? Am I in any of them?"

"I'll find out first thing tomorrow morning," Jessa said.

"It's okay," Fred patted her on the arm. "We're not going to need them just yet."

"I think I'll go out searching in my car tomorrow. I was going to make Grandma Boone's meat sauce, but this is more important."

He nodded, but even in the low light of the moon, Jessa saw something pass over his face. "Do you want some?" she said. "I'm still gonna cook it eventually, and you know I always make enough to freeze and to share."

"Grandma Boone," he said like her name was a joke. "I

don't want any, thanks."

"Mama says she made the best sauce. Do you remember it from your childhood?"

"Nope," he said.

That struck Jessa as strange. "You don't?"

"I do my best to block out that part of my life."

Jessa had noticed over the years that Fred never added to family stories, never spoke about his shared childhood with Dottie. But she always figured it was because he was the boy. Dottie was the story keeper of the family, and that role seemed to gravitate toward women anyway.

"Can I ask why you block it out?" she asked.

"Naw, just believe whatever your mother tells you and leave it at that."

"Uncle Fred," Jessa said, feeling more than frantic. "Is Mama telling me the truth about Grandma Boone?"

He didn't even hesitate. "She has good reason not to."

Good reason not to. Not only did that mean Dottie had been lying, it meant she'd been purposefully covering something up.

Chapter Eleven

As soon as the sun rose above the palmetto trees Saturday morning, Jessa got in her car to look again for Ruby. She would deal with her mother later. Fred refused to tell her more about Grandma Boone the night before, even though Jessa pressed. That was just like him. DeWayne "Fred" Boone was the best secret-keeper on the island. But Jessa also knew that he didn't slip up. He'd given her a clue, and he'd done it on purpose.

Jessa was surprised at how few ditches there were on Goose Island. She drove round and round for two hours, down every dirt road and driveway, but found only three. None of them was very deep and not one had sticker bushes or a dead body.

On her way home, she stopped by Fred's. He was behind the counter cooking an egg for Brooke's mother. Cornelia Warter ordering an egg biscuit from Fred's gas station? Once again, the whole world had gone crazy. The woman was so all about appearances that her dinner ceremonies were a known thing on the island. Every night, she wore a dress to set her fancy dining table and made sure the drapes were wide open for all the neighbors to see. There were always fresh flowers, good manners, and from what folks could see, plenty of food served on the good china with forced smiles and stilted small talk. In all Jessa's years of being friends with Brooke, she'd never been invited to dinner at the Warters' house. Brooke had practically lived at Dottie's every summer, sitting at the old round table at the back of the house with the TV on, laughing about this or that and letting a cat or two lick butter straight from her corn on the cob. But Jessa having a meal with the Warters? Never.

"Hey, Mrs. Warter," Jessa said. "Getting some breakfast?"

"Well, hello, Jessa. You're up early."

Early? Jessa recognized immediately that it was meant to be a put-down. The woman had no idea what time Jessa woke up. Most people would call Cornelia out by saying *I'm an early bird, always have been.* Or jab her with *I see you're up early too.* But Jessa had learned over the years that it was better to play the long game. If you consistently killed people with kindness, they'd either see themselves for what they were and leave you alone out of guilt, or eventually become convinced that you were a rare and wonderful human. A person like Cornelia, once she let a person in, would love and defend them for the rest of her life. The journey to get there, however, would be long and arduous. So, Jessa pretended like she didn't notice the slight and went on acting thrilled to see her, just as she'd always done over the years.

"Did you and Mr. Warter have fun at that Charleston event you went to?"

"Oh, yes," she drawled. "It was just the nicest thing. Some big-name folks were there, you know."

"I'm sure those folks are the ones saying how pleased they are that the Warters attended."

"Well, I should hope so." She pulled her black cashmere cardigan closed over her silk blouse and tucked her arms across her chest. "Now, what is this I hear about a disappearance? Trigger is just beside himself that something like this would happen on the island where we make our home. And I have a vested interest in this because both my daughter and my mother-in-law were right here when it happened." She immediately realized that she'd made a minor faux pas by leaving Jessa out. "With y'all, of course. It is too close for comfort, wouldn't you say?"

"Sure is," Fred said, putting a perfectly fried egg onto a buttered biscuit, then adding bacon and a slice of cheddar cheese. He wrapped it in parchment paper and handed it to Cornelia.

"Thank you, Fred."

As long as Jessa had known her, Cornelia's nails had always been painted mauve, and they still were. "I was hoping you could help me," Cornelia directed all of her charm at Fred, her pointer finger resting against her matching mauve lips. "I would like to be able to address the rumors as they are presented. Do you understand what I mean? There is simply no way to get around the gossip."

"Yes, ma'am," Fred said, looking unbothered. Just like Jessa, he dealt with the public all day and had a thick skin because of it. "What would you like to know?"

"Pardon me if this is none of my business, but these are the things people are asking, and I have no reply for them." She waited patiently as if he hadn't already given her permission.

"Ask away," Fred said.

"I will be perfectly blunt, alright?"

For a third time, he was obliged to encourage her to continue.

"Why is it that you are still single? Have you ever been married or even in love?"

Just like Fred predicted, he was being brought into the discussion. Jessa had to admit she was curious to hear what he'd say. Just like his childhood, he never talked about his love life.

"I had the love of my life once, and I don't want another one," he said.

Cornelia squinted at him. "Fred, now don't you think that is an odd thing to say? I mean, who wouldn't want love?"

"I hurt her, and I hurt myself. I don't ever want to do that again." Fred noticed the look on Cornelia's face at the same time Jessa did, because he immediately added, "Not in that way. I would never physically hurt anyone." He wiped his hands on his apron, then leaned against the refrigerated case. "I have no desire for any life outside of the one I currently have. You can tell that to whoever comes asking. I am accustomed to not having my emotional needs met. I had a terrible childhood and because of that, I do everything I can to protect the women in life—those women being Dottie, Jessa, and Tootie. I don't need any more complications or responsibilities. I don't want any more."

Jessa was shocked at how forthcoming he was with a woman who was clearly intending to pass along this information.

"As far as the single women around here tell it, you don't even date casually," Cornelia said. "So, I suppose that makes sense."

"I have no interest in shallow relationships."

"Interesting." The woman was all judgment. "Now, just so I can say that I asked you directly—you had nothing to do with Miss Ruby's disappearance."

"Correct," he said.

"I know this, of course," she said, "because my daughter was there with y'all. There is no way you could have planned it with all of those witnesses, even though you are a lawyer."

"Right," he said. "Mrs. Warter, I will look you in the eye and tell you the God's honest truth." He focused his eyes on hers. "I had nothing to do with Ruby's disappearance," he repeated, "even though I am a lawyer."

"There," she said, straightening her self-righteous spine.

"I believe you."

As soon as Cornelia left, Fred visibly slumped. "I am not ready for this."

"Well, the good news is, Tootie has pics of all of us at the beach. So, folks around here might do some talking, but you have good evidence that you were with all of us at the time of the crime."

He held up his phone. "Tootie sent them this morning. Never thought I'd be grateful for a teenager's phone addiction."

Jessa didn't want to pry or add stress to an already bad situation, but her curiosity was overwhelming. "I never knew you were in love once, Uncle Fred."

He shrugged. "We all go through it, right? According to my therapist, I sabotaged the whole thing."

"You went to a therapist?"

"I did. And I'm not ashamed of it. They're a dime a dozen out there in New York, you know."

"What happened?" Jessa asked.

"I got spooked. Goes back to being abandoned as a child, apparently."

"Do you mean when your daddy died in the war?"

"That's part of it."

"I wish I could have met him," Jessa said. "Mama says he was a great man."

"I wouldn't know. I have no memories of him."

She'd always had in her head that he was old enough to

remember, like he'd been ten or eleven. But she'd never done the math to figure it out. "How old were you when he died?"

"I was barely two years old."

"He died when you were two?" That made no sense. He and Dottie shared the same father. "Aren't you five years older than Mama?"

Fred untied his apron and hung it on a hook by the oven. "She's not going to be happy with me about this, but I never agreed with the way she hid things from you kids. I'm not going to be complicit anymore. Secrets are like a parasite that kills the host, and you are old enough to know."

"Wait, you're telling me that the war hero I always thought was my grandpa is not my grandpa? Then who is?"

He sighed like the information was physically painful. "If Dottie won't tell you, I will. But I should give her the chance first."

"Uncle Fred. This is crazy."

"Which part?" he chuckled.

"All of it! Ruby disappearing, now Grandpa." She saw a car pull up outside. Fred was about to be busy. Jessa's mind spun with questions. "Who was the lady you used to love?"

"Valerie."

"Valerie who?" The car door shut, and the person was about to enter the building.

"Barton."

Valerie Barton from New York. Well, at least that was something. The rest she would get out of Dottie even if it required torture.

Chapter Twelve

Jessa drove straight to her mother's house. Dottie never locked up, so she was able to walk right in through the front door. She found her mother sipping coffee in the kitchen.

"Mama," Jessa said. "Who is your father, and why did you tell me it was Grandpa?"

Dottie didn't even flinch. "What you don't show won't hurt you."

"The saying is, *what you don't know won't hurt you*, Mother, and it's a bunch of bull. Are you and Fred even related?"

"Of course we are. Grandma Boone was the picture of love and grace."

"I know that. Is she both of y'all's mother?"

"Yes, she is."

"Mama, I have half a mind to go out and buy one of those DNA tests."

Dottie put down her coffee and sat up straight. "They are much too expensive."

"I have a good job. I can afford it. What is it that you

don't want me to know?"

"There are things that neither of us should know."

"Well, I hope you know who you had sex with in order to make me."

"We are not talking about him."

Jessa plopped into a metal diner chair across from her mother. "Mama. Who is your daddy?"

"I don't know who the sperm donor is, and I don't want to. Family is family, Carolina Jessamine, it doesn't matter if the blood is different. I grew up hearing the stories about Grandpa Boone and I liked them, so I figured he's my daddy too."

"I can't believe this, Mama. You don't know who your father is either? Were you ever going to tell me?" Maybe it was true what she'd heard about generational sins—that they repeat through the generations until someone purposely puts a stop to them.

"Carolina Jessamine, I have worked your whole life to protect you from these things. We do not need to dig it all up now. Just let the dead keep on sleeping."

"Did Grandma do the same thing you did? Did she pick out some man just for a baby?"

Dottie shrugged.

"Tell me, Mama. I have a right to know."

"Listen, Tulip can hear us. She's too young."

"She is not too young," Jessa raised her voice. "We should've grown up knowing these things all along. Instead,

I am standing in your kitchen at twenty-five years old not only asking you who my father is but who yours is. Does that not sound crazy to you?"

"It's not important who they are."

"That is for me to decide, Mama! It is important to me!"

Dottie spent some time looking out the window, and Jessa let her. She sensed a shift, like a softening. "I'll tell you about my father," Dottie said. "But I'm not ready to tell you about yours. That would open up a huge can of germs."

Worms, Jessa thought. And why? Even if she knew who her father was, that didn't mean she was going to tell him that he had a daughter. She just wanted to see a picture of him. She wanted to know if he was good at math and if he knew how to smoke a brisket. Could he play the guitar? Did he like to fish? Maybe his life was incomplete because he'd always wished for a daughter.

"After her husband died, Grandma Boone took to the drink," Dottie said. "You think it's hard to be a single mother now? Try surviving alone with two kids all those years ago. Your uncle Fred raised me more than she did."

Disappointment seared through Jessa. Dottie always said Grandma Boone was an angel—the best mother, a great cook, smart, doting.

"It's a sad, wretched story." Dottie slowly sipped her coffee like the hot liquid was going to magically give her the words. "She worked hard all day, and then would get blackout drunk every night. Most often we'd find her passed out on the couch." Dottie paused to sip again. "Folks do things outside of their character when their hearts are full of grief and their bellies are full of booze." Dottie ran a calloused hand through her sleep-messed hair. "She got herself into a pickle a time or two."

"Oh, Mama."

"You see now why I didn't tell you? Who wants to know that kind of thing about their kin? I firmly believe we can change the horrible parts of our lives by telling better stories. Fables and folktales are embellished and imagined versions of the truth. So, what's the difference? Why should you grow up thinking your grandmother got drunk and knocked up when you could think your grandpa was a war hero?"

"You can't just change history," Jessa said, reckoning with the fact that the grandparents who had lived in her heart her whole life weren't at all who she thought they were. "It's not right." So many pieces were beginning to fall into place. The fact that Dottie had no pictures of herself from her childhood, the way Uncle Fred moved home to be near his sister, how Dottie worked so hard for everything she had. "And the meat sauce recipe?"

"It's mine. That woman was too drunk to cook."

"Mama, please don't lie to me anymore, okay? No more stories. It matters. It matters where we came from. I want to know the real Grandma Boone, not someone you made up."

"Well, don't go telling your little sister. Let her stay— Well, I was going to say *let her stay innocent and pure*, but with the way she's been pressing her lips all over every boy in town, I supposed that ship has sunk."

"Will you ever tell us who our daddies are?"

"I wasn't planning to."

"Well, then I'm going to take one of those tests."

"It's not a good idea. You have to trust me."

"Is my daddy a horrible person?"

"No. He is a decent man."

"Then I'm taking the test."

★

JESSA HAD ALREADY bought the ground beef, pork breakfast sausage, bell peppers, onions, and giant cans of diced, sauced, and crushed tomatoes, so she might as well make the sauce. Just as she walked into her house, a text came through from Nelson. *"Can I take you to dinner this week? Have you been to any of the restaurants on Kiawah?"*

Jessa didn't know how to answer. She still felt afraid of him as a result of her dream, and the dancing at the beach had made her feel vulnerable. She absolutely did not want to be anywhere near the man's house on Kiawah. But those thoughts and feelings could very well be way off base. Hadn't she just learned that things weren't always how they appeared? It probably wasn't fair for her to feel that way.

Still, she could pretend for a while that she hadn't seen the text.

This time, when she walked into her house, she immediately checked the milk door. Despite Uncle Fred's advice, she'd left it unlocked.

Nothing was there, just a pantry filled with cans of tomatoes for a sauce that wasn't passed down lovingly through the generations after all. It was double the disappointment that there wasn't another gift. But it made sense, because Nelson was back on Kiawah.

She set out the huge pot she had to make Lowcountry boils and dumped the cans of tomatoes inside, then she started the long process of browning the beef and pork sausage with garlic and onions in her cast-iron skillet. She was making so much that she had to do it in batches. The house was just beginning to smell delicious when the doorbell rang. Now that she lived alone, the doorbell was as bad as a tornado siren. It always sent a shock of fear and adrenaline through her, even if she was expecting someone. She turned off the burner and ran for the door, looking forward to seeing Gates.

There he stood, a suitcase in one hand and a bunch of flowers in the other. "You didn't have to get me flowers!" she said, taking them before she gave him a hello hug.

"What kind of guest would I be if I didn't bring something for the hostess?" Gates smiled down at her.

"Your mama taught you well. And so did mine. Your sheets are clean, and your room is ready." She reached for his suitcase.

"Oh, no," he said. "I will not let you lug this thing inside." He stepped over the threshold, and she locked the door behind him.

"I forgot to ask how long you're out here for."

"You afraid I'm going to overstay my welcome?" He laughed.

"Never," she said sweetly.

"My lease starts in less than a week."

"Starts? Are you renting a place up here?"

"My company is going remote, so there's no reason for me to be in Savannah anymore. Half of my clients are out here, and I can always go back for the others."

"Gates!" Jessa did a few little jumps and claps in the middle of the hallway in front of her guest room. "That's great news!" Truly, it was the best news she'd heard in a long time. "It'll be like our old camp days again. You, me, Brooke, and Nate."

"I like the sound of that," he said.

With all the craziness of recent days, nothing sounded better than her old group together again. "You get settled, then let's call them," she said. "I know we just hung out last night, but I'm already cooking enough for fifty people. Brooke and Nate should come over."

"No moon dances or kidnappings this time," he said.

"Right." *No alcoholics, no lies, no unknown fathers.* "Just us."

Chapter Thirteen

RUBY WAS FOUND. Dottie was so furious she could've ripped apart a watermelon with her bare hands, but Fred was just happy that his employee was okay. Jessa got simultaneous texts from both her uncle and her mother when Ruby unceremoniously showed up for work Saturday afternoon. Jessa and Gates immediately left the simmering sauce and hopped in the car. Not only had Fred been vindicated, but Jessa's nightmare/vision about Nelson had been completely wrong. The whole ride there, she beat herself up for making such an egregious error. Thank God she'd only shared it with Fred. Who was she to imagine an innocent person could do something so horrible? Her silent accusations had been completely unfair to Nelson.

As they pulled into the gravel parking lot of Fred's store, so did Brooke's parents. Trigger Warter got out first and opened the Cadillac door for Cornelia, who did a double take when she saw Jessa and Gates together.

"Hey, y'all," Jessa said. "Did you hear the news?"

Trig nodded with no expression while Cornelia gushed, "Oh, yes. My neighbor, Rayanne Smith, went in for a coffee this morning and came out with some very good news." She clapped her hands together, her huge diamond ring sparkling in the late afternoon sunlight. "We thought we'd pop on over and congratulate Fred."

Congratulating Fred sounded odd to Jessa, but it was vintage Cornelia. In Cornelia's mind, proving the overzealous island gossips wrong was worthy of hearty felicitations.

"Interesting to see you here," Cornelia said to Gates as he held open the front door. She turned to Jessa. "Do you know what happened with Ruby?"

"Not yet," Jessa said. Once inside, their heads all turned toward the woman standing behind the counter with her red hair pulled back into a scarf-tied ponytail that matched her blue work apron. Jessa shot a look at Dottie, who made a sneery pissed-off face from where she stood like a royal guard. If you dared touch her, she might snap your head off. Jessa went up to Fred and hugged him, his beard prickly against her cheek. "Glad it's over," she whispered.

Cornelia, who could small-talk a room of non-English speakers for hours, seemed to have no patience for it today. This was not uncommon when she was around Dottie—Cornelia never had anything to say to her, but she seemed hell-bent on interviewing Ruby. "Oh, honey. We were so, so worried about you! It was a regular crisis out here. Are you okay?"

"I'm fine," Ruby answered. "What can I get you? The special today is a BBQ chicken sandwich."

"Oh my. Nothing for me. Trig? Would you like something?"

He shook his head like he was put out to be there.

Cornelia leaned over the counter and grabbed Ruby's hand. "Where were you, honey? We were beside ourselves with worry. We thought you'd been kidnapped!"

Ruby's eyes went to Fred's before she pulled her hand away. "My boss said I don't owe anybody an explanation." It looked like she wanted to leave it at that, but when Cornelia didn't budge, she went on. "Me and my ex got back together." As soon as she said it, her face changed. She went from a person on the defense to a person deeply relieved. "We figured we'd made a mistake filin' for that divorce. He came out here to take me back home, and I let him. Totally shoulda locked up the store, though. That was my bad."

Cornelia took a step back. "Well, I must say, I am just so relieved that some terrible creature didn't come in here and steal you away."

"Nope. Just my ex-husband."

"And it looks like Fred is going to let you keep your job."

"Well, I was scheduled for today, and here I am." She turned her back to Cornelia and stirred the shredded chicken in the metal warming tray.

"Yes, and of course, you didn't answer your phone because …"

Ruby didn't look at her. "I didn't bring a charger, and I was on my honeymoon."

"Yes, of course, of course. Your last-second, late-evening, no-wedding honeymoon with your ex." Cornelia giggled and smiled at the rest of the people in the room like she was speaking for all of them, like her words were not biting at all.

Ruby stopped stirring and instead put all of her attention on carefully lining up the giant jars of Herb's brand pickled pig knuckles, pickled hot sausage, and pink-tinted pickled eggs.

"All right, Cornelia," Trig said. "It's time to get back home. We've got us a busy day ahead."

Cornelia smiled sweetly at him. "Yes, dear." She followed him toward the door. "Bye, y'all!" She waved like she'd just been voted Miss Congeniality. "Enjoy your day. We're so glad it all worked out."

Dottie aimed the back of her hand at the door as it closed and wiggled all five of her fingers.

"What are you doing, Mama?" Jessa asked.

"It's a flock of birds," Dottie said. "One middle finger just ain't enough."

Ruby immediately did the same thing. Fred followed suit and so did Jessa. The laughter that came as they all wiggled their fingers at the front door was much needed.

Jessa's phone buzzed in the back pocket of her jeans. It was Nelson. Shoot. She'd waited too long to answer his text. Even though she didn't owe him an apology, because there was no way he could've known her private thoughts, she absolutely owed him something.

She turned her back to the room and answered. "Hello?"

"Hey there, baby girl."

Baby girl? The phrase didn't feel endearing—it felt condescending. She hid the annoyance from her voice. "Hi, Nelson."

"I have a surprise for you."

"You do?" Everyone in the room was listening to her conversation, so she stepped outside into the parking lot.

"I got us a room at The Dewberry. Not for this weekend, but for next," he said. "We'll walk around acting like tourists and we'll eat the best food in town."

"What?" She was mortified. She hadn't even answered his text asking her on a dinner date. Now he's talking about staying overnight together? Why would he do such a thing? "I don't know what to say." It felt too soon to have him planning that far ahead.

"Not used to surprises?" It sounded like he was gloating, like he was so proud of his big surprise that it never occurred to him she might not want to stay in a hotel room with him. "I hope you like five-star restaurants. I even set us up for a couples massage."

She was so shocked, she couldn't speak. She'd never had a massage before, but she was pretty sure the folks on the table were naked.

He chuckled. "You're gonna love it."

She quickly worked to suppress the panic building inside of her. "That's so nice of you, Nelson." She pasted a smile on her face like he was standing in front of her instead of on the other end of a phone call. "This is all so fast!" She wanted to say, *I'm not ready for this* or *you don't even know me* or *I'm too afraid of you to do something like that.*

"Plan on wearing your best dress." It was like he'd heard her thoughts and concluded that a chance to dress up would override them. "Don't you worry about a thing. I've got it all covered. Just follow me and enjoy."

Follow him and enjoy. She'd never once in her life done that. "It's so kind, Nelson. Really, really unexpected. I don't know if I can go, though. I have work and my house and …"

"We'll talk about it more over dinner. Wednesday sound good? I'll come pick you up. I'm a gentleman like that." He chuckled at himself. "We'll go to the Ocean Room on Kiawah. They've got world-class ribeye."

"I, um—" She was too frazzled to think straight. A date on Wednesday and an overnight in less than two weeks? It was hard to get past the feeling that she owed him something. "Okay." She would let him down carefully in person on Wednesday. Surely, she could come up with a good excuse for why she couldn't stay in Charleston with him.

Speaking of Wednesday, she had nothing to wear to a place like the Ocean Room. Did she have to go out and find a designer dress? She was sure Charleston had plenty of them, but she would have to ask Brooke for names of what was considered nice. She'd never really paid attention to brand names or fashion trends. She was completely out of her depth.

When Jessa hung up, she could barely get her feet to move. Her simple little life had gotten so complicated lately. Dinner on Kiawah? A hotel in Charleston? She needed to sit down. This was ridiculous. All she'd wanted was for Nelson Tucker to forget about buying the winery. Plus, she still had residual feelings that he was a murderer, even though she knew better. But she had to admit that he was very attractive. It was the same tug-of-war with herself that she'd had since she met him. She leaned against the cinder block of Fred's gas station and tried to calm down. Her heart was panicky—thrashing and snapping like a flag in a windstorm.

The front door opened, and Gates walked out. "You okay?" he asked.

She must've looked shell-shocked. "I'm just"—she took a deep breath—"overwhelmed."

Gates pulled her in for a strong hug. "It's okay," he said into the top of her head. "I'm here if you want to talk about it."

"Maybe later," she said, pulling away. "Right now, I just want to get back to my sauce."

"Then let's get back to your sauce. I'll tell 'em we're leaving." He popped his head into the store and did just that.

Gates opened the passenger door for her, and she gratefully sat. "I'm glad you're here."

He didn't answer, but his face said that he was too. She leaned her head back and settled into the seat. "I think our moon ceremony brought on some weird stuff," she said. "The whole world has gone insane."

"Then let's work on straightening it out."

"Yes," she said, "let's do that." If Gates was going to lead the way, she was ready to follow.

Chapter Fourteen

STANDING AT THE stovetop with Gates beside her, Jessa couldn't fathom saying the words *hotel room*. Had she inadvertently flirted with Nelson so much that he thought she'd be willing to share a bed with him? Even the savory aroma of the meat sauce didn't smell good anymore.

"Dammit!" she said, a little too loud. "I forgot to reach out to Brooke and Nate. What time is it?"

"Coming up on three." Gates put a hand on her shoulder.

They were both wearing aprons and had been taking turns stirring the second batch of sauce in between stopping to watch football on the TV.

"Are you sure you still want to entertain?" he asked. "It's been kind of a long day."

"I really wanted to see them. But we do have work tomorrow."

"A spaghetti dinner sounds good to me. Maybe a movie when the game's over?"

It'd been a long time since Jessa had seen Gates so relaxed and happy. It was like he was sparkling. "I'll cook the noodles," she said. "You make sure Clemson doesn't score on us."

One foot inside the pantry and Jessa stopped cold. There was a gift in front of the milk door. "Gates! Come see this!"

It was a white plastic bag so thin that she could see there was something furry inside. She carefully pulled out the oldest, rattiest brown teddy bear. It had to be at least fifty years old. Maybe one hundred. The mohair fur was worn in spots, especially on his rounded left ear, like a child had rubbed it raw. A glass eyeball hung loose, and there was a hole in the fabric of his paw.

She hugged the bear gently to her chest. "Who could have given me this?" She held the bear out again, in awe of his sweet face and old age. "He's perfect."

She looked inside the bag for any evidence of where he might have come from, then checked every inch of the bear. "Does he have a name? Who did this belong to?" She was talking to herself more than to Gates.

"Looks old," he said, reaching out to touch the bear's paw.

"That's the point! He's amazing!" She hugged the stuffed animal to her chest again. "Where should I put him? I want to be able to look at him, but I don't want anyone to touch him. He's too fragile." She walked around the house, carrying the bear like a baby. Maybe there was more to Nelson than money and good looks. Maybe he knew her better than she realized. If he'd sent that bear, he must have a good sense of who she was as a person.

Jessa almost asked Gates if he thought the bear would be lonely if she put him on the fireplace mantle. But she eventually opted for the top of her dresser where he could sit next to a framed photo of eight-year-old Jessa and Brooke dressed like princesses. Thankfully, she'd stuffed her wallpaper mess into the big outdoor trash can, so the room looked nice, although unfinished, for her new bear.

Gates came up behind her. "Do you remember when you gave me that bottle of peach Nehi back at camp?"

She nodded, adjusting the bear's legs so he would sit upright without falling over. "I knew you liked the peach flavor, and it was the last one."

"God forbid I should be stuck with grape."

"Right? That's what I was thinking."

"But that meant you were stuck with grape, Jess."

"Oh, I didn't really care."

"You even wrote my name on the label."

"I did?"

He looked down on her with a small smile. "All caps in black marker. I still have the bottle."

"You do not!" She laughed and adjusted the ribbon on the bear's neck. "Gates Lancaster, why would you save an old soda bottle?"

"I saved more than that. You remember that scorching hot day? The one where the pluff mud turned hard as stone and you and I both got it in our heads to walk on it? We made it all the way over to the spot by the big bleached-out log."

"No one knew where we were for hours." Jessa remembered it well.

Too well, maybe. It was the dog days of summer and camp was almost over. They were young, probably in sixth or seventh grade. The heat wave would be the last one for a long while. It was always a melancholy time. She was happy to go back home to Dottie and Tulip. She liked their house full of cats and opinions. But it also meant going back to school, which she didn't love. And it meant ten long months until she saw Gates again. She'd snuck away that day to be alone with her thoughts, and he had followed. "We both smelled like briny clams by the end of the day."

"You were hiding behind that log," he said, "holding onto a fistful of slipper shells."

"For Tootie. She liked to make tiny people out of clay and tuck them into the shells like a bed."

"I put them in my pocket when we walked back to camp. Remember? I still have them."

"All that time you were living with Brooke, you still had those pieces of junk?" Even though the bear was perfectly placed, Jessa risked knocking it over to plant a kiss on the top of the small brown head.

"Our time at camp was important to both of us." He shrugged. "All through high school, they were in a bag under my bed. Then when I graduated, my folks gave me a wooden keepsake box, and they've been inside ever since."

Jessa looked into the face of the bear so she wouldn't have to look at Gates. What did it mean that he had kept those things? Jessa needed to talk to Brooke about this; she had no idea if it was a big deal or not. Gates had items from Jessa in a box the whole time he'd been living with her best friend? How was she supposed to feel about that? Long ago she'd learned to stuff her emotions, sometimes even to invalidate them, in order to make them more tolerable. "Well, Gates Lancaster, I never knew you had a sappy side. It is a revelation." She immediately dismissed any romantic notions she might be tempted to consider.

Something in his face made her want to run for the hills. He looked ... soft. That wasn't an outcome she was prepared for. The bear toppled to the side, but she left it and scooted past Gates to the kitchen. Her hands were tingly and her brain fuzzy like she'd just stuck her finger in an electrical socket. These feelings were exactly why she tried to avoid men. A strong man with a soft side stirred up things she'd tried for years to keep tamped down. She had to pull herself together.

The wooden spoon was her lifeline, and the solitary, repetitious stirring of the sauce set her straight again. Gates was back in front of the television watching the game. She looked at him, tall and easy in her house. He might not know it, but he'd been her first crush. If you'd asked her back then, she would have said first love. There was a brief time when she thought he loved her too. Then he'd made her best friend his girlfriend. Still, somewhere in the memories she kept from her consciousness, the ones that remained hidden in her soul, were childhood years of sentimental journal entries, big silly hopes, and a million dreams, wishes, and prayers for the handsome boy at camp.

It all ended when Gates made a decision. He chose Brooke. So, Jessa had bowed out gracefully. She'd pretended to be happy for her friend for so long that she actually was. Seven years Brooke and Gates were together. Seven years of Jessa imagining standing in a pink or yellow or sage green dress beside Brooke as she married the man who used to fill Jessa's heart with desire. She'd come to terms with it. She didn't need a man anyway. Just like her mother. She had a job, she owned her own home, she was fine alone.

She watched him from behind as he sat on the couch. The cut of his hair and the width of his shoulders were so familiar, she could identify him from miles away. Even all of these years later, she knew him like she knew her sister or her mother. She'd seen him tired and dirty and hurt and victorious and mad and hungry and silly and over-the-top happy. She'd thought she'd seen him in love too. But maybe she hadn't. Or ... maybe, possibly, she just had.

The *look*.

"Nelson is taking me to Charleston in a couple of weeks," she threw the words at the back of his head like a panic shot.

Nothing about Gates moved, but the nuance of his body stiffening was enough. "Are you going?"

"I mean, he said he was making reservations at restaurants and even a spa." Hot red sauce splashed from the pot onto her arm. She wiped it off with a kitchen towel.

Gates twisted around to look at her. "That doesn't mean you have to go."

"I've never had a massage before." She was stirring so vigorously, the sauce splashed on her again.

His shoulders slumped forward into the couch like he was physically crumpling. "I shouldn't have brought him here."

"Well, maybe if he likes me, I can talk him out of buying the winery."

"Nelson does whatever Nelson wants to do, Jessa. No one can talk him out of anything."

"I'm sure he's not that difficult."

"Jessa," he sighed. "Don't go."

"How can you say that? He's your friend."

"He's not my friend, Jess. He's a client." He stood and met her in the kitchen. "I'm asking you. Please, don't go."

Maybe it was rebelliousness, maybe it was retribution, but Gates's pleading only served to reinforce her resolve. She was going. And it wasn't because she had an ulterior motive. She might actually like Nelson. Just like her mother, who spent a lifetime paying no mind to what other people thought, Jessa was going to spend the night with Nelson Tucker.

Chapter Fifteen

JESSA AND GATES barely spoke in the days that followed her declaration. The happy sparkle Gates once had faded into a dull gloom. He came to Jessa's house only to sleep for those last two days, missing dinner and claiming to be so tired that he needed to go to bed early. Jessa was tired too. Harvest was a busy time at the winery, with guests from all over coming to witness the process. The temporary harvest crews were there for the nighttime picking when the weather was cooler. During the day, even though most of it was done mechanically, guests were allowed to take part in the sorting—pulling out the damaged or underripe fruit. And, despite the winery using a pneumatic press to crush their grapes, it had always been important to Duke to make harvest a time for community, so Jessa was in charge of organizing all of the guest extras—including grape stomp competitions.

Wednesday morning, Gates had his bag packed and found Jessa in the kitchen to say goodbye.

"Why don't you come out for the grape stomp today?" she said. "I can put out an extra half barrel of grape clusters and I'll be your juice catcher."

He looked at her like she'd just asked him to kill somebody. "I'm moving into my new apartment today. I have too much to do."

"Right. Sorry." She knew that. "Do you need some help?" Those words should not have come out of her mouth. She had a date with Nelson that night. She didn't have time to help Gates.

"I've got it, Jess. It's okay."

She was both relieved and upset by his answer. There was a big part of her that didn't want him to leave—a big part of her that wanted him to join in the grape stomping fun. "Are you going to Brooke's birthday party this weekend?" She knew he was, but in that moment, she needed to connect and smooth things over with him.

"I'll be there."

"Want to go together?"

"Sure."

His lack of enthusiasm was disheartening. "Come here first and we'll take the boat over," she said.

He gave her a thumbs-up, picked up his bag, gave her a halfhearted hug, and left.

Even though the house smelled of the to-go cups of coffee she'd made, Gates left without taking one of them. If there was anything Jessa truly hated, it was failing to make people happy. She'd disappointed him when she dug in her heels about Nelson, and she wasn't sure how to fix it.

All day she felt off-kilter. The chickens, cats, and goats helped, but every time she had to interact with a winery guest, she had to push past the anxiety that leached her strength. She had a date with Nelson that night, and Gates might very well be mad at her. Her brain was like a streetlight switching back and forth from green to red. Date good, no, date bad. Gates mad, no, Gates had no right to be mad. Sometimes she'd be in the middle of a sentence and forget what she was talking about. All day, she found herself sighing deeply and staring off into space. By the time she got home that night, she was completely out of sorts. She let the hot water of the shower pulse against her closed eyelids as she thought through every plausible excuse for canceling the dinner date with a wealthy man who made her more nervous than a cricket in a lizard cage. The problem was, it was too late. It would be horribly rude to cancel now. He lived at least forty-five minutes away and was probably already on the road to come pick her up.

She heard his tires on her gravel first and peeked out the window as his black Range Rover slinked as quiet as a cat to the front of her house. He adjusted his sport coat as he climbed out of the car, then walked up to the door like a gentleman. Not only was this her first real date, but he was a grown man. He owned a nice car and a sport coat. She felt like she was sixteen and about to go against her mother's wishes. It took some strong self-talk to remind herself that she wasn't doing anything wrong.

She hid until the doorbell rang and, like every other time, the sound sent her heart racing. She hated doorbells. And, already, she hated dates too. Her hands were so tingly, she barely felt the knob as she twisted and pulled open the front door. "Hey there," she said. "You look nice."

He looked her over appraisingly, and her safe choice of simple black dress paired with ankle-strapped nude heels suddenly felt dowdy. She prayed he couldn't tell that she'd bought it years ago from a thrift store in case she needed something to wear to a funeral.

"You're gorgeous," he said with a smile.

She hadn't realized she'd been holding her breath until she suddenly let it out. "Thank you." Funny how one word—*gorgeous*—changed her whole opinion of herself. She instantly felt ten times more confident.

He held out his hand for hers. "You ready for some good food and beautiful views?"

She took it. "I am."

If she'd known the conversation in the car would be as easy as it was, she wouldn't have been so nervous. It wasn't hard at all to fill the space with words—his, mostly, but that was what she preferred. No question seemed to be off-limits, and by the time they reached the end of Kiawah where the Ocean Course sprawled against the sea, they were both laughing like old friends. She knew all about his ex-girlfriend, Regina, who brought her little dog along on all of their vacations and made him pick up the poop. And there was Shelley, who cried all the time and tried to make him feel like the bad guy when she was the one who created all the drama. Most recently, there'd been a bikini model named Harley. He likened her to the apple in the Garden of Eden, convinced that she was put on Earth solely as a temptation. Every woman from his past taught him what to look for in a partner and what kind of women to stay away from. This winding path led him to Jessa. He said she was a refreshing change. He might be the same thing for her—he was fresh and new, with no childhood history or hurt feelings. She was free to be whoever she wanted to be. And the restaurant was the fanciest she'd ever been to. The Ocean Room was part of The Kiawah Island Golf Resort at the Sanctuary Hotel, which Jessa had heard of but never dared visit. She'd been to a million restaurants on her Atlantic beaches—sticky ones with fresh seafood and sandy tables, but never to one with valet parking and crystal goblets and aged steaks where the ladies dress code was cocktail dresses and gentlemen must wear long-sleeved shirts with collars—jackets recommended. Nelson handed his keys to a valet while another man opened the passenger door. The man offered her a hand as she stepped out, and she'd never felt as feminine, or as special, as in that moment. Nelson placed his hand on the small of her back and led her in.

There were three forks on the table. She knew what to do with the salad fork and the dinner fork but had no idea why there was both a fork and a spoon above her plate. She kept quiet and put her napkin on her lap, waiting for Nelson to open his menu. Instead, he turned his attention to her.

"Are you going to look at the menu?" he asked.

"I was waiting for you to go first."

He chuckled. "Are you afraid of doing something wrong?"

The pointedness of the question embarrassed her. "No, I just—I was trying to show good manners."

"You wait for the host to pick up their fork before eating, not for your date to pick up his menu."

She felt the redness spread from her cheeks down her neck as she picked up the thick leather menu and opened it.

He quirked an eyebrow at her. "I think there's something alive inside of you, but your personality is holding you back."

"I am very much alive, thank you." She smiled sweetly to cover the fact that his words hurt. Was something wrong with her personality?

"No, I mean there is more to you, but you won't let it out. Do you ever push back? You need to free yourself."

"You make it sound like I'm a baby loggerhead stuck underneath the sand. I am fully here, out in the open, living my life."

"You don't seem to have many opinions."

Why was he suddenly picking on her? She focused on the menu. There was no way to defend herself from his statement—mostly because it was true. She didn't have many opinions. She tended to see things in shades of gray. It was a wonder to her how other people could be so loudly opinionated, how they could view issues as black-and-white. It had never been that way for Jessa. Her whole life she'd wondered why people did things, and what made them behave the way they did. She tended to approach people with curiosity rather than pigeonholing them into good or bad or mean or annoying. For the most part, she believed that people did as well as they could with what they were born with and what they knew. Life was both nature and nurture.

But maybe she was wrong. Maybe she did need to be firmer in her choices. "I don't like prime rib," she said, even though it wasn't the truth. "You should get that, and I'll get the trout."

"Oh, so you do have opinions." He laughed at her. "I was going to start with the seafood tower, but if you don't want an appetizer, we can skip it."

She found it on the menu. It was $250. That was more than the cost of her entire dining room set. "I don't want an appetizer, thank you." There was no way she would let a man spend that kind of money on her. *There—a true, honest opinion.*

Chapter Sixteen

NELSON ORDERED THE seafood tower even though she asked him not to. It was so extravagant, Jessa felt like she had to eat every last caviar deviled egg, her share of the tuna poke, half of the lobster tail, and what Nelson left of the king crab salad. She was okay leaving the shrimp and the oysters, though; those didn't feel special enough to be worthy of stuffing herself like an animal with no stretch receptors. By the time they finished what ended up being a four-course meal, she was so bloated and uncomfortable that she'd started sweating. Nelson wanted to go for a walk on the beach, but she was afraid the exercise might cause more intestinal distress. What she needed was some white clay, but surely he wasn't aware of that particular Southern remedy and would think she was not only backward but stupid. If he didn't already.

"I think I need to get home," she said after he paid the bill and began leading her toward the darkened beach. "I'm sorry. I don't usually eat this much. It was all just so delicious."

Without saying a word, he took her hand, turned

around, and led her back inside to the lobby bar. He pulled out a chair for her, and she sat down without question. He returned carrying two glasses of whiskey, each with a piece of ice the size of a large golf ball. "This will help," he said.

At that point, she was willing to try anything. She was as swollen and distended as a washed-up whale in the sun. The brown liquid burned on her lips as she sipped it.

"I must really like you," Nelson said, like the words were easy for him. "I don't even want to hook up with you right now."

She coughed as the words hit her ears and the liquid hit her throat.

He moved his chair up against hers and rubbed her back as she tried to pull herself together.

"Sorry," she squeaked. "It burned my throat."

"You're okay."

She'd had two glasses of wine with dinner and now she was drinking whiskey. She wasn't sure how okay she was.

"What are you afraid of?" he asked out of the blue. "Do I make you nervous?"

"I don't know." Her voice sounded strangled, but at least the coughing had stopped.

He kept staring at her, his hand solid on her back, waiting for an answer.

Maybe it was the pressure to have an answer, or maybe it was alcohol, but she experienced a moment of clarity when she said, "I guess I'm afraid that if a man makes me too happy, he can also make me sad."

"So, you're afraid of being sad?"

She slowly took another tiny sip, then answered. "Yes."

"Are you afraid of me?"

"A little," she said, noticing that the other low bar tables that were previously occupied were now empty. The only other person in the room was the bartender. She felt Nelson's warm hand against her cheek, bringing her attention back to him. With gentle pressure he turned her head, and before she could think, his lips were pressed against hers, warm and firm. She followed his lead and held still as he carefully kissed her over and over again, pausing against her lips long enough for her to smell his skin, long enough for her to enjoy it. It wasn't her first kiss, but it felt like it. Years ago, when the leaves were on the cusp of crispy and the sun was losing its summertime warmth, she'd kissed Gates the same way. Just like tonight, the Atlantic lay guard beside them and the softness of his lips made promises that everything would be okay. And just a few days later, Gates had made Brooke his girlfriend.

"I have work tomorrow," she whispered into Nelson's lips.

"You can stay with me tonight. I'll drive you home in the morning."

Jessa was not the kind of girl who would spend the night with a man on their first date. Just the thought of it alarmed her. "I can't do that."

Nelson pulled back. "I have a guest room. It's not like I'm going to take advantage of you."

"I know. It's just that I'm new to all of this." The truth was, she fully expected him to try and manipulate her into something.

He pushed away his half-full glass of whiskey. "I've got water in the car. It's been hours, and I've had enough food that I can drive. I'll take you home."

His response shocked her. "Thank you." Maybe he really was a gentleman.

"And you know what?" He pulled out the chair for her. "You're smarter than you think you are."

Jessa was stunned. He'd just made a direct hit in the best way—squarely in the center circle of her biggest insecurity. "Do you really think so?"

He took her hand. "I know these things."

"Maybe you shouldn't have to drive me all the way home tonight." What would be the harm of staying in his guest room? Maybe it was time she started behaving like everyone else. Maybe it was time to grow up.

"Nope. I'm taking you home," Nelson said. "You need to know that I listen and take your feelings into account."

Even though the last line sounded like something out of a psychology textbook, it was a smile of relief and gratitude that she gave him. One that meant she'd just taken a baby step toward trusting him.

★

JESSA SLEPT WELL in her own bed that night. It could have been the whiskey or maybe the full belly, but when morning arrived, she felt rested and ready to exit her warm cocoon and see what the day had in store. The winery would be crawling with tourists hoping to take part in the winemaking process, and Dottie was on the schedule to bring the food truck. The special was porkstrami on a pretzel bun with cheese and mustard—Jessa's favorite. It was overcast, and the chill in the air felt like a reminder that even though she felt better, she still wasn't in control. As a matter of fact, she was more out of control than ever. Both Nelson and Gates had the power to make her sad. But control was something her mother liked, something Nelson seemed to like, but wasn't something Jessa had to have. She would be a ship on the ocean, rolling with the waves, watching the horizon, and doing her best to stay afloat.

The drive in to work, welcoming guests, running the grape stomp, and leading tours felt like a reprieve from all of the intrusive thoughts. She floated somewhere above herself, looking down at the person pretending to be her. Nana was the only thing that felt real. She was there with a new crystal bedazzled nametag: GRACE WARTER, MISS SOUTH CAROLINA. She'd changed the date from 1959 to 1975. Jessa did the math. If Nana was eighteen in 1975, she would now be in her mid-sixties. Everyone knew both Grace and Duke were fully into their eighth decade. A small laugh escaped as Jessa watched her convince a little girl to take turns pushing each other on a tree-tied wooden rope swing. Nana whooped with joy as her bell sleeves and long skirt billowed and flowed with each glide forward and back. The little girl and her parents beamed like it was perfectly normal for an old folk to play with a young one.

Ever since Nana decided to be an unofficial employee of the Saltwater Winery, not only had she gained Duke Bradley as a boyfriend, but people returned over and over again just to see her. Nana bobbed around the property with her white hair and strange outfits exuding the kind of confidence a person only had if they didn't care what others thought. She sang Frank Sinatra and Lady Gaga songs in the tasting room, led conga lines around the old oak trees, and bullied people into buying cases of wine. Nana hadn't been around when Brooke and Jessa were growing up, but now that she was widowed and living in Brooke's parents' backyard cottage, she'd become the Warter family ambassador. Trig and Cornelia were even supposed to make an appearance for the harvest that year.

Away from Nana, Jessa reverted back inside her own head. Every time she spoke to someone, she found herself looking at their lips, remembering what Nelson's felt like when he kissed her. Had she been any good at it? She considered telling Nana about her date to see if she had any advice, but it would be impossible to drag the woman away from the visitors. Anyway, she had time. Her Charleston stay with Nelson was more than a week away. It was Gates she'd be seeing Saturday night for Brooke's party. She'd know then if he was mad or not.

Jessa grabbed a sandwich from Dottie and holed up in her office during her lunch break where she searched online for the components of a good kisser. There must be good hygiene, it said, as well as attraction, comfort, passion, and communication. The whiskey covered the hygiene part—both she and Nelson smelled and tasted of alcohol. She took a bite of her sandwich and enjoyed the tender pastrami-spiced pork inside of the dense pretzel bread made gooey by the cheese and mustard. It was better than the salad and trout she'd had at the fancy restaurant.

Let's see, she went on. The attraction was there, but the rest she wasn't sure about. Comfort? No, she wasn't really comfortable kissing someone in public, particularly him. Passion? No, she'd been too nervous for that. Communication? Did they have that? Not really. As much as she knew about him, he still knew very little about her. It felt like he was always judging her, trying to make her fit into the mold of what he wanted her to be. But he was a catch. Anybody could see that. If she had a father, he would be so proud. If she had a father, he would proudly walk her down the aisle at their wedding. He would say something like, *Well done, my love,* or *You picked a good one.* And he would plan to take Nelson fishing and to football games and he would share his best BBQ recipes and tell him what stocks to invest in.

There was a knock at her office door, and she realized she'd been holding her breath. "Come in." The door swung open, and there stood Tulip, her face stained with tears.

Jessa jumped from her desk. "Tootie! Aren't you supposed to be in school?"

"I left."

Jessa braced herself. Something bad must have happened.

Chapter Seventeen

JESSA HELD HER little sister in a tight hug as Tootie's words spilled out like water over a failed dam.

"Everybody hates me," she sobbed. "Just because Chloe likes Jacob doesn't mean he is off-limits to everybody else. It's not fair. She can't call dibs."

"What happened, Toots?" Jessa led her to a chair in front of the desk, then walked around and sat down.

"Well, Everly told Chloe that I kissed Jacob, and now Chloe is spreading rumors about me. Everly is such a backstabber."

Clearly, her little sister had way more experience in the hook-up department than Jessa did. Which was fine. Because she was a *prude*, Jessa had managed to avoid this sort of high school drama.

She made a mental note to make sure she didn't put any shame on her little sister. "You're right. People can't call dibs. Is Chloe your friend?"

"Not really. I mean, everybody knows everybody else, right? But it's not like I've ever been invited to her birthday parties or anything."

"Okay, so acquaintances."

"What she is to me doesn't matter, Jessa. The stupid snitch told on me. Maybe you can be all *whatever* and *she's probably been hurt by someone else*, but I can't. And I won't."

Jessa felt her sister's words like a knife to the heart. They backed up what Nelson had said. There was something wrong with Jessa's personality. She was too danged nice.

"Now everybody's talking about how I tried to steal Jacob from Chloe. So, I went up to Jacob and told him he needed to fix this. And do you know what he said?" A high-pitched squeak escaped as her tears started back up. "He said I probably had some sort of a virus same as a computer." She dropped her head into her hands, then finally looked back up. "He said I was gross and to leave him alone, when just two days ago he was begging me to meet up with him. I have the texts to prove it. Freaking liar."

"There is nothing gross about you, Tootie. You are one of the most perfect people I know."

"I wish I was as pretty as you," she sobbed.

"You're prettier and smarter."

Tootie gave her sister a small wet-faced smile. "Don't tell Mama I'm here."

"The school probably already called her."

She thought about that for a second. "Well, Mama can't get mad. I have As in all of my classes."

"Then you might as well go show your face and get yourself some lunch. You can always come back and hang out here if you want."

Jessa handed her sister a tissue and watched as she slinked to the door and blew her nose, head down as she shuffled her feet. She was adorable, a cute teenager with a dimple on her left cheek and a wide smile. And, just like Dottie had planned, she was exceptionally smart—brilliant even, especially when it came to schoolwork and whatever her latest passion happened to be. But emotional intelligence was not her strong suit—the poor girl regularly got way too caught up in drama. She was right about calling dibs, though. It wasn't fair. But it had to be taken into account anyway. Just like all of those years ago when Jessa had called dibs on Gates. It took her years to forgive Brooke for taking him, but she'd finally gotten there. She'd overcome the feelings of entitlement, anger, and resentment. It took work, and it took choosing to love her friend despite what felt like a betrayal. It also took letting go of her feelings for Gates. She slumped into her chair as, for the first time, she considered what had happened years ago from a different point of view. Would Tootie have kept her mouth shut if Gates had kissed her, professed his feelings for her, then turned around and made her best friend his girlfriend? No. Tootie would have made a stink bigger than a row of tipped-over outhouses. Gates would have known exactly what he'd done wrong. But on the other hand, Brooke would probably not be her friend anymore. By being nice, Jessa had been able to keep both people in her life.

Jessa wanted to pull out her brain and stomp on it. Just as soon as she thought she was getting clarity, her thoughts got all muddy again. Which way was correct? Attack a situation head-on, or keep quiet and ride it out?

By the time her shift was over, Jessa had determined that she was a disaster. Not having strong opinions and trying to see the best in people might help her get through the day with a smile on her face, but was it strong and courageous? Would she have any impact on the world? Was she truly as weak as everyone seemed to think? Her thoughts were like a hammer beating her to a pulp from the inside.

Once home, she had to do something to distract herself. Either she would tackle peeling off the rest of the wallpaper mess from her bedroom walls, or she would brave cleaning out the storm cellar underneath her house. She needed to clear it out before the next weather event came around. Hurricane season spawned tornadoes, so she'd been lucky so far. The space was like her current state of mind—messy and dank and filled with spiderwebs. She needed to organize it so she could store her beach stuff and bicycle. Then she could finally put her car in the tiny one-stall garage.

She parked by her front door and went around the side of the house. The cellar door was built into the ground next to the foundation. Someone had once painted the heavy wooden boards white, but they were now a chipped grayish color with huge rusty iron hinges and a padlock latch that had long since been missing the lock. She'd mistakenly stacked her wood pile too close to the left side of the door, so when she swung it open, it rested against the logs. Thankfully, there was still enough space to access the narrow concrete steps into the dark space.

The old painted door felt sticky, like years of sun and rain had degraded it into glue.

When she was first thinking about buying the house, she'd stuck her head in and found shelves of long-expired home-canned food. Now, as she took a few steps into the darkness, she found the old browning jars of okra, beets, carrots, and green beans still there. Maybe whoever lived in the home before her didn't want to go back down there either. They'd left moldy stacks of magazines next to car parts, with an old sewing machine piled on top. The space was as small as a closet, probably made only of dirt at first, and when the water table kept rising, concrete was added later. It was cold like a root or wine cellar. Maybe she should stockpile canned food down there too—if there was ever a hurricane that wiped out the one bridge to the island, she might need it.

After changing into a pair of old sweats, covering her hands with garden gloves and her hair with a knit cap, she hurried outside to get as much done as she could before the sun turned off the light. If she didn't think about the spiders, it wouldn't be so bad.

The concrete steps were pockmarked and crumbly, and the wind blew leaves down the hole ahead of her as she entered. She moved steadily into the darkness, her hand on the wall as a guide. The first thing she grabbed was an old folding chair. It had dust so thick it was as if the concrete walls had steadily rained down on it for years. She pulled it to the top and tossed it outside, then headed back down for more. It was good exercise, and she hummed to herself as she worked. When the area to the left of the wooden entry filled up with old junk, she tossed the car parts to the right near the wood pile. The goal was to clean out the inside of the cellar tonight and the outside tomorrow. She didn't know the names for half of the things she threw over the door aside from a labeled box of dashboard wires, a tire iron, and several mismatched hubcaps. Surely, her arms were getting stronger with every toss and her thighs firmer with each trip up and down the stairs. She'd grown confident in the old stairs now, so she jogged up and down, tossing each part over the door like a shot put. The sun was fading fast, and if she kept moving quickly, she might have everything except for the old jars of food cleaned out by the time it set.

As she hopped down the stairs, she heard the pile of metal objects shift outside, then the tell-tale scraping of bark and wood. She stopped cold and looked up just as her log pile tumbled. There was one last glimpse of light before the door smacked closed. Black was instantaneous. She felt her way up the stairs and pushed against the door. It wouldn't budge. Not the tiniest bit. Her log pile had locked her in. It may as well have been a car or a two-ton rock. There was no way out. And her phone was inside charging on her kitchen counter.

"Help!" she yelled. "Help!" She pushed against the door again and again and again. It was useless, she knew. "Help!" Her home was in the middle of two acres. No one could hear her. She sat on the cold hard stairs, unable to see any part of her own body. It was too dark for her eyes to adjust. She'd felt alone before, she'd felt abandoned, but she'd never experienced such a futile desperation for another person to be there with her.

Any person.

Chapter Eighteen

As soon as Jessa didn't show up for work in the morning, someone would come looking for her. She reminded herself of that every time panic threatened to overtake her, but it didn't help the emptiness in her belly or the fact that everything in this black hole was hard and damp and quickly growing colder. As night fell, everything was going to get worse—the cold, the night creatures, the intense desire for freedom, and the hollow soul-deep loneliness. Why didn't she bring her phone with her? God, if only. One little thing, the tiniest wrong choice, and she was stuck underground like a corpse.

The stairs felt like the safest place to be. She'd seen them clearly each time she'd gone up and down, so at least she knew what was there. Leaning up against the wall, she pulled her knees to her chest. That afforded a tiny bit more warmth and made her feel safer. She pulled her knit cap over her ears. That helped too.

Long ago, Jessa had learned that dreams were a great way to escape the drudgery of life. When she was little, she looked forward to going to bed every night because she planned in advance what she was going to dream about. Her mother had always considered visions to have real-life meaning and consequences, but to Jessa, dreams were wishes. One night she would dream about singing on stage with a famous country star and another night she was decorating her room and filling her closet with everything she longed to have. She hadn't planned out a dream for years. Growing up had a way of snuffing out childhood fantasies.

She tucked her head into her knees and imagined herself on the beach in the sweaty humidity of a Lowcountry summer. She and Brooke wore matching pink gingham bikinis as they watched the clouds roll by, casting shadows on the sand and intermittently making it easier to see.

It wasn't helping. Thinking about the beach made her feel the chill of the cellar even more.

She readjusted her position and put her feet on a lower step, leaning her side against the wall instead. Maybe she should think about something uncomfortable. There was always summer camp—the thin mattresses on metal springs, cabins without air-conditioning, and the fact that she'd never felt lonelier despite being surrounded by people. But if she thought about Camp Dogwood, she would have to think about Gates. And she didn't want to think about Gates.

Thinking about Brooke felt good, though. She smiled when she remembered the time Mr. Warter built a treehouse in Brooke's backyard. It was straight out of a fairy tale, better than what she imagined Disneyland to be. The treehouse wasn't pretty, not like the playhouses in Charleston that looked like miniature plantation homes. It was just pieces of wood sawed by hand and nailed together on the middle branches of a huge angel oak. The oak had thick branches that reached all the way to the ground, so Brooke's father nailed blocks in a line leading from the lowest branch up to the platform like a ladder. By the time he added the roof, winter was setting in, but that didn't stop Jessa and Brooke from spending the night outside. They pulled every comforter they could find out of closets and from beds, making themselves a cozy nest in the tree. Then they piled up a corner with moon pies, potato chips, beef jerky, and cans of RC Cola.

It was the night sounds Jessa remembered best—the frogs that *chirred* like crickets and the noticeable absence of loud summer cicadas, Spanish moss hitting against spent oak leaves and knocking them into the breeze, the gentle *swoosh* of the salt marsh tides, the creaking of the nailed pieces of wood, and the soft breathing of her best friend. For years, the treehouse had been their happy place. That first summer when the mosquitoes came alive again, they'd been chewed up so badly one night that they were forced to go inside before midnight. The next day, a mosquito net magically hung like a teepee from the ceiling. Other things were added over the years as well—a pulley system to heft up six-packs of soda and, when they were lucky, a plate of lunch or a snack from Cornelia.

Jessa had always felt lucky to have Brooke in her life. Like any small town, they'd met as soon as they could walk. Dottie and Cornelia had never been particularly friendly with each other, but that was to be expected considering they came from different social classes. They were cordial, and that was enough to allow Jessa and Brooke to play in the sand together at the beach or run around giggling on the playground at church. They'd been drawn to each other from the beginning. Their first day of kindergarten, when Jessa brought the baby blanket she called her *bubbie* and the teacher made her leave it on a shelf, it was Brooke who came to her rescue. They held hands almost every day for a week as Brooke helped Jessa to adjust. She never left her side.

Tears slid down Jessa's face, and she caught them with the back of her hand. Brooke's birthday party was Saturday, and she should do something especially nice for her.

All night, Jessa relived her childhood. In those twelve hours, she went through almost every emotion—fear, anger, sadness, anxiety, calm, frustration, anticipation, embarrassment, gratitude, regret, hope, doubt, and even happiness. Her life wasn't perfect, but she loved it. It may not be fancy like Nelson Tucker's, but it was rich nonetheless. And maybe it was time she shared it with someone. Maybe it was time to finally let someone in.

She never slept—it was impossible on the cold concrete stairs. It felt like she'd been there two weeks when the wake-up *trills* and *chirps* of the birds finally told her the sun was rising. Someone would be here soon to rescue her. She needed to listen carefully so she could make a loud ruckus as soon as they arrived. What she didn't expect when she finally heard the sound of a car approaching was a male voice she couldn't quite place.

"Hello? Is anyone here?"

She was already beating on the cellar door. "I'm here! I'm stuck in the cellar!" she yelled as loudly as she could.

"Is that you?"

"It's me, Jessa. Help! I'm in the cellar!" She felt around until she found something metal and banged it against the door hinge as hard as she could. The metal clanking was much louder than her fist on the wood.

Thank God, the voice was getting closer. "Where are you?"

"Under the wood pile! It's covering the door!"

"I'll get you," he said, and she heard a log being lifted and tossed away. "Are you hurt?"

"No! I'm okay!" She was so relieved she shook like a puppy in a snowstorm.

Finally, sunlight filtered through the slats of the old wooden door, and with each log moved, it felt like a weight was lifted from her body. When the door opened with a rusty groan, she was right there ready to escape. It felt like a rebirth.

The first thing she saw as her eyes adjusted was a pair of brown leather oxfords and creased navy-blue slacks. Then a crisp white work shirt covered with streaks of brown and sweat rings. She was fully standing before him when her blinded eyes finally allowed her to focus on his face. "Mr. Warter?"

Trigger Warter took her into a warm hug. She cried as he held her, despite the awkwardness. Brooke's dad was her rescuer. Jessa had spent all night thinking it would be one of her coworkers or her mother. She'd never considered him.

"You're freezing," he said, reaching for the navy blazer that he'd slung over one of the old folding chairs. He put it over her and overlapped it in front, the padded shoulders sticking out twice as wide as she was.

"How did you know to look for me?" she asked.

"The winery called Brooke, and when she couldn't reach you, she called about a hundred people, including me. She's on her way, but I could get here faster."

"Thank you," she said. "My log pile fell when I was trying to clean things out down there."

Down the road, she heard the loud honking of a horn. They both watched the driveway, knowing full well who was about to arrive. Dottie's big yellow food truck was coming in hot, honking her way down Jessa's long gravel driveway. Mr. Warter put his arm protectively around her.

Dottie barely put the truck in park before she ran at them like a linebacker, tackling her daughter out of Trig's arms and into her own. "What in the blazes happened to you?" She held Jessa out for inspection. "You look like you got caught up in a dust devil."

"I'm okay, Mama. I got stuck in the cellar."

Dottie abruptly turned to Trig. "Thank you for your help."

"My pleasure."

It was clear that Dottie meant the thanks as a dismissal, but Mr. Warter didn't move to leave.

"We don't mean to keep you," Dottie said, turning her back to him.

"You're not keeping me," he said.

There was something else he almost said—something else he wanted to say. Jessa was good at sensing those things.

"Okay then," Dottie said. "I tell you what. We're gonna head inside, and you just feel free to go on home. Go ahead and tell Cornelia you're a dadgum hero, alright? If she asks, we'll say the same."

Trig made no move to leave. Jessa felt like maybe he was the one who needed a hug. "I can't thank you enough for coming out this morning," she began, walking toward him. "I'm sure you had other things to do."

"Nothing this important," he said, looking more tender than she'd ever seen him before. Her whole life she'd known him to be mostly stiff and uninterested—it was odd to witness this whole new side of Brooke's dad.

"That's nice." Dottie smirked. "She certainly is important. And you're probably late for a meeting."

"Mama!" Brooke frowned at her. "Why are you being so

mean? He just saved me."

Mr. Warter stepped forward like he was about to say something, but Dottie stepped firmly in front of him. "Don't."

"Mama! What is going on with you?" As soon as she said it, Jessa knew the answer.

Chapter Nineteen

A LINE OF cars streamed onto Jessa's property like a funeral procession. First Fred in his truck, then Brooke, and in a Cadillac at the end of the line was Cornelia, Nana, and Duke. As each person joined the half-circle standing around the mess of logs and cellar trash, Jessa felt like she'd been tossed into the ocean on top of an ominous dark spot. It wasn't until Gates's car came up the drive that Jessa felt like maybe there was a lifeguard.

Dottie welcomed Fred with *He told her*. To Brooke and Gates she said, *Brace yourselves*. And to Cornelia, Nana, and Duke she said absolutely nothing.

Each person took turns hugging Jessa as they arrived, and they all asked the same questions. "Are you okay?" and "What happened?" She stiffened when her mother and uncle squeezed her.

Jessa told the story over and over again. "I was cleaning out the cellar and my log pile fell and blocked the door."

People were satisfactorily horrified every time she answered that she'd been there all night. But the real tension came with the knowledge that something else was going on.

It was Brooke's presence that made Jessa tremble. All night, she'd been grateful for her best friend. But would her best friend be grateful for her? Brooke looked as lost and confused as Jessa had been.

"Something's up," Brooke said. "What is it?"

Gates joined the group without a word, standing closest to Jessa. Brooke's eyes went back and forth between them, then landed back on her father.

Dottie spoke up. "Who wants to say it? Carolina Jessamine already knows."

"Well, *my* daughter wasn't supposed to know. Ever." Cornelia was as dramatic as a soap opera actress. "Trigger, this is all your doing. I told you she would find out."

Brooke figured it out in the same way Jessa had. No one had to say it.

"You're Jessa's dad?" She looked more stunned than mad, her eyes moving from her father to every Warter in attendance. "Nana? You knew?"

"Well, I—" Nana raised her bony shoulders in a shrug, then pulled off her floral hair bonnet and held it to her chest like a treasure, her white hair resembling rising smoke. "My heavens, you know I cannot tolerate secrets, but I'd have been put through the wood-chipper if I said anything."

"Blame your father," Cornelia said with a noticeable lack of compassion for what her daughter must be experiencing.

"How long have you known, Cornelia?" Brooke had fire in her eyes.

Cornelia took a step backward.

"She's known from the beginning," Trig said. "We all have."

Brooke finally looked over to where Jessa stood, still wearing her father's blazer. "You just found out too?"

Jessa nodded. "We're half-sisters." The words were barely loud enough to hear.

It was the moment of truth. The rickety bridge that connected their families was either going to be reinforced or detonated.

"Y'all are just now telling us this little piece of news?" Brooke turned to her parents. "Our whole lives we've been related and y'all kept it from us? What did you hope to gain by that, huh?"

Jessa hadn't seen him move, but suddenly Gates was just inches away from her side.

Brooke shot her fury straight at her father. "What did you do, Trigger? How did this happen?"

With one look, Trig tossed the responsibility for answering to Cornelia.

"Now, that is something our family will discuss in private," she said.

"Son of a dang it," Dottie said. "No. We're gonna get it all out in the open right here and now. Cornelia got cold feet is what happened."

Cornelia huffed and turned on the sweetest Southern accent she could muster. "Now, all y'all know how these things go—we were babies, just children. We had no business getting married that young."

Dottie huffed right back. "You were twenty-five, Cornelia, and so was I. Cornelia canceled her wedding two weeks before it was supposed to take place. I was bartending at the time, and Trigger came in needing someone to talk to."

"Wait. I thought you planned me," Jessa said. "You said you chose a man because you wanted me to be pretty."

"Naw, I was just trying to throw you off track."

Jessa's knees felt weak, and she was grateful Gates was there to help hold her up. So, she wasn't bred to be pretty. Not only that, but Mr. Warter was a smart man. A very smart man and a successful one too. "Can we all go inside? I need to sit down."

Cornelia balked. "I've got something in the oven at home. I best get back to it."

"Oh, don't go starting up with your lies now. We all know there is nothing but grease in your oven." Nana pointed a finger toward the front door. "Get inside and be a part of this. We're all family now."

"Should I leave?" Gates whispered.

"Please stay." Jessa started to take his hand and then stopped herself, thinking of Brooke and the fact that she and Gates had been a couple for years. Now that Brooke was her sister, she had to be even more careful about crossing lines. Ex-boyfriends were off-limits. Even as friends. "On second thought, I'm so sorry, Gates. Yes, maybe you should go."

It was the first time her house was full, every chair at her kitchen table was taken, and all but two of the people were blood-related. Duke and Cornelia were the only outliers.

Jessa went straight to the sink for a big glass of water, then took a wet paper towel and wiped the dust and dirt from her face while everyone around her spewed their opinions, completely caught up in their own perspective. Not once in the five minutes they'd been inside had anyone thought to comfort Jessa. She wished she'd asked Gates to stay. She needed someone to care about her.

Trig took a seat on her couch, clammed up like his mouth had been superglued shut. But Cornelia spoke loudly and with gusto. "Now, look here. We have done right by this child. Who do you think bought the food truck, huh? And who do you think paid for all those years at that expensive summer camp? Do not let it go unnoticed that we have done our part."

Jessa watched Cornelia like she was still in the dark of the cellar, blinded by daylight. All her life, Jessa had stuffed and invalidated her own feelings in order to try to see things from other people's point of view. It was what made her kind and thoughtful. It was what made people look at her with awe and say, *I didn't think I'd like you because you're pretty, but you might be the nicest person I've ever met.* Niceness was accomplished in her life by putting herself dead last. The whole room of people were counting on that. Counting on her to go with the flow, accept without question, and keep any opinion she might have to herself. Well, that era was about to be over. It was a new Jessa who climbed out of that cellar.

"I'm your stepdaughter, Cornelia." Jessa interrupted loudly. "And for my whole life, I was never allowed to stay at your house for dinner. God forbid anyone should see a Boone sitting at your dining room table."

"Those dinners are for family." Cornelia realized what she'd said as soon as it came out of her mouth. "You know I didn't mean it that way."

Jessa turned to Trig and straightened her spine. "I am twenty-five years old. Do you realize that?" She looked back and forth between Trig, Cornelia, and Dottie. "All these years I've been wondering who my father was." Her heart thudded so viciously it threatened to come up into her throat. "Do you remember when you built the treehouse? I was up there with Brooke almost every day, and you hardly ever spoke to me. Do you really think that's fair?" Her voice shook with the truth of it.

The room was quiet. "That's right," Cornelia said. "He built a treehouse for them too."

"Shut up, Mother," Brooke said, moving to stand next to Jessa. "Hey." She put her hand on Jessa's shoulder. "I love you. You've always been my sister, even when we were just friends. None of this is fair to you. I see that."

Jessa put her hand on top of Brooke's, grateful for the connection.

"Can I say something?" Dottie stood and Fred tried to pull her back into her seat at the kitchen table. But Dottie wasn't having it. She was ready for a fight. "He could have taken you away from me. He could have gone to the courts when I didn't have a penny to my name. Especially after he and that witch over there got married after all, and I found out I was pregnant a few months later." When she was met with blank stares she added, "Not that he would have married me, I'm not saying that."

"There is no need for name-calling." Cornelia rolled her eyes. "My word. Had I known he'd gotten another woman pregnant, I wouldn't have gone through with the wedding."

Trig didn't flinch. Not in the slightest. Neither did Nana or Duke. It seemed Cornelia's displeasure with her husband was nothing new.

"It was horrible of all y'all to keep this from me," Jessa said as another thought occurred to her. She turned to Mr. Warter. "Are you Tootie's dad too?"

Trig shook his head.

"Look, this isn't something we did to you. It's just a thing," Dottie said. "Men don't have to know if you don't want 'em to."

"But clearly, you told him."

"I needed a little help. And don't you judge me for it neither. I'm the one who raised you and made a home for you. I'm the one who did all the work."

Jessa couldn't hide her anger. "Who's Tootie's dad?"

Uncle Fred shook his head before Dottie said, "That is a discussion for another time."

Jessa immediately turned on him. "Uncle Fred, if she won't tell me, you have to."

Fred's countenance was very lawyer-like despite his beard and overalls. "Like I said before, I'll give her the chance first."

"Alright, then. Mama? Tell me."

Dottie sighed loudly. "I will tell you. But not right here in front of all these folks. I'm done with this attack."

"Then I am coming over this afternoon, after I get some rest," Jessa said. "Fathers are not *optional*, Mama. They are important. You should know that. You grew up without one too." Her voice broke and she wiped the tears away, replacing them with righteous anger. She was finally allowing the words she was thinking to actually come out of her mouth. She looked straight at Trigger Warter, who barely raised his eyes to meet hers. "You don't care about me, do you? You never have."

"He did plenty for you," Cornelia answered for him.

Jessa dashed to her bedroom and locked the door. She hated Cornelia. Trigger Warter's money, or whatever it was he'd paid for, had nothing to do with any of it. This was about a daughter's basic need to have a father who cared about her. A father who was invested in her. A father who protected her and provided a happy life for her. He was supposed to take the time to know her. He was supposed to be a decent person.

Screw them. Screw all of them.

Chapter Twenty

JESSA TOOK A shower and climbed into bed after Duke gave her the day off and the last guilty person finally stopped knocking on her bedroom door and left her house. It was a relief to have them gone. Brooke offered to stay, but more than anything, Jessa just wanted to sleep. She texted Nelson: *"So much to tell you."* She was asleep seconds after she tucked her sheets beneath her chin.

Four hours later, she awoke to her alarm, feeling like she needed at least twelve more hours of rest. *Trigger Warter is my father. Trigger Warter is my father.* It was like her brain was on repeat trying to convince itself to believe it. *Trigger Warter is my father.*

There were several texts from Nelson. *"Is everything okay?"* Then hours later: *"Gates told me. I'm taking you out tonight. Be ready by six."*

He hadn't given her a choice. Usually, she was good at reading people, but not Nelson. She had trouble anticipating what he would do. That made him mysterious. It also made her want to figure him out.

She pulled her still-damp hair into a messy bun and

found a pair of clean jeans and a gray SALTWATER WINERY sweatshirt. She stepped outside and immediately noticed something was different. The pile of old chairs she'd tossed from the cellar were no longer there. She jogged to the side of the house and there was her wood pile, perfectly stacked several yards from her cellar door. All of the trash was gone and even the autumn leaves had been raked into a neat pile. She pulled open the in-ground door; the musty dark space was empty and swept clean, even the rotting jars of canned fruits and vegetables were gone.

Jessa texted her mother. *"Do you know who cleaned up my yard?"*

Could it possibly be Mr. Warter trying to make things better? Trying to show he cared?

A message popped up. *"Gates."*

Of course it wasn't Mr. Warter. She'd been right when she said he didn't care. Jessa let the door slam as she went back inside, then dialed Gates. "Did you clean my cellar?" She didn't bother with hello.

"I didn't want you to have to think about it anymore. I still can't believe you were stuck in that hole all night."

"Gates! That's incredible. It's so nice of you."

"Not really. It's just housework. I'm renting, so I might as well help with yours."

"No, no, really. I needed that. I can't thank you enough."

"Well, you just did. And it's enough."

She walked back to the kitchen and sat at the head of the table. "Thank you for coming back. I'm sorry I didn't have you stay. I was trying to think about Brooke and her family and …"

"You were right, Jess. It would have been weird to have me there. How'd it go?"

"Good question. It seems that my mama and Mr. Warter had a drunken night together after Cornelia called off their wedding. Then Cornelia changed her mind and went through with the ceremony after all. A few months later, Mama found out she was pregnant. Pretty sure Mrs. Warter was pregnant by then, too, since I'm just a few months older than Brooke. My mama made a deal with him that she wouldn't tell anyone if he would help pay for my upbringing."

"That's what you know?"

"Pretty much."

"You want some company tonight?" he asked. "I can pick us up some BBQ, and we can watch a movie. You can talk about it all you want."

"Can't. Nelson's taking me somewhere. Not sure where."

There was a long pause. "Be careful, Jess. I don't want to tell you what to do, but—"

"Then don't. I have opinions, you know. I can decide for myself." She was going to have opinions if it killed her.

"I know that, Jess," he said softly.

"Well, other people don't seem to. I'm done with being

nice all the time."

"Okay. Just …"

"You already said to be careful, and I heard you."

"Right."

"I'm going to hang up now. See you later."

"Yup." He hung up.

Was this how it felt to be blunt and forthright? Had she just been courageous? It felt strong, but it didn't feel good. But maybe she just needed to get used to it—grow that proverbial thick skin. Change was supposed to be difficult.

Gates was stuck in her mind as she drove to her mother's house. He'd cleaned up that huge mess and all she'd done was shut him down. She waffled between feeling proud that she'd held a boundary and horrible for not properly appreciating him.

"Mama?" she yelled as she opened the front door to the low-slung brick house and walked in.

Immediately, two cats welcomed her with tails high and loud meows.

"Tootie?" she called before bending down to pet them.

Aside from the cats, the only sounds from the house were the old clock ticking on the wall and the wind chimes outside the back door.

"Mama! Tootie!" She'd figured the food truck was parked in the back where Dottie sometimes left it, but when she looked out the kitchen window, it wasn't there.

"Where are you?" she texted Tootie.

"Working the baseball game with Mama."

Dottie hadn't mentioned she was working that afternoon. The woman had purposefully let her eldest ill-begotten daughter believe that they would have a family discussion. She'd lied and avoided telling them the truth. Again.

For Jessa, anger usually equaled tears. The tears then led to feelings of shame and frustration, which led to more tears. It was like her body betrayed her. She normally wouldn't allow herself to yell or act out, so the emotions ran down her face instead. This time, she would refuse the tears. This time, she would feel the anger.

A glance in Dottie's foyer mirror showed Jessa's hair had dried into unflattering waves and the cowlick she always blow-dried straight down formed an awkward straight-up swoop at her forehead. If she was going to survive the night, she had to get herself into gear. Nelson would be at her house to pick her up in less than two hours. The last thing in the world she wanted to do was go to some fancy restaurant and make small talk.

She texted him. *"Want to have dinner at my place instead? Very casual. I'll make pasta."* She was a good cook and knew that she could scrape up enough from what she had in the house to make a decent meal.

"Sure," was all he said. No *thank you* or *I'm excited to try your cooking.* Maybe Nelson's dry, uninspired answer was a good thing. It added to her commitment to change. No

more being a pushover.

From Dottie's refrigerator, she took two eggs and half a block of cheddar cheese. Then she zoomed home, battling to block out everything except what was in front of her—dinner and Nelson.

★

HER HAIR WAS freshly washed, glossy, and lightly curled, her skin highlighted with sunny pinks, her eyes vibrant with the same sky-blue hue of her sundress. She'd rolled out lasagna noodles and hand shredded the cheese. A Saltwater Winery white was chilling in the refrigerator. By the time Nelson arrived, she should have the lasagna in the oven, the store-bought elbow noodles cooked, and the bechamel-based cheddar sauce melted. It might sound strange to have two pastas, but at every good Southern buffet there were always at least two choices—and it was practically a requirement that one of them be macaroni and cheese. It was a lot of food, but she wasn't yet satisfied. They needed something green. A few yards from her house was an overgrown plot where someone years ago had tended a garden. It was something she would get to working on eventually, maybe once she finished the inside of her house. But she recalled seeing squash there once, so she traipsed outside to look. Finally, the universe appeared to be on her side. There were clumps of huge leaves with healthy green zucchinis underneath—at least five of them, along with tons of yellow blooms portending more. A watermelon rotted nearby, and dark purple eggplant grew up around it. She felt like she'd just happened upon a treasure. The garden moved to the top of her fix-it list.

She chose two of the best-looking zucchinis to wash and slice. She would sauté them in butter and salt until they were brown. That way, their flavor would be less vegetable-like.

By the time the doorbell rang, Jessa had the kitchen table set and two wine glasses on the counter. Her heart flip-flopped at the sound, and she walked on numb feet to answer the door. When she said "hello," she sounded breathless.

Nelson stood on the front porch, tall and confident, holding a bouquet of daisies and a bottle of red wine. She immediately thought how nice it was that he had brought her flowers twice—once through the milk door and now at the front. He handed them to her, and she hugged him from the side, her head barely above his armpit. "Thank you. I'll put them with the others." Never before had she accumulated three sets of flowers—one from Gates, and now two from Nelson. Her vase was overflowing.

"Gates said you got some big news today," Nelson said as he followed her into the kitchen. He put the wine on the counter, and she thanked him for it as she stuck the daisy stems in with the assortment of pastel-colored blooms and white roses.

"Red or white wine?" she asked.

"White."

She pulled out the white she'd put in the fridge. It was a thirty-dollar bottle of wine—a nice one. She recognized what he brought as being extremely cheap. Like, under five dollars kind of cheap. No wonder he chose her wine. Strange that he would spend hundreds on a single seafood appetizer, then turn around and present a bottle of swill. Especially since he had a leather sommelier's journal and fancied himself an expert on wines.

Nelson took a seat on her counter stool while she poured them each a glass. He swirled and slurped the wine to ensure it was up to his standards before he took an actual drink. "So, from what Gates said, your new daddy's got money."

Her heart sank. Was everything about money for him? Was the bottle of wine he brought an indication of how much he thought she was worth? Or was he just some strange combination of cheap and extravagant? She ignored his comment, but a feeling of intense vulnerability washed over her. She wasn't going to play the game anymore. Tonight, she would ask Nelson to back off from buying the winery. If he agreed, then, and only then, would there be a possibility that she might be willing to date him.

Chapter Twenty-One

NELSON ATE ALL of the macaroni and cheese and half of a piece of lasagna but didn't touch the zucchini. He drank three glasses of wine and only asked Jessa one question about her father. "Do you think he put you in his will?"

Normally, Jessa would have been exasperated with a person who was so clearly obsessive about money. She would have been completely done with Nelson Tucker ... except for that he seemed nervous. Yes, Mr. High and Mighty, Mr. Rich and Suave, was *nervous*.

"Nelson," Jessa asked, sipping at the same glass of wine she'd had since the beginning of the meal. "Why did you want to go on another date with me? You said you were used to dating supermodels and CEOs. I'm just an island girl."

"Listen," he said, tapping his fingers on the table. "I've got five sisters. They love to light me up and give me hell for every little thing I do. I noticed right away that you're not like that. You probably step over ants on the sidewalk." He laughed. "And you cook a mean mac 'n' cheese."

"Remember playing that ice-breaker game at the Dogwood? You said there were eight kids in your family?"

"Yeah, I've got a big family. Grew up on a farm."

"I thought you were from New York." Nelson Tucker grew up on a farm? How was that possible?

"I went to school in the city, and I have a place there now, but I grew up on the Mississippi Gulf."

Instantly, she saw him in a different light. "No way! I never would have guessed that you were Southern."

"It's not something I go around bragging about," he said. "I worked hard to lose my accent."

Jessa rested her elbow on her big wooden table. "What did y'all grow on the farm?"

He hesitated before he answered, "Earthworms."

She chuckled and covered her smile with her hand. "You can't be serious. Next, you're gonna say you raised fire ants and cockroaches."

"I'm not kidding."

Jessa could tell by the way his face fell when she made her little joke that he truly wasn't kidding. A shift in the balance of power was threatening, and she felt herself gaining momentum. She needed to settle the air before he got defensive. "Oh, shoot. I'm sorry. I've just never heard of an earthworm farm before."

"It's quite lucrative."

"As fertilizer? Or bait?"

"The castings from the red wigglers make great compost."

So, Nelson Tucker grew up on a poop farm. She tried

not to look amused while it dawned on her that maybe she'd misjudged him again. She'd always seen people from big cities like the cities themselves—braggarts with their tall buildings and smorgasbord of businesses screaming to be visited and revered, begging for their self-importance to be affirmed. Maybe Nelson wasn't that way at all. Maybe the man could cast a line and gut a fish. Maybe he'd brought his own cooler cup to the local bar and sipped beer on a hot day while kids ran free out back. Maybe he listened to stories from leathery men with tattooed hands and names like Tank and Ace from long ago days in the military. That would be a Nelson she could relate with. That would be a Nelson she could like without question.

Nelson looked like he would rather be in a fancy restaurant than stuck in an old bungalow with a girl who was gaining steam with her questioning.

She saw her opportunity, and she took it. "Can I ask you something?"

He nodded again.

"Are you really considering buying the Saltwater Winery?"

"Yes." He lit up when he said the word. "You know, that winery is Duke Bradley's second career. He was retired when he started it."

Of course she knew that. She worked there. She kept her face passive.

"He took a *risk*. I respect him for that. It's been a big

payday for him. But let's face it, someone needs to take that place off his hands before he ruins it."

Jessa skipped over the offensive *ruining* part to ask a more important question. "Is he ready to sell?"

"Doesn't matter. Money talks. I've got an investor lined up. We can make that place nice, like a Napa winery or some place in France. We call that low-hanging fruit in the business. It's easy to see where we can make improvements—the whole vibe needs to change. We'll handle most of it with marketing."

"Libby does the marketing now, and I think she's pretty good." As abrasive as Libby's personality might be, she did a darn good job getting the word out and branding the winery as both rustic and high-quality.

He chuckled. "We've got people for that. Like, a whole department, not just one little girl."

Jessa felt her hackles rise. Libby was no little girl.

"The first thing I'm going to do is get rid of all the vermin wandering around. They give the impression that the place is rinky-dink. No one wants a redneck winery."

"We have a great pest control company. There aren't any vermin."

"Those two old goats and the chickens. Aren't there some cats too?"

She felt her face grow red. This was supposed to be a person who grew up on a farm? Farm folks appreciated animals. "They are not vermin. They live there and the customers love them. It's not redneck at all."

"They're filthy."

The man who grew up with earthworms thought goats, chickens, and cats were filthy? "Have you talked to Duke about it yet?" She worked to keep her voice light.

"Not yet."

What gave Jessa hope was the fact that Duke didn't need the money. The man was happy to stay at Nana's cottage and get free breakfasts from Cornelia. He didn't have children to leave an inheritance, and he owned everything he wanted. "So, do you just make an appointment and then tell him how much you want to buy it for? Is that how it works?"

"We try to be a little more sophisticated. I'm gonna schmooze him first. Get him to like me."

"Did they teach you how to do that in school?"

"It's a God-given talent, baby." He smiled proudly. "I get whatever I want."

"So, like manipulation techniques?"

"Masterful manipulation," he laughed. "No, no. I just know what appeals to people. You've got to get at their ego. People will do whatever I want if I just push the right buttons. You understand? You have to figure out what their currency is."

He leaned back in the counter stool so far, she was afraid he might tip over backward.

"His wife died, right? See, I did my homework. She is part of his currency. So, if we promise to keep that garden or name a wine after her, that will be meaningful to him. Get what I'm saying?"

Jessa was more horrified with every word that came from his mouth. Nelson planned to take advantage of Duke.

"Also, Duke's an old fart. So if I convince him that letting us grow the brand will be his legacy, he'll like that. Everybody wants to be remembered. The other great thing about him is that he has no heirs. Once he corks off, we're free to do whatever we want."

Jessa had to put down her wine glass—it was visibly shaking in her hand. Between her father being Mr. Warter, Dottie not keeping her word, and now this, she'd had enough. She was definitely done being nice. "You are a horrible person."

He was taken aback. "What?"

"You're going to take advantage of Duke? You're going to lie to him? And then what?" She hadn't raised her voice like that since she was a child. She burned with the ferocity of it. "Would you really fire Libby? Not to mention, me and my mother? You're going to kick Skip and June out of their home? And the cats and chickens?"

He laughed. Nelson had the audacity to *laugh*. "I'm a businessman. That's what we do."

"I don't believe that. There are businessmen and *women* who actually care about people. There are people on this planet who actively try to make it better." Her voice shook as she spoke.

"Like your dad?" He chuckled in a series of judgmental grunts. "You're living in a dreamland if you think he didn't step all over people to get where he is."

Nelson did *not* just bring up Trigger Warter. She seethed. "You realize I've known he is my father for less than a day, right? Where is your heart? Do you care about anyone other than yourself?" So much for her plan to sweetly manipulate him. Now that she'd given herself permission to be angry, it burst forth like a fire hose.

He stood and grabbed his bottle of cheap wine from the counter. "And here I thought you were actually nice."

"Not anymore, I'm not. I'm done with people lying and manipulating. I'm done with selfishness and greed."

"Yeah," he said as he opened the front door. "Well, it sounds like you're mad about your daddy and instead of yelling at him, you're putting it all on me. Pretty only goes so far, you know. This is not an attractive side of you." He shut the door, and a second later, pulled out of her driveway.

Her stomach clenched like she'd been gut-punched. Had she just made a huge mistake? Not only had she failed to convince Nelson not to buy the winery, she'd sent him running away.

Jessa immediately texted Gates, hoping he was in Charleston. *"Can you come out to Goose Island?"*

Chapter Twenty-Two

As soon as Nelson left, Jessa had a good cry. Her thoughts were all over the place. He was awful, right? He was the enemy. And yet, he wasn't. She had to admit that she'd been softening toward him. She liked his kisses. What began as a manipulation might be having the unintended effect of tearing down her walls. She'd given him her attention, made him a priority, and forced herself to get to know him. It was hard to hate a person who was becoming known to her. The moment he'd uttered the words *earthworm farm* he became more three-dimensional. Nelson Tucker might be more like her than she'd realized. The fact was, he wasn't evil—maybe just off-track. Maybe what he needed was someone like her in his life. Maybe he was trainable. Only now, thanks to the one and only time she'd allowed herself to lose her temper all over someone other than Dottie or Tootie, he was certainly convinced she was awful.

She felt like the whole world was pressing down on her like the stone of a gristmill, grinding her to bits. She desperately needed to get out from underneath all of the questions that weighed so heavily. Vulnerability might be considered a strength, but in that moment, it was turning her inside out. She was wearing her fragility on the outside like a too-small see-through out-of-date party dress. Something needed to be done. If she couldn't deal with Nelson in that moment, she would deal with her mother.

Jessa got in her car and drove directly to Uncle Fred's gas station. The whole way there, it felt like her heart was in her throat.

Her old camp buddy and current coworker, Libby, was walking out as Jessa walked in.

"Hey!" Libby said much too cheerfully.

"Hi, Libby. Can't talk now."

In a rare act of kindness, Libby held the door for her and didn't say another word. Gossip about Jessa's dad must have reached the winery employees already. Jessa went straight to the sandwich counter. There were two customers in the store, and Fred was flipping a chicken breast on the griddle with his back to her. "Uncle Fred," she said over the piped-in seventies music and sizzling food. "Can we talk?"

He didn't bother to turn around. "Meet me out back in ten minutes," he said. "And flip the sign to CLOSED."

Jessa sat on the deck of his houseboat with Whiskey at her feet until Fred ambled out to meet her. "You all spun up?" he asked.

"Nelson just left, and Mama is a disaster and Mr. Warter? Trigger Warter is my dad? I don't know which way is up right now."

"One thing at a time. Talk to Gates," Fred said. "Talk to him about Nelson, alright? A man with an ego as big as Nelson's usually turns out to be small."

Jessa nodded. "I already asked Gates to come out." That was probably good advice. Gates knew Nelson better than any of them. "Will you tell me about Mama?"

"It's a lot for one day," he said. "Are you sure you want to hear this?"

"You know what I think, Uncle Fred? I think it sucks to be in limbo. At least if I knew the truth, I could deal with it. Wondering and trying to fill in the blanks is messing with my head."

"But knowing can be hard too."

"Well, I'd rather know. I don't care if it's hard."

He pulled up a beach chair and sat beside her. "I have to warn you that your mother might show up and interrupt us. She's been feeling puny about all of this, and you know what happens when that woman gets deep in her feelings—Lazy Daisy Dottie morphs into the Histrionic Hulk. You want a beer?"

Jessa said yes for the beer and tried to send a strong mental message to her mother to stay away. Fred returned a minute later with his little red cooler. He popped open a bottle for her, then spent some time petting Whiskey and looking pensive as he collected his thoughts.

Gravel crunched as a car drove up and parked. They could hear someone tugging on the locked front door of the store. "Do you think that's Mama?"

"Naw, she'd have hollered for me by now." Fred took a swig of beer. "So, here's the story. Dottie'd been working as a bartender and living in a nasty old apartment with your Grandma Boone—by that time, our family didn't own land anymore and Grandma Boone couldn't function without half a bottle of vodka in the morning, much less pay bills and put food on the table."

"And that's when Mama had me," Jessa said.

He nodded. "Dottie having a child out of wedlock did not help the Boone reputation in these parts, I can tell you that. But as much as everyone was telling your mama she couldn't raise you, you know how she is. *Can't never could* was what she'd say. There was no way she was gonna give you up."

Jessa always thought her mother had tricked a man. The revelation still felt impossible after a lifetime of believing her mother was selfish and conniving. "She really didn't do it on purpose."

"No, she didn't do it on purpose." Uncle Fred put a hand on her shoulder. "It was never some sort of devious plan like she tells it."

"She didn't even have a place of her own."

"I thought I'd have to send her money," Fred said, "help her to rent a place or something after Mama died and the Social Security stopped. Then ol' Trigger Warter stepped up. That house you were raised in? That was one of his rentals, and he signed it over to her. I don't know if Cornelia knew about that part. She still might not know. Now, I get that it might have been a hush house. He might have been buying your mother's silence. But it was a house just the same."

Jessa had never thought about it. Not once did she wonder why Dottie never talked about having a mortgage. It'd been paid off from the get-go. Trigger Warter might not have been part of Jessa's life growing up, but he did put a roof over her head.

"DeWayne!"

Dottie's annoyed voice flew at Jess and Fred like a bullet through the night air. "I know y'all are out there gossiping about me." She must've been walking fast with how quickly her voice got nearer.

"Carolina Jessamine, if you have questions, you need to come straight to the horse, got it?" She was now climbing up the old marine ladder onto Fred's deck.

"Is that right, Mama? 'Cause I've been asking you my whole life and you have never given me an answer." Jessa made no move to welcome her mother on board. Her cell phone was a good distraction. It had been buzzing over and over again in her pocket, so she took it out and set her eyes on it instead of her mother. It was Gates calling. She texted him that they were behind the gas station in the houseboat.

"Need a beer, Dorothea?" Fred asked, already handing her one. "I was about to tell her about our mother."

"Good Lord. Imma need the whole case." Dottie unfolded a chair and sat across from Jessa. Big dog Whiskey and little squirrel Roscoe were now the centerpiece and the footwarmers for the circle of three.

Having her mother there stirred up the blackwater swamp of Jessa's emotions, and she considered getting up and leaving out of spite. She wouldn't say a word; she'd just get up and go. She could always apologize to Uncle Fred later. She didn't want her mother's defensiveness, or more of her lies. But she didn't move fast enough. Fred was already talking.

"Your grandma fell in the bathroom and cracked her head before you were born," he said.

Dottie popped open the bottle and took a lengthy swig of beer. "I found her."

"If you don't mind my sayin' so, Dot, that set you back a bit."

"Those weren't the happiest days, that's for sure."

"Mama, you never told me that," Jessa said.

"I think I speak for us both when I say it wasn't exactly a wallop," Fred said. "We weren't too upset about it. Our mother's passing was a blessing."

Dottie took another swig of beer and agreed.

They all sat quiet with their thoughts for a while. The sun was fading, and a lone cricket struck a chord, inciting the rest of the insect band to join in. Even a couple of hoots rang out from a nearby owl gearing up for a nighttime hunt. It would have been a beautiful evening if Jessa's stomach wasn't in as many knots as one of Dottie's macrame plant hangers.

"Carolina Jessamine, I hope you can see that there is good reason why we didn't tell you this story sooner," Dottie said.

"Not good enough reason the way I see it. I've been an adult a long time now." She shook her head like her mother was exasperating. "I want the whole thing—all of the daddies—yours, mine, and Tootie's. And make it fast. Gates is on the island, and I told him to meet me here."

"This is not a conversation to be had in a hurry," Fred said. "Frankly, I think it would be better to hold off."

If it had been Dottie saying that, Jessa would have pushed back. But she had a different sort of respect for her Uncle Fred. She trusted that he knew what he was doing. "Tell me something, okay? I need you to give me something."

Both Fred and Dottie nodded, so Jessa bit her tongue and waited while they all surrendered to their own thoughts, the cold taste of beer, and the soft snoring, chirping, and rustling of the creatures around them. Dottie looked like she was meditating on her beer bottle. She stared at it so hard her eyes were somewhat crossed.

Jessa took another deep breath as she waited for them to speak. She recognized how surreal her day had been. This time last night, she'd been stuck underground in the cold wondering if the cellar would be the spot where she died. Then she was rescued by the man who had abandoned her at birth. The one who had been living down the road in the same house as her best friend. Now her mother was across from her sinking deeper into her nylon chair looking perfectly serene, like she had nothing to be ashamed of, like she'd done nothing wrong. The woman wouldn't admit to her bad choices if they lunged at her like a gator and bit her on the butt. Had she loved Trigger Warter? Was the night Dottie and Trigger made her the one and only time they'd slept together?

Jessa jiggled her legs like she'd had too many cups of coffee. To top it all off, she was nervous about Gates showing up. Of all the swirling emotions she was feeling, why was one of them the jitters about Gates?

"Mama, at least tell me why you did it. Why did you get with him if you knew he was supposed to marry Cornelia?"

"I got with him because of my mother, but I let him off the hook because of Cornelia," she said. "I knew my place, and I knew yours. Don't think for a second that your shiny little face would have been on the Warter family Christmas cards. Cornelia would have made your life a living hell."

"What did Grandma Boone possibly have to do with you sleeping with a man, Mama? That doesn't sound right." There would be no dancing around it. Jessa was in a hurry and ready for answers.

"Grandma Boone was all about aspirations and expectations," Fred interjected. "She put them on us so much that we finally figured out what they truly were." He cut his eyes to Dottie. "Her sort of expectations were just resentments made in advance. She never expected us to live up to them, she was purposefully setting us all up for disappointment."

Dottie nodded. "It's not like I planned to get with Trig. I never even thought about what he could do for me at the time," Dottie said. "He was just someone I knew. He was from a family my mother respected. I felt an air of change around him, and I thought that hopefulness came from meeting my mother's expectations, if you can imagine that. I was actually excited to tell her that I slept with Trigger. Turns out, whatever I was feeling wasn't for her. It wasn't even about him. The good thing I sensed was you."

Dottie had always said things of that nature. If there was one thing she exceeded at as a mother, it was making her daughters feel wanted.

"So, you never loved him," Jessa said.

"No, I never did. But I never hated him either."

Chapter Twenty-Three

JESSA SAT WITH the new information while Dottie and Fred told stories of Grandma Boone, all of which added up to a troubled woman with a big problem. None of Dottie's happy childhood stories had been true—she'd been creating a narrative for her daughters so they would believe they came from good, upstanding stock. Dottie had decided that if she didn't like her history, she would change it for her daughters. All the stories were just talk anyway. Heck, people didn't know for sure if the actual history books they taught in schools were correct. People were people and they told tales to make themselves look better. The truth was, Tootie's mother and uncle grew up with a woman who wished to be more—a woman who kept herself down with addiction and put all of her wants and needs onto her kids. It wasn't a childhood of war heroes and meat sauce recipes like Jessa had been told. It was a childhood of poverty and emptiness and the only slimmest threads of hope. When Fred left with a college scholarship he'd earned through hard work and exceptional smarts, Grandma Boone trampled over Dottie like a two-ton elephant let loose from its rope. Trigger

Warter's brief attention turned out to be Dottie's opportunity to escape. Trigger Warter, even though he married Cornelia, was the best thing that ever happened to Dottie Boone.

The streetlight in the parking lot was on, and the old painted SUNBEAM BREAD sign on the side of the building glowed in the spotlight. Every nerve was on edge as Jessa waited for the sound of Gates's car. By the time he arrived, she was exhausted. Her body had no more adrenaline to give. She was completely wiped out. His tall shadow hit the SUNBEAM BREAD sign before he walked past, and Dottie yelled for him to join them on the deck of the boat.

"I was hoping to steal Jessa away from y'all if that's alright," he said, easily peering over the hull without climbing up. His short hair, muscular physique, and confidence made him look like a hero from the cover of a romance novel.

"Sure." Jessa jumped up, eager to climb down the ladder.

"Hold up." Dottie acted like she was sniffing at the air around her. "What is that?"

"What is what, Mama?" Jessa took to the ladder while Gates stood ready to catch her in case she slipped and fell.

"It's the air around y'all. Just like I sensed before. There's something here. Can you smell it, Fred?"

"Dottie, the only thing I can smell is yeast and hops."

"Jessa, I feel it in my hands."

"But it started with your nose, Mama, so that means it could blow over."

"I said it's in my hands now." When Dottie felt something in her hands, it required action.

Jessa was on the ground now, walking as quickly as she could away from the boat with Gates following closely behind her. "Shake 'em out, Mama. It's nothing. See y'all later." She practically ran around the building to Gates's car.

He opened the passenger door for her, and she climbed in.

By the time they were both in the car, he'd already made himself clear. "Don't go to Charleston with Nelson. Don't stay overnight with him." He whispered the word *overnight* like it was dangerous. "I should never have brought him here. It's my mistake, and I'm so, so sorry."

"I'm pretty sure that trip has been canceled," Jessa said. "We had a fight."

Gates looked confused. "You don't fight with people," he said.

"I got fed up with being nice."

"Well, thank God." Gates exhaled loudly. "Remember when Ruby went missing and our first thought was that Nelson might have something to do with it?"

"I mean, that only lasted for a second. Clearly, he didn't deserve it."

"But why did our minds go to him?"

"I don't know." The car was on, but they still hadn't left the parking lot.

He shifted to face her. "There's something off about him."

"I don't think that's it," she said. "We jumped to conclusions because we didn't know him. We don't know anyone like him." Her words felt true and right, even though the dream she'd had about him as Ruby's murderer was still burned into her memory.

That dream was completely unfair. Nelson had done nothing to deserve it.

"I know plenty of people like him," Gates said. "Nelson grew up with tons of money. I know he told you about the earthworm farms. I promise you he wasn't out there getting his hands dirty. The town is named for his family, and he's like the prince of it."

"Please don't tell me it's called Tucker Town."

"Tuckerville."

That brought about a giggle. "Okay, but he left that and became a successful businessman, right? He's making his own way." As she said the words, she wondered why she was defending him. Finally, she'd had an opinion, she'd held her ground, and now guilt was making her second guess herself. Nelson had definitely come across as conniving, but maybe she just didn't understand the business world and what it took to make money. Maybe she was too soft.

"Jessa. Maybe I don't have a good reason to stop you from seeing Nelson, but I care about you. If he still wants to take you to Charleston, please don't go."

Jessa liked the fact that he said he cared. "I'm an island girl who didn't go to college. I live in a tiny cottage with thrifted furniture and two acres of weeds." She thought of her mother using a one-night stand to get herself a better life. She thought of how much Trigger Warter would probably be proud of her for getting a guy like Nelson. "You know what, Gates? I shouldn't have gotten so mad at him for thinking about buying the winery. Like he said, it's just business. I was letting my emotions get in the way. And as soon as I found out he grew up on a farm, I realized that I really didn't know him at all. I'm just making up stories about him in my mind. It's not one bit fair to him."

"Well, I'm not making up stories about him. I'm doing what people do when they use their God-given intuition to keep themselves safe, and I'm telling you, you shouldn't stay with him."

It didn't go without notice that the very person who was badmouthing Nelson was also the one who brought him to the island. "Maybe he's the best thing to ever happen to me," Jessa said. As much as she didn't want to be like her mother, maybe that was the lot she'd been given in life. Maybe she needed a man to rescue her.

"Maybe he's the worst."

They were both quiet. Jessa had wanted to download all of the things that had been going on in her life lately and get Gates's advice. Or, if she was really honest, she wanted to feel his support and compassion. Now, she was stuck on the thought that Trigger Warter would be proud of her for winning over a guy like Nelson. Trig and Nelson were the same, weren't they? They knew about money and investments and the finer side of life. Surely, Trig would be more likely to embrace her, invite her over, and call her his daughter, if she was on the arm of an equally successful man. Nelson could, by his earnings alone, change her standing in society.

She must apologize to him immediately and do everything she could to make things better. "I'm sorry," she said to Gates. "You're such a good friend and I appreciate you so much. I just keep making mistake after mistake and now I've got to fix them. I'll call you soon." She barely said goodbye when she got out of his car.

"Jess," he began, in time for her to slam the door.

Getting home was a blur. She could hardly remember driving at all, she was just suddenly opening her front door. She didn't want the dinner she'd made for Nelson. She put it all in glass containers and shoved it into the refrigerator. In the pantry was a box of Ding Dongs. Chocolate for dinner would be just fine. If there was one good thing about living alone it was that there was no one around to judge. One step past the kitchen, and she saw it—another gift pushed through the milk door. "Nelson," she said aloud, picking up the box.

She took it to the kitchen counter and untied the thick white ribbon, then carefully removed the pearlescent white paper. The box said CROGHAN'S JEWEL BOX and inside was a crystal camellia bowl. A typed note said, IN THE MIDDLE

OF WINTER, THE CAMELLIA BLOOMS. IT REMINDS ME OF YOU—ABLE TO FLOWER AND SHINE IN THE HARDEST OF CIRCUMSTANCES.

Thank God, she'd been forgiven.

Immediately, she texted him. *"I am so sorry for my rudeness. You are right. I was upset about my father and I took it out on you."* Then she added, *"I don't usually behave that way."*

Nelson texted back immediately. *"We all have bad days."*

She almost invited him to Brooke's birthday party the following night, but she'd already planned to go with Gates. If Gates canceled, she would invite Nelson.

Jessa should have slept immediately. It'd been a long and emotionally draining day. But she got caught up in searching out every last photo of Trigger Warter from her camera roll and from Brooke's social media. She spent hours zooming in and staring at his face. She had Dottie's light eyes, but Trigger's wide, toothy smile. And, although she'd never noticed before, upon finding hundreds of photos of her and Brooke side by side, they definitely resembled each other. It was their face shape—high cheekbones and a delicate chin.

When she awoke, the soft early morning sun was streaming through her window. It felt like a milk door surprise, like the sun was saying *Here's a gift for you—a brand-new day.* The best part was, it was Saturday, and she had Brooke's birthday celebration at the Dogwood that night. She needed a good party.

Chapter Twenty-Four

"I TELL YOU what," Nana said as soon as Jessa climbed the hill from the boat dock, "the Dogwood is growing like a dandelion weed. I don't know how my granddaughter plans to have a birthday party with all of the people coming in off the water looking for food and pretty little spots to relax. It's not even the season! Just wait until it's warm again. My little auditorium won't be large enough to fit 'em all in. We're going to need more chairs, at least." She took a breath and studied Jessa. "What's going on with you, dear? Your face is pale, and those dark circles are not becoming."

Jessa acted chipper as she said, "Nothing's going on. I'm fine."

Nana squinted at her. "You are not fine. And you're here alone. Where's that fancy-pants boy you've been seeing?"

"I'm not seeing anyone right now."

"Bless your heart. What happened?" Nana was the queen of the well-placed *bless your heart.* It meant she was on to her. Nana was a consummate pro.

"Nothing happened."

"Right," Nana said. "Nelson Tucker was his name, I believe. I will make sure my Duke knows that you are no longer seeing him."

"Well, I might be," Jessa began. "I might be seeing him again later."

"Dear heart, I can see more with one eye than your mama claims to see with two."

Jessa chuckled good-naturedly. "Things are just a little crazy right now."

"Tell you what," Nana said, taking Jessa's hand and squeezing it tight. "Cornelia's making pork chops Wednesday night. I'll have her put on another one. Why don't you join us for a nice family dinner?"

"Oh." Jessa nearly choked.

She knew full well that Cornelia's dinners were sacred—they were showtime, like the large front window of their formal dining room was a movie screen for all of the neighbors to watch. Jessa had been best friends with Brooke her entire life and she'd never been allowed to stay. Not once.

"I don't think they'll want me at dinner."

"There's nothing to hide anymore, dear. You are a Warter as much as the rest of us. If you're not ready, I understand. But if you see fit to join us, wear a dress and be at the house by six. I promise, you are most welcome."

Jessa watched Nana walk away, feeling more alone than ever. She'd finally gotten the invitation she'd always hoped for. Now she had four days to get in the right head space to go.

Jessa approached the dining hall, the doorway flanked with balloons of pastel yellows, greens, pinks, and purples. The room was full of unfamiliar faces. It was clear that Brooke and Jessa were both in the *scatter* and *make new* phase of their lives. So many friends Brooke and Jessa had in common were now living elsewhere and couldn't make it to the party, and new friends that Brooke had made without Jessa showed up. There were no more built-in friend groups and entire lives in common. No more *if you invite one, you have to invite them all.* Friendships were now about going with the flow and accepting the new and different. Jessa tried to remind herself that change was good, but she couldn't help but feel relieved when Gates walked in. They were supposed to go to the party together, but neither of them had reached out to coordinate the ride. She should have felt badly about that. Or maybe he should have. Either way, he still felt like her buoy in the water—her solid thing to hold on to while a mysterious new sea swirled around her. That was the benefit of being friends for so long—one little tiff would never ruin all those years of knowing each other.

She made a line straight for him. "Hey! Did you see Brooke's cake? She's doing a pull, and you know how much I love a good charm. I still have that old bracelet from when we were little, and I like to add …"

Gates interrupted her without a smile. "You should get the antlers." Then he walked away.

The antlers? That was the charm meant for a person who

needed to take the reins in their life. It meant they weren't in control. *Rude.* So much for the new and improved Carolina Jessamine Boone—the woman who spoke her mind and didn't run her life according to other people's feelings. She stomped off in the opposite direction and quickly realized she was headed straight for Cornelia and Trigger. That required an abrupt about-face and out-the-door.

Just like her old days at camp, she made her way to the jumping rock where she could sit with her legs dangling over the water and be alone with her thoughts. That peace and tranquility lasted about seven and a half seconds. "Jess!" Brooke yelled from the top of the hill. "Jessa, get over here!"

Jessa didn't want to answer her best friend. She wanted to sit with her sickening feelings of confusion and loneliness. She wanted to wallow in her suffering and, for the moment, blame it on everyone else. But Brooke was her best friend, and it was her birthday, so Jessa was obliged to answer. "I'm not here!" Jessa yelled back. "You can't see me."

Brooke was jogging down the hill. "You know you're not invisible unless you eat the steamed carrots." It was a reference to a game they used to play at camp when they were forced to eat whatever vegetable was slapped onto their plastic plates.

"Give them to me. I will eat ten thousand of them. Give me the nasty carrots so no one can see me."

Brooke was standing on the edge of the water looking at Jessa. "We're about to do the cake pull and you're my best friend, so you have to pull first."

"Pull for me."

"Jess. I know this is hard. I know that my folks are here and that things are messy right now. But the only way past this is through it. Come with me. We'll do it together."

Funny how Brooke was under the mistaken assumption that Jessa was upset about Trigger and Cornelia when the fact was, she was more spun up about boys. Good God in heaven, she was back to the days of wondering who she was and whether anybody liked her. Her life was completely turned around.

"I'm coming," she said, slowly standing. "Did you label the ribbons or is it a free-for-all?"

"Mine is labeled. Everyone else gets to choose."

"Awesome," Jessa said, certain that with her luck, she would tug on the ribbon attached to the golden antler charm stuck deep within the filling layer of the cake while Gates stood there gloating.

Almost any other charm would be preferable. Usually, she got something like an Eiffel Tower, which was fine, because she did like to believe that travel was coming. And she prayed she wouldn't get a bird because that meant she'd be next to have a baby and she would never, ever follow in her mother's footsteps. The charms had no real meaning, of course, but Jessa was just superstitious enough to care about which one she pulled.

Twenty-five of Brooke's closest friends, including Cornelia and Nana, stood around a small circular table holding a three-layer cake decorated with icing flowers and a large golden twenty-five on top. Hanging from in between each layer were pastel-colored ribbons streaming down the sides. Nana was in possession of her silver bedazzled microphone, so as soon as Brooke and Jessa walked in, she fired up the announcements.

"Cake time!" Nana declared. "Now, we've got twenty-five gals here for my granddaughter's twenty-fifth year. Each one gets a pull. Carolina Jessamine will start us off, and we will end with Brooke."

Jessa stepped up and chose a lavender ribbon attached to the second layer, noticing that the pink ribbon labeled with Brooke's name was the only one coming from the small top tier. She pulled straight out, bringing buttercream frosting along with a charm that she immediately put in her mouth to clean. Thank God, she'd pulled the key. It was supposed to signify that a brilliant love awaits. If she'd pulled that charm back in the old camp days, she would have been certain that love would be Gates. Now, she wondered if maybe it was Nelson. Her eyes scanned the room to see if Gates was watching, and she found him in a far corner with his back to the cake talking to someone. Nelson.

It hadn't occurred to her that Gates might invite him. Certainly, Brooke hadn't. It didn't seem right considering Gates had made the big declaration that she shouldn't go to Charleston with the man. Now he was inviting him to a party where he knew she'd be? It made no sense. And why hadn't Nelson told her he'd be there?

Typically, Jessa would paste a smile on her face and say hello like there was nothing wrong in the world. She'd done it for so long that it was easy to make her voice the tiniest bit high-pitched and imbue it with enthusiasm. But she wasn't playing those games anymore. She was in her strong girl phase, her *don't mess with me* era. As soon as Brooke pulled the final charm, Jessa would walk right up to Nelson and ask if she could have a word. In doing so, she would purposefully ignore Gates and give him a taste of his own medicine.

It was always interesting to see which girls loved the limelight. Some had their ribbon chosen well in advance and when it was their turn, they'd pull, then either lick the charm clean or wipe it with a napkin, exclaim over whichever one they got, and be done. Others kept the attention on them as long as possible, pretending to shop for a ribbon, they'd lift and inspect it, then peer at the cake as though they could see between the layers. One even looked around at the other girl's charms to guess what she might be getting before she actually pulled. It was all a test of Jessa's patience.

Cornelia pulled a conch shell, Nana pulled an elephant, and finally it was Brooke's turn. Jessa was engrossed in her own thoughts, practicing what she would say to Nelson, when Brooke pulled her light pink ribbon. She immediately stuck the charm in her mouth. When she took it out, Nate had miraculously appeared beside her—down on one knee.

Nana grinned from ear to ear, while Brooke and Cornelia went from shock to tears in tandem as a sparkling engagement ring hung on the ribbon in Brooke's hand. Jessa watched Trigger's face. He didn't look surprised, he looked proud. Nate had probably asked his permission. Every good Southern man asked for his future father-in-law's consent before popping the question. *Trigger Warter.* Would Jessa's future man ask his permission too?

She watched her best friend hug and kiss Nate, her face beaming joy and excitement onto him like a floodlight. They were a good match. Dottie would say a fated one. Jessa switched her focus to Gates, who was watching the scene with the tiniest smile on his face, his hair badly in need of a trim—one particular curl flipped in front of his ear and reminded her of Cornelia's hair-sprayed swoop that lay against her right cheekbone. Jessa felt outside of herself as if she was seeing the people around her for the first time. Who were they, really? What forces molded and influenced them? Were they happy?

Cornelia and Trigger hugged Brooke simultaneously, then opened their arms to Nate. It was a touching family hug, and Jessa was hyperaware of the fact that she wasn't a part of it. Just as she felt herself begin to shrink, an arm fell across her shoulders and Gates pulled her into his chest. He held her especially tight and especially long but never said a word.

When she finally took a step back, she could breathe

again. "Thank you," she said.

Again, he said nothing, but he looked at her in a way that said he understood. He understood that she felt alone and ostracized. She reached up and tucked the rogue curl behind his ear. She loved Gates Lancaster. She would always have love for him.

Nelson sauntered his way over to them, a sour set to his mouth. "Hey," he said like he was going to offer his hand to shake, then didn't. Instead, he stuck both hands in his back pockets and bowed his chest. "Nice party."

"Hi, Nelson," she said. "I didn't know you were coming to this."

Did he realize that he had subtly stepped in front of Gates and forced him to take a step backward? Jessa watched as Gates shrugged before leaving them to join the crowd congratulating Brooke and Nate. Jessa needed to join them too.

"Surprise," he joked.

She took a beat before bringing her eyes to Nelson's. "I think I should apologize again. I overreacted about the winery and about what you said about my father. I never should have said those things to you."

"It's all good," he said, looking away. "I didn't cancel our Charleston reservations if that's what you're wondering."

She didn't want to admit that she was wondering that exact thing. "I just want to make sure you understand."

"I mean, I don't usually put up with crap like that, but I

know you had a rough day, so I'll overlook it."

"Thanks," she said, feeling like she should be pleased, but for some reason, wasn't at all. "I need to go hug Brooke and Nate."

Chapter Twenty-Five

THE HOUSE WAS still and quiet when Jessa walked in. She turned on the light in the foyer and locked the door behind her. She should probably get a cat. Coming home to an empty house was lonely. She could easily take one of the many cats from her mother's house, and Dottie might never notice. She chuckled at the thought and flipped on the light to the kitchen.

There, in the pantry, was a package. A stinging adrenaline surged through her. Wrapped in plain brown craft paper, it could hold a copperhead inside for all she knew. She picked it up and shook it. Definitely not a snake. It was somewhat light, and nothing jiggled or knocked around.

She sat down on her kitchen stool with a *clunk*, placing the box on the counter. She used her shears to cut the ribbon, then tore off the paper like she wasn't afraid at all. It was a nice white cardboard box, one with strong sides and a proper lid. She pulled it open and inside was a creamy soft blanket. It felt like some sort of silky blend, something she could certainly never afford. It probably came from some fancy millinery in New York. Movie stars and billionaires probably had blankets just like it. Nothing of that quality would ever be sold at the places she shopped. She pulled it out and wrapped it around herself, then moved to the couch, where she turned on the television, cuddled up, and tried to feel some peace.

She really, really needed a cat.

Just as soon as she snuggled deeper into the couch, her doorbell rang.

She hated that stupid bell.

Someone jiggled the handle like they were going to let themselves in, but she had it locked up tight. Her instinct was to hide. But her car was outside, and the television was loud enough to hear. Whoever it was, knew she was there. "Who is it?"

"Gates."

Sure enough, when she opened the door, there he was, a specimen of fitness and good looks, with concern all over his face.

"Are you okay?" Jessa asked, stepping aside and opening the door as wide as it would go.

Surely, Gates felt some sort of regret for his ex-girlfriend of seven years getting engaged.

"I wanted to ask you the same thing." He came inside just far enough for her to close the front door.

"I'm super happy for them," Jessa said.

"Oh." He paused like he had to mentally catch up. "Yeah, me too." He led the way to Jessa's couch and sat.

She still wore the new blanket like a shawl as she sat beside him.

"Nelson's investor pulled out."

Jessa had never considered something like that might happen. "Who was his investor?"

"His dad, I think."

"Do you know why?"

"Apparently, he prefers to focus on a different type of farming. Something other than wine grapes."

"So, as simple as that?"

Gates nodded.

She stared at the black screen of the television, then down to her little stone fireplace beneath it as she let the information sink in. Nelson wasn't going to buy the winery. Since saving the winery had initially been her secret motivation, she'd just been freed from her duplicity. She didn't have to be disingenuous anymore. Nelson was now just a guy. A guy who happened to be interested in her. A guy who she couldn't quite figure out. A guy who seemed like the answer to her dreams one minute and an absolute nightmare the next.

"Listen," Gates began. "Nelson is a nice guy. He really is. I feel like I have to tell you that."

Jessa squinted up at him. Why did Gates feel it necessary to tell her that Nelson was a nice guy? Not to mention, he could have texted or called instead of dropping in unannounced.

"Do you want to stay in my guest room tonight? You don't have to drive all the way back to Charleston."

"I didn't bring any clothes. But, yeah, if you don't mind."

"I told Mama I'd go to Uncle Fred's tomorrow for breakfast. You want to join?"

"You know I do."

"Wanna watch a movie?" she asked.

"Yes." He seemed to melt into the couch. She took off the blanket she was still wearing and spread it across both of them.

It was nearly three A.M. when she awoke on the couch with her head on Gates's chest. He smelled familiar and … safe. Was it even possible for a man to smell safe? She listened to his soft breathing and felt his heartbeat against her cheek. Was it his confidence? His strength? She thought about that for a while. No, what made her feel safe was his affinity for her. He'd proven over the years that she was important to him, and she trusted him implicitly. Without a doubt, she knew that he would be devastated if something happened to her. They'd been friends for so long that he was like a brother. She stopped at that thought. No, he wasn't like a brother at all. She'd told herself that when he was dating Brooke. She'd tried to make it her truth. But it wasn't. She'd never had sisterly feelings for Gates. There had always been more.

She should jiggle him awake. They should both walk to

their respective bedrooms while they still had the chance to get some more comfortable sleep. Instead, she snuggled closer, closed her eyes, and stayed.

The next morning, Jessa awoke with her head still on Gates. He was awake, scrolling on his phone with one hand. She lifted her head.

"Stay cozy," he said in a sleepy voice. "You don't have to get up yet."

"What time is it?"

"Six thirty."

She rested for another minute. "Hey, Gates?"

"Mmm-hmm?"

"Did you bring Nelson to Brooke's party?"

She could feel his breath change and his heart rate increase. "I think I mentioned it to him, but I didn't invite him. And I didn't bring him there."

She could tell by the way he said it that there was something more. "What aren't you telling me?" She sat up so she could look him square in the face.

He looked guilty. It was the same look he had years ago when he'd kissed Jessa and then turned around and made Brooke his girlfriend.

"Gates. Tell me."

"Nelson said that he'd give me the account if I helped him get you."

"Get me?"

"As his girlfriend. He said it the first time he met you at

the winery."

She jumped up, her new blanket puddling on the floor. "So, this whole time you've been using me? You've been trying to throw me at him for money? Is that why you told me how nice he is? You're trying to convince me to be his girlfriend?"

"No, Jess. That's not it at all." Gates's hair was charmingly messy, and it only served to make her angrier.

"Why did you tell me not to go to Charleston with him if he's so nice?"

"Because—"

"No," she interrupted. "Don't even bother." She leaned into the anger even though it brought hot tears along with it. "Leave, Gates. I want you out of my house."

"Jess, I need to tell you—"

"Then tell me fast because I am fixing to pitch a big fit. A huge one."

"I chose Brooke because I thought you were too good for me."

"Well, I'm sure my *best friend* will be thrilled to hear that." Her face felt as hot as red coals.

"You're dangerous, Jess. You always have been. My heart isn't safe with you."

"I see. You care for me so much that you dumped me for my best friend and are now trying to force me to be a man's girlfriend so you can get his money. Yep, that's love all right. Nice work."

"Jess, please listen."

"No, you listen, Gates. Not only did you break my heart ten years ago, you reinforced to me that men are bad and can't be trusted. Now, all of these years later when I'm finally healing, and finally opening my heart to trust again, you do the same thing in a different way. I am so stupid."

"Don't say that."

"Leave, Gates."

Gates reluctantly walked to the foyer. "Jess, I brought it up because I want to tell you something. Please let me explain."

"I don't want to hear it." She opened the front door and waited for him to walk through it. As soon as he was on the other side, she slammed it shut. No more sweet Jessa. She was going to be strong even though it felt clunky, mean, and out of control. It didn't matter that he said he'd once thought she was too good for him or that she was dangerous. He deserved everything she'd said and more.

Once she heard his car leave, she went to the bathroom and brushed her teeth. Her hands shook and every time she looked at herself in the mirror, she had to fight back tears. She'd allowed Gates Lancaster to break her heart again, and in the process, she'd lost Nelson too. She couldn't be Nelson's girlfriend now, even if she wanted to. They were both sneaky liars.

Chapter Twenty-Six

It was a sweatpants and messy bun kind of Sunday morning. The church crowd would still be packed beneath the steeple in the little wooden church next to the sea, so Jessa was free to meet her mama and Uncle Fred at the gas station. She didn't bother with mascara or lip gloss. As far as she was concerned everybody and their brother needed to mind their own business.

A few minutes later, she parked next to Ruby's car. *Huh.* Ruby usually worked the night shift. There were a few other church-skippers in line for breakfast, so Jessa greeted all of them as she took her spot at the end. On Monday, the patrons would switch over to the tourists who stopped in on the way to the winery. Uncle Fred's little gas station was beginning to get a reputation as a hidden gem.

"Hey, Ruby!" Jessa said when she caught Ruby's eye.

Ruby immediately looked away. It struck Jessa as strange. They certainly weren't friends, but everyone on the small island went out of their way to at least be cordial. Except Duke. But that was expected. Had Jessa done something to upset her?

"Is Fred out back?" Jessa asked. "He usually works the mornings."

"I'm fillin' in," Ruby answered without looking at her. "Got himself some personal stuff happening, I believe."

The only personal stuff Uncle Fred had going on must involve Dottie. Who else was there? Considering the recent news about Trigger Warter, it probably involved Tootie too. Which must be why they'd asked her to breakfast.

The bell on the front door jingled as it opened, and like everyone else, Jessa turned to see who was walking in. Her heart nearly stopped. It was Nelson.

He seemed surprised to see her, then walked over and gave her a quick hug. "Good morning."

"You're on the island today?" Seeing him brought up all of the feelings from the night before. He was a liar. Instead of pursuing her like a normal person, he'd been bribing Gates behind her back. But this was no place to make a scene. She wasn't going to take on Nelson Tucker in the middle of her uncle's store on a Sunday morning. The man in front of her stepped aside, making it her turn to order. She smiled sweetly at Nelson and moved forward.

"What can I do for ya?" Ruby smirked and waited with her hip jutted out.

"I'd love a bacon biscuit and a cup of fruit. Also, a medium coffee with cream but no foam." She kept a smile on her face despite sensing hostility.

"Pig biscuit, melon, fat cow, no head." Ruby repeated it

like Jessa was supposed to understand her verbal shorthand, then turned and got to work.

"Thank you," Jessa said. The more someone was rude to her, the more she felt compelled to be nice.

Jessa stepped aside so that Nelson could have his turn at the counter. "The winery is closed today," she said, assuming that was why he was in her neck of the woods.

Then it occurred to her that maybe he'd come all the way to Goose Island to leave a gift at her milk door. She smiled sweetly at him and realized she'd never seen him so casually dressed. He was in jeans and a quarter-zip top—one that didn't have the logo of a fancy golf course like he usually wore.

"I just came for breakfast," he said.

They watched Ruby work. She was a pretty lady, probably in her early thirties. There was not a wrinkle on her pale skin, and with her hair pulled back in a scarf-tied ponytail, she looked especially young. Jessa wondered what Ruby's husband was like and whether she was still happy that they were back together.

The woman worked skillfully. She had the coffee going while she assembled the biscuit and had Jessa's order ready in just a few minutes. When she handed the bag and the hot paper cup across the counter, Jessa noticed that Ruby wasn't wearing a wedding ring.

"I've got to go out back for a little family meeting," Jessa said, wondering what gift Nelson had left for her at home.

"We'll coordinate later," he said, and began giving his order to Ruby, who no longer looked annoyed.

Jessa went out the back door thinking that *coordinate* was an interesting word to use. Very businesslike. Coordinate what? Their weekend together?

It was chilly that morning, so Uncle Fred and Dottie weren't outside on the open stern of the houseboat as usual. As a matter of fact, Fred had cleaned up the folding chairs and it appeared as if he'd even washed the boat.

Jessa climbed the ladder and found Fred, her mother, and some other person seated inside at the tiny space next to the galley kitchen. "Good morning," she said, placing her biscuit, fruit, and coffee on the table in front of the only empty seat. She turned to the unknown woman sitting next to her uncle. "Hi, I'm Jessa."

"Valerie," she said, holding out a dainty, red-manicured hand.

She was a beautiful woman with bright eyes, warm brown skin and a genuine smile. She was dressed in a smart beige sweater set paired with gold accent jewelry. She looked like one of Charleston's elites.

Jessa instantly knew the name. Valerie Barton. The woman Fred used to love. "It's so nice to finally meet you."

Valerie flashed a playful smile at Fred. "What did you tell her about me, DeWayne?"

"Not enough," he said, his eyes crinkling at the corners like her presence brought him joy. Then his eyes switched over to Dottie and his smile faded.

Something passed between them, and Dottie nodded her approval.

"Jess, Valerie is Tootie's aunt," Fred said.

Jessa took some time to process the statement. "So, you're her father's sister?"

"I am."

No wonder Tootie had the most beautiful skin tone, like a toasty little biscuit, especially in the summertime. "Mama. Who is he?"

Dottie shrugged. "I never knew him."

That was the most ridiculous statement Jessa had ever heard. "Right, Mama. It was an immaculate conception from the spirit above. You had nothing to do with it."

"She's telling the truth," Valerie said. "She never knew my brother."

The whole thing was very confusing. "Does Tootie have any idea what's going on?"

Dottie stiffened. "Not yet. We'll get to that later."

"You didn't know him? Mama, I have so many questions for you, I don't know where to start. It's like you've been living one life in front of us, but behind our backs you're out robbing banks and working the streets."

"Working the streets?" Dottie chuckled.

"You know what I mean."

"And you bet I've been out robbing banks, that's how I got my Ferrari and my condo in Paris."

Jessa's head was spinning. "How did you have a baby with a man you never met?" She was completely overwhelmed with the *who's my father and who's your father, and who's Tootie's father* drama. There were too many missing daddies.

"Hold up, now." Fred straightened his back and seemed to flip a switch in his brain that allowed him to fully engage in the conversation. "Before we start cursing the family, it's not what it looks like. We've got our share of dysfunction, but your mama's not at the center of it." Fred could always be counted on to act as the mediator. "My sister is a damn good mother." As soon as he said it, Dottie leaned back in her chair, allowing her brother to take over the story.

"We're not debating that, Uncle Fred."

Valerie spoke up. "When DeWayne and I were fresh out of law school, we went to Charleston one Christmas. My brother, his name was Vance, was mad as a hornet, and no amount of talking could get to him. At that time, my mama had ovarian cancer. And, you know how some folks age faster than others? Well, my daddy was as hunched over and skinny as a bent scarecrow."

"Her mother had her hands full," Fred said.

Jessa was listening, but all she could think was that Vance was the name of Tootie's father.

"The cancer was the kind that didn't come with many symptoms," Valerie said. "By the time she knew she had it, it was already too late. Poor Vance didn't know how to handle her loss except to be mad."

"We got walloped when Valerie's mother died." Fred reached out to hold Valerie's hand. "And her daddy died of a broken heart two months later."

"I was suddenly responsible for my brother. I was all he had."

"And that's when Mama met him?"

"I told you I didn't know the man!" Dottie raised her voice.

"Here's what you need to know," Valerie said. "On the day Vance was born, he went without oxygen for too long. There was brain damage because of it. He couldn't go to school like the rest of us, and for a long time, we didn't think he could hold a job."

Fred jumped in. "But he was strong, and he could follow directions, so he eventually got work at the docks."

"Mama! You had sex with a disabled man?"

"Carolina Jessamine!" Dottie threw a bottle cap at her. "Shut up and listen!" She sighed like she'd been put-upon and didn't appreciate it. "Do you remember when we got Tulip?"

"Of course! You said you were going to the hospital to have a baby, and you came home with her."

"And had you ever seen me pregnant?"

"I don't remember."

"I did go to the hospital. And I did come home with her. I just didn't birth her."

The truth sank into Jessa's body like the fangs of a venomous snake. Dottie wasn't Tootie's biological mother. "Oh my God. Oh my God, Mama. Tootie's not my sister?"

"She is," Fred said. "Just not by blood."

Jessa immediately moved on to the next burning questions. "Who is her mother? And where is Vance now?"

"He died in an accident at the docks years ago."

Poor Tootie. Poor, poor Tootie. At least Jessa knew her father. She was even having dinner with him on Wednesday night. Tootie never would.

"And her mother? Where is she?"

"That's a little more complicated," Valerie said.

Chapter Twenty-Seven

THE WINERY WAS busy when Jessa arrived on Monday. Harvest was still going strong, and seasonal workers crawled around the acreage, focused on the task at hand. Jessa knew many of them from years past. It was a symphony of good mornings as she went about feeding the cats and goats and releasing the silkie chickens. It was overcast and drizzly, and that made her more excited about Salty Dot's Food Truck working the winery that day. It wasn't for the food either. More than anything she wanted to hug her mother and hold onto her like she used to when she was little. Things between them hadn't magically become perfect between them from one revelation, but Jessa was experiencing again the reason why the world was gray to her. As soon as she started seeing relationships or issues as black-and-white, she was reminded that things weren't always what they seemed. All it took was some new information for her to see clearly that she hadn't been fair to her single mother. For the first time, she had a glimpse into how strong Dottie was. Not because she had strong opinions, and not because she raised her voice or talked back. She was strong because she cared, because she took on the hard work of a baby girl when no one else would. Jessa cringed at how she'd accused her mother of wretched things. The truth was that Vance had been a low-functioning man who happened to also be exceptionally good-looking. While working as a dock worker, a local addict had taken advantage of him. He had a pension and a decent income, but he didn't have the awareness to know when he was being used.

Fred and Valerie had saved Tootie from that horrible woman by literally paying her off. She'd planned to use Vance for his money and his daughter as blackmail. As far as they knew, that woman was somewhere in Louisiana. They'd lost track of her years ago.

Tootie might never recover once she found out. Her dad was dead, and her mother wasn't Dottie. As a matter of fact, her biological mother was an addict who might very well be dead too.

Jessa set down the bucket of chicken eggs she'd been collecting and pulled her phone from her pocket. There was a text from Nelson. *"Heading to the island again today. You at the winery?"*

Why would he be coming out this far again? He'd just been on the island for breakfast a day ago. Plus, his investor had pulled out. As far as she knew, he had no reason to come to the winery except to see her. *"Yes,"* she answered.

When she'd gone back home on Sunday after all of the revelations from Fred, Valerie, and Dottie, she'd been expecting something at her milk door. But there was nothing. That meant Nelson's presence on Goose Island for breakfast that morning was a big, fat mystery. She hadn't seen him for the rest of the day. And no one would drive all the way from Kiawah no matter how great Fred's biscuits were.

Dottie's big yellow truck pulled into the winery parking lot around eleven. Jessa left her office and ran outside as her mother was setting up the chalkboard sign with the words HAM, BLACK-EYED PEAS, COLLARD GREENS, AND CORNBREAD.

"Peas for pennies, green for dollars, and cornbread for gold," Jessa said as she approached.

"I'm making money today." Dottie smiled warmly at her.

"Did you put a carrot in those black-eyed peas?"

"I always do. I'm not gonna have my customers tootin' around like brass instruments. This is a winery, not a marching band."

"I won the lottery with you, Mama."

Dottie held her arms wide open before Jessa's sentence was finished. "Don't think that I ain't got regrets, all right?" Dottie said into her ear. "I wish I'd been able to give you a daddy. I really do. I'm just not the type to do a man's bidding."

"I know, Mama." Jessa was still in awe at how the anger she'd struggled with for years dissipated like fog on a hot day as soon as she discovered that Dottie had taken on the care of an abandoned child at the request of her brother and his girlfriend. Then she made that child believe she'd not only had her on purpose but bred her to be smart. She did it because she was determined that Tulip grow up feeling wanted. And because Tulip's biological father was not, through no fault of his own, conventionally smart, Dottie made sure that intelligence was never an issue for her daughter. And it worked.

"Do you think both of Tootie's parents are dead?" Jessa asked.

"Oh, no. Tulip's mother is alive and well right here," Dottie said, pointing at herself.

"You kept this to yourself all these years, Mama? You let people believe that you purposefully tricked men to get pregnant?"

Dottie aggressively grabbed a tissue from the box and blew her nose. "It was important to me that you had a strong mother, and that you both felt wanted."

Wanted? Yes, Jessa had always felt wanted by Dottie. There had never been a question about that. Tootie too. Their tight little family, with all of their quirks and problems, had always felt solid and right. The question was, would they still feel that way after Tootie found out?

"It's not a rule that a woman has to have a man in order to be happy, you know," Dottie said.

"I know, Mama." But Jessa also knew that having a man

around helped sometimes.

The whole reason Uncle Fred moved to the island was to be available for his sister and her daughters. It all made sense now—he felt a responsibility for Tootie. So did Valerie. At the time Tootie was born, Fred and Valerie had huge student loans and full-time jobs. It felt impossible for them to take on a new baby when they were building their careers. But Fred's sister could. Dottie's only requirement was that no one knew that Tootie wasn't actually hers. "How did people believe you if they never saw you pregnant?"

"Carrying a little extra weight around my midsection worked mighty well in this situation," Dottie said. "And I always did love a big T-shirt." Dottie shrugged like it didn't matter, then added, "It might be that folks kind of expected that sort of thing from me."

"I'm sorry, Mama," Jessa said.

All her life, Jessa had never considered the fact that her mother was quietly enduring years of being looked down upon, of being talked about, when the truth was that she'd actually been doing something so selfless that it was downright heroic.

"Do you think her mother tried to find her?"

"I don't think so. She was never really interested in the baby once she got her money. But we were careful. That's one of the reasons why Valerie moved away. We couldn't have that lady tracking her."

Dottie took Jessa back in for another hug and whispered

in her ear, "Why is Nelson Tucker hiding by that tree and looking at you like a heron about to spear a fish?"

Jessa's stomach turned sour. There was another issue to deal with. No matter how nice he was, or how misunderstood, Jessa was not going to be Nelson's girlfriend in order for Gates to get his account. As a matter of fact, she didn't appreciate that she'd been brought into their business dealings to begin with. The old Jessa would have ignored it all and quietly put distance between them, but the new Jessa wasn't going to look the other way.

Jessa walked right up to Nelson in his dark-fitted suit and RayBan sunglasses. "Don't you have work to do?" She didn't bother smiling.

"I make my own hours."

"And you needed your morning wine-tasting?"

He leaned against the tree and crossed his arms. "I just ... I feel like we need to talk."

"You're right."

He looked surprised that she'd agreed with him. "What do you need to talk to me about?"

"How you were trying to bribe Gates to get a date with me. You told him you would only give him your account if he set us up. That is sneaky and it makes you a liar."

He looked hurt. "How did I lie? Just because I didn't tell you? You should be flattered."

"Well I'm not. I don't want to be manipulated and pushed into something."

"I don't need to manipulate or push people into anything." There was no remorse, not even the slightest hint of regret in his voice.

"Can't you see how it's wrong?"

"How is it any more wrong that setting someone up on a blind date?"

"Because you held your account over his head! You were forcing him—and me—into it!"

"I don't need to force anyone to be my girlfriend. Do you see how offensive that is? How could you say to me?"

What he was saying actually made sense. Her anger was quickly losing steam. "I'm sorry," she said. "Maybe I'm wrong."

"Can we sit somewhere?" he asked.

Jessa was supposed to be working. "I don't have much time, but sure."

The sixty-degree day felt warm in the sun, so they found a spot at an unshaded picnic table. Nelson unbuttoned his suit coat and leaned onto the old, weathered wood. "I like you, Jessa. You need to know that."

"I like you too." It was true. She didn't have any reason not to like him.

"You're not the kind of girl who would go out with a man for his money."

"Of course not. Never. I'm very happy with my life the way it is."

"But you're still going to Charleston with me."

She didn't understand why he'd just said that. "People date and spend time together to see if they're compatible, right?"

"Do you really want to add me into your life?"

Jessa watched a squirrel chase another one up a tree. "I can't answer that yet. I'm still trying to figure out who you are."

"You know that I'm not looking at buying this place anymore, so your whole thing about me bribing Gates is null and void."

"Right." She was realizing how much she'd over-reacted. The fact was, Gates had told her not to got to Charleston with him. There might have been a behind-the-scenes deal in the works, but Gates never really tried to force them together, aside from telling her that Nelson was nice.

"And you're still going to Charleston with me?"

He had to bring it up again? "Why do you keep asking me that?"

"Because I don't believe in wasting my time."

"I can't promise you that, Nelson."

He ran a hand through his hair. "I don't want you to see Gates again."

"What?" She leaned back so far, she nearly fell off the bench. "Why would you say that?"

"Because I want you to be my girlfriend."

He couldn't have asked in a more unromantic way. "Gates has been my friend since I was a kid. I can't just suddenly stop talking to him."

"He told me he stayed over at your place."

Heat spread across her cheeks. So, that was why he came all the way out there? "Well, he used to stay with the Warters, but now that he's not dating Brooke anymore, there's no bed for him on the island."

"So you gave him yours."

"He slept on the couch." So had she, with her head on his chest, but she opted to leave that part out. "He knows he can always have my guest room."

"And yet he slept on your couch."

"What are you accusing me of, Nelson?"

"Just be mine, Jessa. And stay away from him."

"I can't do that, Nelson. He's my friend."

"Do you like me enough to be my girlfriend?"

How to answer when she really didn't know? This vulnerable side of him was new. What other sides of him had she not yet seen? "I think so. Probably. I mean, we don't know each other that well."

"Then let's just start here, okay? With the probably." He stood and moved to the spot next to her on the bench, sitting as close as possible. His arm was around her and the thick fabric of his suit jacket was so warm it was almost hot. His cologne smelled musky as he kissed her on the temple. She wanted to kiss him. She wanted to make up for the fact that she may have been wrong about her accusation, so she turned and met his lips. The way he kissed her back, the way he claimed her as both a victory and a relief, she was aware that, even though she hadn't technically said *yes*, she was now Nelson Tucker's girlfriend.

Chapter Twenty-Eight

THERE WAS A tour group scheduled that afternoon. Thirty people were taking the ferry from the Dogwood Resort and requested a behind-the-scenes lesson on winemaking. Jessa led them from the fields to the sorting table, citing all of the facts she'd learned over the years. Grapes didn't ripen once they're picked so it was important to pick them at the right time. Wine grapes were never washed—it would ruin the fruit concentration. The thicker-skinned grapes were destemmed, and the grapes for white wines went into the pneumatic press. She was peppered with questions and loved the challenge of fielding them.

The group was tasting young wines out of steel containers when Nana swept into the large concrete room like a peacock attempting to fly. She wore a royal blue gown and had one white curl that stood straight up on top of her head. "Well, hello, y'all," she addressed the group. "I am Grace Warter, Jessa's grandmother and the pseudo-wife of the winery's owner. And yes, I say *pseudo* because we are married, only not legally. Anyhoo, that is neither here nor there. I will be taking over this tour so that our Jessa can handle some other business. Alright? Now, y'all finish your sippin', and we'll get moving along." She whispered to Jessa, "Duke wants to talk to you."

Jessa said her goodbyes to the group quickly, a little off-kilter from Nana publicly claiming her as a granddaughter and met Duke out front. He stood like an old hunched-over cowboy using a sweet gum branch as a cane.

Once she was close enough, he put a thick hand on her shoulder. "We have acres of grape vines around here," he began, "and we hear it all through them."

Jessa smiled at what was probably a joke he'd used hundreds of times over the years.

"You're like your grandmother," he said. It was surreal to be compared to Grace Warter. Nana still felt like Brooke's grandmother, not hers. "Men want girls like you. Now, I'm not saying they're against you, but they are always, *always* out for themselves. I am an old man, and I know this."

He studied her face as if to make sure she understood him. She had no idea why he was talking to her about men, but she nodded to show she agreed with him.

"It's a shame," he said. "A man's ego is his downfall. We don't know what we've got until it's gone, you see?"

The only way the conversation would make sense was if he was trying to warn her about someone. "Are you talking about Nelson?"

Duke leaned in and whispered, "I know what he wanted to do, and I know he was about to make me big promises.

What he didn't know is that my legacy is set. Right here at this winery. I do not need another dollar or another thing in this world, and when it is my time, I am quite content to go."

Jessa had never heard Duke Bradley speak so many words in her life. His purplish lips quivered with the ferocity of his feelings. "I hope you stay here a long time, Mr. Bradley."

"Well, your Nana is helping see to that."

For the first time in her life, Jessa wished she wasn't so tall. She wanted to show him the respect of being smaller, of looking up to him in the way he deserved, but in his back-hunched state, she had an eagle's view of his comb-over.

"Now, I have a favor to ask of you." His watery eyes drifted up. "Your grandmother is performing at the Dogwood tonight. Most people don't give a lick, but believe it or not, she's nervous. I need you to get your people to come out for it, and I need you to clap loudly for her."

"Like Dottie and Tulip?"

"And Fred and anyone else you can. I know I haven't given you much time, but I need some excited folks in the audience and y'all are the best we've got."

"Are Trig and Cornelia going to be there?"

"I asked, but you know—if they don't feel like it, they won't go."

Jessa hadn't mentally prepared to see Trig and Cornelia until Wednesday night at dinner, but if Duke was asking, she would do it. "Yessir. Absolutely. I'll get everyone I can."

"Excellent." He attempted to wink at her. "I think you're supposed to wear a costume."

As soon as Duke walked away, Jessa was on the phone with Brooke. "Who's coming to the show, and do we really have to wear a costume?"

Brooke began the list with Gates and Libby, then went on to add a bunch of names Jessa only vaguely recognized.

"What costume are you wearing?" Jessa asked.

"You know our little duck Zippy who follows us around? Well, Nate and I figured we'd be a whole duck family. We've got feathery tails and beaks and orange feet."

"I think I'm going to barf." Jessa laughed.

"Right?" Brooke sounded ecstatic. "It was Nate's idea. So freaking cute."

"And why are we dressing up?"

"Nana slept through Halloween this year and didn't get to wear her costume, so she made a declaration or a proclamation or a pronouncement—whatever the word is."

"Demand." *Vintage Nana*, Jessa thought, once again reminding herself that she shared DNA with the woman. It was a pleasant feeling to remember it. "And the show is …"

"One woman, that's all we know."

Oh, boy, Jessa thought, *Nana really is going to need us there.*

"I'll get everybody. Save us some good seats."

"You got it, sister," Brooke said. It was a phrase repeated to many of their friends, but that time, it hit particularly hard. "I mean it," Brooke said as she realized the deeper meaning at the same time. "You got it, sister."

Jessa hadn't been off the phone for thirty seconds before Gates called. She hesitated to answer it. Not only had Nelson asked her to stay away from Gates, but things hadn't ended well the last time she saw him. She was fully aware that she had no right to be mad at him anymore. Now that she was Nelson's girlfriend, it made no difference why Gates had brought him into her life. "Hello?"

"Hey," he said, sounding sheepish. "Brooke told me about Grace's show. Are you going?"

"Yes."

"We need to talk," he said. "And it's so much shorter and easier to get to the Dogwood by boat. Can I ride with you?"

Nelson was going to be pissed when he found out. "We'll make room." Not only was Gates now going with her, but she had no intention of inviting Nelson.

It was a race against the clock, but in a little over two hours, Jessa managed to get Gates, her uncle, sister, and mother to the dock and safely into the jon boat without tipping it over. Gates took control of the outboard motor and Jessa sat at the bow, laughing every time she looked behind her. Tulip was dressed in a blue beanie, denim jeans, floral shirt, and she'd blacked out one of her lower teeth—she'd dressed as their mother, and Dottie thought it was hilarious. Leave it to Dottie to not take herself too seriously.

She'd had to be that way her entire adult life as she stood back and let everyone believe she'd done things she hadn't. A renewed wave of respect and appreciation came over Jessa. Her mother was amazing.

Gates had them going full-out toward the Dogwood, and they all held down their hats and their hair in the wind, dodging saltwater droplets on their way across the sea. Gates was decked out in camouflage with a red-and-black checked trapper hat that covered his ears. Once Dottie had seen Tootie's costume, she'd put away her teddy bear onesie and worn a matching outfit. So, it was a boat filled with a hunter, two toothless Dotties, Fred in his dark blue jumpsuit as a gas station attendant, and Jessa in ponytails and an old, faded Camp Dogwood T-shirt and jean shorts.

Jessa didn't get to the Dogwood Resort as often as she'd like. So, every time she went, there was something new. This time it was the lights. Twinkling throughout the trees was an upgraded version of what they'd done two years ago for Libby's wedding. There were string lights wrapped around the thick arms of the old oaks, and lanterns hanging artfully among the Spanish moss. Short pathway lights illuminated the wide sidewalk down to the water and tall black metal lamp posts flanked the dock.

The place was beautiful, high end, and professionally decorated. Brooke had even added granite countertops in the bathrooms, trendy new furniture, and enormous chandelier lights in the old cafeteria. But the bones were still the old

Camp Dogwood. Brooke and Nate came down to meet them, and Jessa laughed as they duck-walked three in a row with their real-life duck, Zippy.

They looked like ghosts from a time gone by. And in a sense, they were. Anyone who was aware of Nate's background knew that the Dogwood was hallowed ground for him—a reclaimed legacy from his long-lost family. His life with Brooke was a prime example of the kind of good that God always brought from the bad. A solid life and relationship had been built inside a heart that had been cracked wide open and mended back together, the scar tissue stronger than before. Jessa never thought of him as having a limp, even though he'd been born with it, so she was, for a brief second, surprised when his walk had a little hiccup. "We're so happy you're here!" he said as Brooke took Jessa into a tight squeeze and patted four times, holding on a few beats longer than normal.

"It's Nana time!" Jessa said.

"You still look like you did when you were fifteen." Brooke held her at arm's length to get a good look. "In the best way."

Nate was already laughing about the two Dotties, and it quickly turned into a loud guffaw.

Brooke noticed and joined in the laughter. "Gates, please tell me you're not a duck hunter."

Gates shrugged and made an apologetic face. "I only hunt the plastic ones. And, you and Nate always won at that game, so I guess I should've come as a loser."

"You could never be a loser," Brooke said.

Something passed between the three of them. To Jessa, it felt like a tacit, mutual understanding about the seven years Brooke and Gates had spent together and the two years they'd been rightfully and happily apart.

Jessa was surprised at how relieved she was to have witnessed their moment.

"Well, come on, y'all," Brooke said, leading them toward the Grace Warter Pavilion. "We've got appetizers, entertainment, and a buffet dinner afterward."

Sure enough, when they walked inside, among the ten or so people scattered throughout the stadium seating, Trig and Cornelia were in the front row with tiny white plates of hors d'oeuvres on their laps. From the look of Trig in his fall-colored plaid button-down and Cornelia in her burnt orange dress and oversized pearls, they hadn't worn a costume.

"Well, there you are," Cornelia called out, straining her neck to see who had just walked in. She set her plate on the seat as she stood. "I have been so looking forward to seeing you, Jessa!" She took Jessa into a hug, and her arms felt like they were made of air with the way they barely touched her. "Aren't you just so pretty? So, so pretty." The smile was with too many teeth, and Jessa had the distinct feeling that Cornelia was playing to an audience.

"Thank you," Jessa said, stepping back.

She'd purposefully worn little makeup to go along with

her little-girl hairstyle.

Cornelia held her by the shoulders. "Just so pretty," she repeated. "It's like you're finally getting to be the woman you always thought you were." A strange thing to say while Jessa was dressed as a child.

A strange thing to say, period. Leave it to Cornelia to smile wider as she shanked her victim with words. Did she mean that Jessa always fancied herself a Warter? Was she inferring that Jessa thought she was better than Dottie and Tulip and Fred? *The woman you always thought you were.* It wasn't the truth. Not at all. Jessa might have wanted to know who her father was, but she'd never aspired to be a Warter.

Trigger stood beside his wife with the most awkward smile Jessa had ever seen. And his eyes were watery. She didn't know what to make of it. Maybe he had allergies. "Hello, Mr. Warter." She extended her hand.

He didn't accept it—instead, he took a step forward and briefly hugged her. One of her pigtails got caught in the button of his shirt.

"Shoot," she said, trying to pull away.

She lost several strands of hair in her panic to dislodge them. She was free, but he had several long blonde hairs hanging from the front of his outfit. She pulled at them awkwardly.

"Leave them," he said. "I like them."

Was her whole life going to be a series of strange, uncomfortable run-ins with the Warters? Jessa would never be a good enough actress to pull off being happy about it.

Chapter Twenty-Nine

THE REST OF the Boone family avoided the Warters by going straight to the food table as soon as they got inside.

Tootie's plate was filled with shrimp and cocktail sauce. "Let's sit in the back so we can sneak out if this sucks," she whispered.

Jessa wished leaving was an option. Not only was she completely embarrassed from her run-in with Mr. Warter, but she felt like everyone was looking at her. Yes, she did resemble Trigger Warter. No, it wasn't her choice, and no, there was nothing she could do about it.

She looked up from her plate full of shrimp and raw oysters, and with one glance at Gates's face, she felt better. Despite how they'd left things, it still felt like a miracle that she and Gates Lancaster had the Dogwood in common again. He was still the most handsome boy in the room, only he was a man now. They needed to talk soon and put what happened at her house behind them. Their friendship was too strong to let something like that come between them. She turned her focus back to her plate of food. The long-held feelings she had for Gates would probably never go away, but she was definitely safer with Nelson. *If a man makes me too happy, he can also make me sad.*

They sat in the back row with Dottie, Fred, and Tootie eating their fancy food and sipping on champagne.

Tootie leaned over to whisper to Jessa, "You can have them."

"Your shrimp?" Jessa asked. "Are you done?"

"No, the Warters. I don't want them."

Jessa shook her head and whispered back, "I don't want them either. Except for Brooke and Nana."

Tootie stuffed another shrimp into her mouth. "I'll keep Aunt Valerie."

"Toots. Stop talking with your mouth full. It's bad manners."

Tootie opened her mouth wide to give Jessa a view of the chewed-up shrimp inside. Jessa made a face at her. How did Tootie know Valerie was her aunt?

There was a boom and an ear-piercing screech, like a microphone had been turned on too close to a speaker, creating painfully loud feedback.

"Welcome, one and all," came Nana's voice from somewhere off stage. "To the best burlesque show this side of the Mississippi."

"Hold up," Dottie said, leaning over to Tootie and Jessa. "Did she just say *burlesque*?"

"Mama, hush." Tootie pushed her away.

"Oh Lord," Jessa said under her breath. Was this really her family?

The whole place went dark, and a single spotlight flooded the stage. Grace Warter stepped into the light wearing a sky-blue leotard adorned with pink fringe and silver sequins. A short black wig brushed against her ears, and a light blue feather was clipped onto the side. White thigh-high boots completed the ensemble, and the heel height was clearly giving her problems. Jessa feared for the woman's dainty bones with every step she took.

In complete silence, Nana turned her back to the audience, raised one finger high into the air, then two, then three, and to the sound of tinkly bells, she jiggled the big pink bow on her hindside. Then she faced the audience again, stuck one arm out to the side and with one sensually curling finger, invited someone onto the stage. It was Duke in a tux carrying a microphone and a stool. He placed the stool behind her, handed her the microphone and ducked back out of the spotlight.

"I took the liberty of changing the lyrics to a little song they used to sing back in the war days," she said with confidence. "This one is for my granddaughter, Brooke. And, y'all, pay no attention to the stool, all right? It's on account of these shoes. In case I need to sit."

The tune to "Boogie Woogie Bugle Boy" came over the loudspeakers and Nana's hips wiggled to the beat.

"She was a little bitty baby from Goose Island Way. She

had a special daddy, yeah he was my babe. He's now the top man at his job. But once he made a mistake, and there was Dottie to pay."

Jessa searched for Brooke in the dark. What was Nana thinking? She was airing her family's dirty laundry under the guise of a song? It was horrible! Brooke must be upset. She leaned over to Dottie. "We should leave."

"Heck no. I wanna see where she's going with this."

They'd missed the next line and caught the tail end of "She's the Brookie Wookie Brookie-doo of our family."

Excruciating. Cringey. That was what it was—even though Nana did have a nice voice and incredible stage presence. The secondhand embarrassment was painful.

"A Brooke, a Brooke, a littley baby Brooke," she sang.

"Turn on the lights!" came a loud male voice. Whoever was the light board operator heard the man and flipped them all on at once. "Where are you going with this, Mother?" Trigger stood like a general about to charge onto the stage.

"Whatever do you mean, Trigger my dear?" Nana said with great innocence, her lips rubbing up against the microphone screen. The sound was still up high.

"Why are you doing this?" he shouted.

Jessa caught sight of Brooke holding tightly to Nate's arm in the corner of the room.

"I am simply celebrating my granddaughters," Nana said sweetly. "And do you know what else I'm celebrating, my dear? The fact that our little Brookie Wookie has a sister. I have two granddaughters! Count them! Two!" She held two crooked fingers in front of her wide smile. "Which means you have two daughters. If you would just let me get to the end of the song, you would see that I end it on a high note." She giggled. "That was a pun, wasn't it?"

"Get off the stage, Mother. The show's over."

"I am so sorry if I upset you, dear. But the show is not over. Next, Duke will be singing a lovely little piece I wrote just for him."

Duke's voice bellowed from off stage, "I don't need to sing it!"

Nana shot a look stage left that could have withered a kudzu vine. "Get over here." She pointed to the spot beside her, and a few seconds later, stooped Duke with his shiny white comb-over entered the stage and stood beside her. "Cornelia, Trigger, Brooke," Nana demanded. "You get up here on this stage too."

Brooke was the first to comply. She sweetly flopped her wide orange feet up the stairs to join her grandmother. "Cornelia and Trigger, right here." Nana pointed to a spot nearby.

Cornelia was as pasty as a turkey sandwich, and Trigger looked like he wanted to relive his running-back days and make a full-speed dash out the door. But Nana had given them no choice, so they obliged. Jessa prayed Nana had a solid plan or the wealthy Warters of Goose Island were about to be laughed at for all eternity. There was nothing like money to make folks want to knock a family right off any pedestal they might be teetering on.

"Remember what I said a while ago about saving face?" Gates whispered to Jessa from his seat a row ahead of her. "Get ready to be called up on stage."

"You think so?"

He nodded. And, sure enough, in a voice as sugary as sweet tea, Nana invited Jessa to join them. But it wasn't just Jessa. She invited Tootie and Dottie too.

The three of them scooted out of their row and made the long walk to the stage single file with Jessa in the lead. There were no thoughts in Jessa's head at that point. The two Dotties and the summer camper were fully in Nana's hands.

Nana put the microphone onto the stand and took hold of Brooke's hand, then reached for Jessa's. The three of them were upstage while the rest of the family stood behind them like a group of backup singers. The lighting director killed the main lights and kicked on the spotlight. The bright beam hit directly into Jessa's eyes, making it impossible to see the audience, and for that, she was glad. She knew, at least superficially, half of the people in the room. Including Libby, who was part of her childhood friend group and now her coworker at the winery. So, come Monday, even her friends back at the winery would know all about whatever was about to happen.

"Now, one thing I love about the Lowcountry," Nana began. "Is that when you look at it on a map, the inlets and waterways appear like the limbs of an oak tree. Water flows through those channels just as sure as the ocean has waves. It was flowing before we existed, and it will continue after we leave. We are but the tiniest speck in that current, flowing this way and that, until our time is done. Or, if you rather, you could liken our lives to the grains of sand beneath the surface. We are merely one among many." She paused. "Audience? Am I right?"

"Yes, ma'am!" someone yelled loudly above the murmurs of affirmation.

"So, just like looking at the Lowcountry from far away, let us all take many steps back and look at our lives." She paused again. "Have you done it? Now, in your mind's eye, I want you to zoom out some more." Nana squeezed Jessa's hand. "What do you see?"

"A mess," someone said, and a few people chuckled.

"Our lives should look like a tree, same as our waterways." Nana scanned the audience like she was trying to make eye contact with every person there. "And the branches of the tree are made up of people. Some we choose, and some we don't. But it is our responsibility to keep those branches strong. We don't cut them off. We don't poison them. And when a new branch grows, that tree shares its strength, its nutrients, and its very spot on the planet."

A few folks actually clapped. Jessa glanced behind her, and Cornelia's face wasn't nearly as pale. Maybe it was the heat of the spotlight, but Trigger looked less like he wanted to cut and run too. The two Dotties looked less annoyed. So, Jessa allowed herself to trust Nana a little more.

"I realize y'all are here to be entertained, but there are folks with us who are worth recognizing. In light of recent developments, I suggest we all take this time to honor and appreciate our families. They are our very own tree, the bigger the better. The more branches, the more people we have to love." She waved toward Duke, who had snuck off to his hiding place in the wings. "Duke Bradley, come back out here." He waddled over to her, and Brooke and Jessa stepped aside to give them center stage. "Most of y'all know that this particularly handsome branch and I have merged our trees together. And I'm sure all of you can see that we are old." She took his hand. "Here's what I'm trying to get across to y'all. Some folks are born into a family and other folks choose them. Because life is short, it is imperative that we make a big impression on the people who matter while we still can. Carolina Jessamine Boone, come back over here and stand with us."

Duke bowed like a gentleman and offered her his spot.

Nana dropped Duke's hand and took Jessa's. "Dearest Jessa, you were given and now you are chosen too. And as the matriarch of this family, I declare the merging of the Boone and the Warter trees. That means that we accept you, your mother, and your sister into our place in the world. Like trees, we will share our nutrients, we will shelter you in times of crisis, and we will not"—she turned to make brief eye contact with Cornelia—"spread falsehoods or wish harm upon you. Ever. No one will poison our well."

Trig stepped up from behind them and put a hand on Jessa's shoulder, then he leaned over and kissed his mother on the cheek before taking over the microphone. "Sometimes it takes a mother to remind a person what's important. I"—he cleared the emotion from his throat—"am a very lucky man. I am not always what I should be. I can do better, and I will. Because of the particularly special branches on my tree, I am the luckiest man on Goose Island. I am proud of every person on this stage." He turned to look at each person, one by one. And when he got to Dottie and Tootie, they both smiled, each with a missing bottom tooth.

"Mother, let us skip the burlesque and move on to dinner. I'm sure we're all starving." He took both Jessa and Nana by the arm, and after meeting with some stubborn resistance about leaving the stage from his mother, moved them both along.

And with that, a giant branch-filled tree made their exit.

Chapter Thirty

"DON'T GET ALL happy about what just happened up there," Dottie whispered into Jessa's ear as they waited in line for dinner. "You know as well as I do that the Warters are all about the show. This won't amount to a hill of queens."

"Beans, Mama. And I know—like you said about Grandma Boone, expectations are just resentments made in advance. I don't expect them to accept me. They've known I'm his daughter for all of these years and never treated me like family, why would they start now?"

"Exactly."

Dinner was an Italian buffet of lasagna, salad, and garlic bread—an elevated version of what they used to have at camp. Jessa, Gates, Nate, and Brooke found a table for four away from everyone else and met there with their full plates of food. It wasn't lost on Jessa that they were sitting in the same room where they'd spent so many summers eating, doing crafts, and dancing. The old cafeteria was the hangout on rainy days and the one spot where she was sure to see Gates, even if they had differing activities scheduled for the day. He was always easy to spot because he was a head taller than most of the other boys. It was a full-circle moment, and the old butterflies in her stomach came alive when she thought of him as her crush from ten years ago.

There seemed to be a tacit understanding that any lengthy discussions of what had happened on stage should be avoided. Brooke was clearly on the side of Jessa and Nana and seemed to have quickly come around to the idea of having her best friend as a sister. It was best to save any deeper talks for a time when the room wasn't filled with guests who'd just been served up a heaping helping of family drama.

"Wanna go for a walk?" Gates asked after their bellies were full.

"I do."

Outside, the sun had set and the pathway torches, twinkle lights, and lanterns all glowed yellow. It was chilly, and Jessa's old T-shirt was thin. Gates must have noticed she was cold because he took off his camouflage hunting shirt and put it on her. His body heat was still in the fabric and the smell of him made her tingly. She tried not to look at him in his white T-shirt that was tight around his biceps and highlighted his toned midsection. But her mind and heart were filled with desire for the man walking beside her.

"Jumping rock, okay?" he asked.

"The jumping rock is perfect." It was a private spot where they could dangle their legs over the ledge and watch the water from up high.

"I shouldn't have thrown you out of my house," Jessa began as they made their way down the path.

"Don't even think about apologizing. It's my fault. Everything with Nelson is my fault. I should have shut him down the minute he mentioned you."

"That's true. I'm not a bargaining chip."

"You never were in my mind," Gates said. "I never wanted you to date Nelson. It just ended up looking that way. Behind the scenes, I was trying to steer him in a different direction."

Talking about Nelson quelled the excitement she'd felt just moments before. Jessa had been raised to believe that if a woman was taken, she shouldn't spend time alone with another man—it was practically taught at school. The fact was, she was probably, evidently, presumably, Nelson Tucker's girlfriend.

"Are we friends again?" Jessa asked, her shoulder bumping into his arm as they walked side by side.

"Always."

It made her mad that Nelson had told her to stay away from Gates. She'd been friends with Gates for too many years; they'd been through too much together to let someone come between them. She needed to spend time with Gates that night, to be close to him, to repair what she'd come close to losing—again. Walking alone with him in the place where they'd grown up together, where every summer they arrived young and left considerably older, felt surreal. She didn't mean to say it out loud, or maybe she did. Either way, her inner thoughts came out in a whisper. "Why am I feeling this way?"

"What way?" Gates stopped in front of her. They hadn't yet made it to the moonlight on the big, flat rock. It was dark where they stood, but he was so near that she could see him clearly.

"I shouldn't say." She felt her cheeks flush.

But he knew. He absolutely knew. Their attraction filled the space between them. She needed to tell him right then that Nelson was her boyfriend. She needed to stop whatever was about to happen before it was too late. But she didn't want to.

Gates didn't wait even a second. As soon as the words left her mouth, he had her in his arms, their bodies pressed together, his nose touching hers.

"Jess." It was more of a breath than a word. His lips touched hers, softly at first, then with more pressure. He took peeks at her and she at him as he kissed her over and over again. "Do you know how long I've wanted to do this?" He was breathless.

"As long as I have?"

His lips were on hers again. He was eager, like she was fresh water and he'd been thirsty for years.

"Jess," he breathed again, just inches from her mouth.

Just like Dottie used to warn, once the toothpaste was

out of the tube, you could never put it back in. Now that the kissing had begun, she didn't want it to stop. They could hear the party in the distance. There was music playing and voices down by the water. But none of it mattered. She needed to be as close to Gates as possible.

Maybe it was the aftereffects of Nana's big show, or maybe it was living the reality of a desire she'd stuffed down deep for years that caused Jessa's emotions to run high. She thought she'd blocked everything out. She thought she was living in the moment. So, when hot tears slid down her face, she hoped Gates wouldn't notice.

But he did. He held her face in his hands and looked at her lovingly. "Hey, you okay?"

"I don't know what's wrong with me."

"You don't have to know," he said, touching her cheek with the back of his hand. "Sometimes you just need to be held safely in that place where you're hurt. I want to be that person for you, Jess. I will hold you through everything."

"I'm afraid I'm going backward," she said. "I feel like the old me with you, and I've been trying to be tougher." But what she was doing wasn't tough or strong or brave.

It was wrong. And she needed to tell him.

Gates chuckled. "You've always been strong, Jess. It's in the way that you're soft and caring—how you see the best in people. Please don't put up walls or feel like you have to change."

"I am changing, though. I have changed." She took a

step away from him.

Gates looked worried.

"All of those years ago when you chose Brooke? You hurt me, Gates."

He visibly shrank. "I did. I knew it too. I couldn't see it for what it was back then, but I do now."

She waited for him to say more.

"I was a weak little boy, and you had this mysterious power over me. I was afraid, Jess. I didn't want to get hurt."

"So, you hurt me instead." She saw the distress on his face and added, "It's not just because of you. It was Mama, too, and my lifetime of wondering and feeling like I was different."

Gates took a tiny step closer, but she held him at bay.

"I've been trying to figure out how to stop being a pushover. I need to be more opinionated and stand up for myself. I need to get mad sometimes. Really mad. But it doesn't feel good. It's not working."

Gates smiled that *I see you* smile.

Jessa felt dizzy. "You've always been too risky, Gates. But something about being with you right here, right now—I don't feel scared."

"Thank God," he said, leaning in for another kiss.

She stopped him. "Gates. If I'm going to be strong. If I'm going to be a good person, I have to tell you something." Everything in her screamed that she shouldn't say the words—that she should simply solve the problem without him knowing. But the moral part of her insisted—the part that felt shame for not making a clear decision. The part that had inadvertently made a commitment to Nelson Tucker. The part that knew Gates would find out and might never forgive her.

He stepped away from her again, the worry lines on his face deepening. "Tell me it's not Nelson."

How did he know her so well? How could he always guess her feelings so accurately? "It's Nelson."

He held her by the shoulders in a way that was protective and concerned. "Are you okay? What did he do?"

"I'm fine," she said. "He asked me to be his girlfriend."

Gates's grip loosened and his arms fell to his sides. "Please tell me you didn't say yes."

"I didn't say it, but it was implied." She couldn't meet his eyes.

He ran his hands through his hair. "No, Jess. No. I can't believe it."

"Gates." His name was a whisper. "Why did you go out of your way to tell me he's a nice guy? I thought you were trying to get us together. I thought you wanted his account."

"I don't want his damned account! I just wanted you to be happy. I still want you to be happy. I was trying to be a stand-up guy. He liked you, and I didn't want to lie to you. It needed to be your choice, not manipulated by me or anyone else." He shook his head. "I'm such an idiot."

They turned from the jumping rock and walked back the

way they'd come. They were still friends. She knew that. But the loss burned hot. It felt like the same mix of sadness and grief over lost opportunities that she'd felt years ago when camp came to an end. But this time it was her fault.

Chapter Thirty-One

"THERE YOU ARE!" Brooke came running down the hill toward them. She'd ditched the orange duck feet and looked like a canary with yellow feathers stuck to the top of her head. "Where've you been hiding?" She passed Gates and stopped smiling when she got to Jessa. "What's wrong?"

"Nothing," they said in unison.

Brooke led Jessa up the hill with Gates a few steps ahead. "I feel like I barely had any time with you, Jess," Brooke said. "We've got to make some plans for when there aren't a bunch of other people around."

"Yes, please. I hope that all the talk about me tonight didn't ruin the night for everybody."

Brooke took the band of yellow feathers from her head and placed it on Jessa's. "You're a duck now too. Part of this crazy family whether you want to be or not."

Jessa hugged Brooke so tightly that Brooke burst out laughing. She patted her four times, and they walked arm in arm the rest of the way up the hill—Jessa with yellow head feathers, and Brooke with yellow tail feathers.

Back at the main building, it was time for all of the

Southern women to start in with *I'm not going to keep you* or *I'm going to let you go now* as they extricated themselves from conversations. Brooke and Nana were practically accosted with goodbyes and thank-yous as the guests all simultaneously headed for their cars or boats.

"I'm riding home with my friend Everly," Tootie said.

"I thought she wasn't your friend."

Tootie shrugged. "She said they can take Mama home too. Aunt Valerie came by a while ago to get Uncle Fred. Now you and Gates can be alone."

"Y'all don't have to do that. I don't even know where he is."

"What kind of sister would I be if I didn't help you?"

"You'd still be a good one."

"Well, if I want to be alone with a boy, I expect you to help me."

"I will not promise that, Toots. And anyway, I don't really want to be alone with him."

"Whatever," Tootie said. "I'm not blind. Y'all need to talk."

Jessa raised her voice as Tootie walked away. "Tell Mama to meet up at Uncle Fred's."

Somewhere on the dark ocean with Gates manning the outboard motor, Jessa lost her head feathers. Maybe a shark would mistake them for a duck and have himself a meal of yellow-dyed feathers, glue, and a plastic headband. She was cold and damp by the time they got to Gates's car, so he turned the heat up high and drove down the tree-lined road in silence.

Jessa was toasty warm on the outside, but by the time they got to Fred's, she was stiff and colder than ice on the inside. It felt horrible to have Gates upset with her. He hadn't said a word the entire ride. After all of the years she dreamed of kissing him again, it had finally happened. And she'd ruined it.

It was a relief to see Fred's store dark and his parking lot empty. The light was on inside the houseboat, and Jessa and Gates slowed their walk when they caught sight of Fred and Valerie in a slow dance together. In all her life, Jessa had never seen Fred show affection to any woman outside of their immediate family. He had Valerie in a swaying embrace with his cheek against hers. The look on his face was the way Dottie used to look on Christmas mornings when she sat on the couch with her hot chocolate watching Jessa and Tootie open their gifts. All was right in Fred's world. Jessa hated to spoil the mood.

They waited a few minutes, and once the dancing stopped, they purposefully stepped heavily and spoke loudly on their walk up to the houseboat ladder. Whiskey started barking, and Jessa called out, "Uncle Fred?"

"Come on up!" Fred and Valerie came outside and began unfolding beach chairs for everyone.

"I heard it was quite the party," Valerie said.

"Very dramatic." Jessa climbed up the ladder, expecting

Gates to follow behind her.

"Nice to see y'all," Gates said with a little wave from the ground. "I'm just dropping her off. Gotta head on home."

"Why don't you stay?" Valerie said. "I'd love to get to know Jessa's boyfriend." She winked at Jessa and smiled. "I heard."

"I'm not him," Gates said simply, then walked away.

Jessa thought about chasing after him, but something stopped her. Her emotions were all over the place and couldn't be trusted.

"I am tired-er than a hundred-year-old dog," Dottie said by way of greeting when she and Tootie showed up. She climbed up the boat ladder and the whole boat tilted slightly on the concrete blocks. "That was some party. First Grace Warter makes us think we're gonna get an old lady striptease, and then she makes people stand with her while she talks about trees. We were all put through the dinger. I tell you what."

"Wringer, Mama," Tootie corrected, climbing onto the deck behind her mother. Jessa noticed that Tootie's black tooth paint had long since been accidentally swallowed, and her knit hat was probably left in the car.

"At least you weren't off kissing boys this time, Tulip Boone," Dottie said.

"I'm not the only one kissing boys, you know." Jessa recognized the sass in Tootie's voice and was afraid she was about to call her out for kissing Gates. Jessa shook her head at Tootie in a silent *please don't tell.*

"Aunt Valerie?" Tootie said with a tone of accusation.

"Me?" Valerie's mouth fell open, then quickly turned into a smile.

"Everybody wants to know."

"If I've been kissing DeWayne?"

Tootie nodded.

"She ain't lying," Dottie added.

"A lady doesn't share that sort of private information," Valerie said. "But seeing as we're talking about building a house together, yes, I have been kissing your uncle. If I'd had my druthers, I would have been kissing him for the past fifteen years."

"Why weren't you?"

Telling Tootie the story would be a slippery slope. No one wanted to tell her that her father couldn't be trusted to keep her safe or that Valerie had wanted to raise her—but raising Tootie would have meant abandoning her disabled brother and staying in debt. Tootie didn't know that Dottie never slept with Vance, or that, as a matter of fact, she'd never even met him. Was it right for her to know that Dottie had stepped up to adopt a baby girl born of a damaged man and a greedy woman because her brother asked her to? A brother who had battled guilt and regret over the situation for years? Those emotions festered and blistered and oozed in DeWayne Boone until he up and left his high-powered job and moved to a tiny island in the Atlantic to be near his sister and her kids. He'd once said he didn't move here for a simpler life—he moved here for a richer one. And, as far as Jessa could tell, that was exactly what he got.

As much as Jessa believed that secrets were a poison that rotted a person from the inside, she also believed that adults must put the needs of children before their own. Tootie was in high school. That was hard enough. If these devastating secrets picked the lock and pushed their way out of the box where they'd imprisoned them, maybe they should wait for Tootie to be older when it happened. She wanted to do whatever was right but had no idea what that was.

"Now, Tootie, why do you think I asked you to call me Aunt Valerie?" she asked, before immediately answering her own question. "It is because I plan to stay."

Uncle Fred looked slightly thinner, a little more toned, and what used to feel like a rain cloud between him and everyone else had somehow lifted. "We're glad about that," Jessa said simply.

Fred leaned back into his beach chair. "We should have been here all along." It felt like he was a fraction away from saying that he should have raised Tootie. That he should have married Valerie and made it work.

"You're here now," Jessa said.

"Yeah," Tootie piped up, "And we know you'll always be here for us no matter what." For Tootie, it was still *us,* and maybe it needed to stay that way.

Fred seemed to purposefully take in their words, like he

needed them. He needed his sacrifice and his effort to be seen, no matter how many years too late. "Watching over you both has never been a burden, but the greatest privilege in my life."

Valerie reached over a stack of large architectural drawings and patted his hand. "God's perfect timing," she said.

"Right. So, it seems like a good time to explain what we have spread out in front of you."

"We can see what they are," Dottie said. "Are we talking a house for the two of you, or are you opening up a restaurant?"

"I was thinking that, if Valerie will have me, maybe we could finally pick up where we left off," Fred said. "I always promised her a Lowcountry house with a wraparound porch and room for a garden."

"I've had these house plans since we were in college," Valerie added. "The same ones you see right here."

"Where are you planning to build?" Dottie asked. "Don't you live in Charleston, Valerie?"

"I do. And I think it's time I rent out that place, make a little extra retirement money, start cutting back on my hours at work, and help DeWayne run the store. We want to build right here on this land."

"Yay!" Tootie clapped. "Can I have the houseboat?"

"We'll see about that," Fred said.

The house had three bedrooms, four bathrooms, and a large island in the kitchen. Between the two of them, Valerie and Fred could afford something much grander, but they wanted their long-awaited dream. The little Lowcountry house on paper had been living in both of their minds for so many years that they said they had no choice but to make it a reality. Jessa watched Fred and Valerie interact. She watched them point and laugh and talk about soaking tubs and garage cabinetry. They were like two halves of the same person. Just like Jessa and Tootie would always be like Dottie, genetics or not. They'd grown up with her. She'd influenced the way they saw the world. Dottie knew it. And she'd done her best to give them everything she could. Jessa used to think that she and Tootie were the only people who knew Dottie's tender side—how loving and affectionate she was at home—that she cried at sad movies, and sang sweet songs to them when they were sick or couldn't sleep. Out in the world, Dottie was a fire hydrant—poised to douse flames, solid enough to stay unmovable when something smashed into her, kind enough to spray down kids in the summertime heat, and tough enough to take it when a dog lifted its leg and pissed on her. But Fred knew her tender side too. He'd known all along. And Valerie did too.

"Who here is making me feel sappy?" Dottie asked. "Is it you, Jessa? Somebody is sending out an energy that is stirring up my emotions like a blender. I know you love me, all right? Cut it out before I start crying."

"It's me, Mama," Tootie said with no discernible sass in her voice.

"It's me too, Mama," Jessa said.

"Me too, Dorothea," Fred said.

"And me," Valerie said.

Dottie huffed loudly. "Y'all cut it out! Jeez. Carolina Jessamine, make yourself useful and get me a beer."

"Yes, ma'am," Jessa said, filled with wonderment at how a bruised and broken heart could still be filled with so much love.

Chapter Thirty-Two

SUNSHINE CUT THROUGH the aged glass of Jessa's bedroom window creating colorful prisms from the ceiling to the hardwood floor and across the foot of the bed. Jessa was snuggled in deep, cocooned in her comforter. Someone on the island had a fire going, and the nostalgic smell of the woodsmoke helped soothe the anxiety that washed over her the minute she opened her eyes. It was Wednesday but the week had been so long that it felt like it should be Friday. Tonight, she would have dinner at the Warters'. In between, she would be vacillating between more thoughts of Gates and Nelson—most of which made her stomach hurt. Gates hadn't reached out since leaving her at Fred's on Monday night, and there was less than a week left until she was supposed to go to Charleston with Nelson. Just the thought of it made her want to hop on the earliest flight to Australia or China or Zimbabwe and disappear. She texted him that they needed to talk.

Jessa wasn't early to work that day, so many of the employees were already at their stations when she arrived—gift shop cashiers and tasting room hosts, janitors, seasonal workers, and winemakers. She freed the goats and chickens and set out food for the cats. Maybe she wouldn't go to the Warters' house for dinner after all. Nana had said it was optional. Instead, she would build a fire and make some hot tea, maybe use some of her homemade sauce on a baked potato with cheese on top, then settle on the couch for a movie—something funny with a touch of romance. She would decide all that later. What she was looking forward to the most that day was her mother coming up the road in the big yellow truck. When Jessa finally heard the telltale crunch of truck tires on the gravel, she went running outside and climbed into the food truck from the doors in the back.

"What's wrong with you?" Were the first words out of Dottie's mouth.

"I just need a hug, Mama."

Dottie dropped everything and hugged her daughter. "What is it?"

"Just as soon as Nelson is my boyfriend, it turns out that Gates likes me too. My life is a mess."

Dottie sucked in her breath like she'd just had a major revelation. "Goll durn it. I am not listening to the air anymore. Tootie said something was going on with Gates, but I didn't believe her. I thought the air was all around Nelson, and I tell you what, the feeling was so good and so strong that I was willing to forgive that clown. That danged air lies to me all the time." She nearly hit her head on the rack of potato chips over the window with how hard she was shaking it. "Now, you know Nelson and Gates were standing mighty close together down at the beach. It's hard to tell where the feeling's coming from when you're outside with the wind and all."

"What are you saying? Do you think I'm supposed to be with Gates?"

They both smelled burning french fries at the same time. "Dagnabbit! Get those things out of the fryer." Jessa pulled the basket of brown fries out of the oil and dumped them in a nearby trash can. Dottie put on gloves and began pulling apart rib meat. "I don't know."

Jessa opened a bag of frozen shoestring potatoes, poured them into the metal basket, and slid them into the boiling oil.

There was already a line forming outside, so Dottie stuck her head out the window and took the first person's order. Then she stomped back to the tiny prep area and spoke loudly. "You will live a full and a happy life, Carolina Jessamine. Ya hear? I don't know which man is right for you. I'm getting all kinds of signals that don't make sense. But this I know for sure. You will take risks and you will love people and you will not use my mistakes as an excuse." She threw a bun onto a paper plate and topped it with a mound of meat. "You are more than the way you look. And so am I. And so is your uncle Fred, and your sister. If you want a man in your life, then find one who can see past everything to who you really are."

It felt like Dottie was talking about Nelson. Did he even know her outside of the fact that she was pretty?

"Mama, do you ever want a man in your life?"

"Don't be ridiculous. I will never be on some desperate hunt to find a man. I've got my family." Dottie pulled out the basket of freshly cooked fries and poured salt all over them. "But I've been thinking. You know how you got stuck in that cellar? One time I was cleaning out the gutters and the ladder wobbled, and I thought to myself that once you and Tulip are off living your own lives, I could get hurt and no one would know. I might fall off a ladder and no one would find me until I was dead on the deck."

"We should have been talking about this stuff all along." Dottie's nonexistent love life had always been the untouchable topic, the incomplete story.

"Yeah, well, if I wasn't working so hard holding onto all of these durn secrets, we would have."

"Right." There was no use laying in to her about how she never should have kept such toxic secrets to begin with.

As if Jessa's little sister had anticipated something going down, an old red pickup pulled up and Tootie hopped out from the passenger seat.

"Toots! Aren't you supposed to be in school?" Jessa asked, climbing out of the truck.

"How many times do I have to remind y'all?" Tootie thanked the young man and waved him away. "I am the best student they've got. No one is going to question me for skipping."

Dottie leaned so far out of the window, she could easily have fallen out. "Tulip Evergreen Boone, what in the tarnation are you doing here? And who was that boy?"

"Don't start with me, Mama." Tootie put a hand on her hip like the sassy teenager she was.

"And don't you sass mouth me, young lady," Dottie said as she placed a stack of napkins on top of a paper bowl of food and handed it to a person in line. "Get your little behind back to school."

"The school day's almost over, and the prissy posse is on a rampage, so I skirted out of there."

"The mean girls are still at it?" Jessa asked.

Tootie rolled her eyes. "It's like this, see—boys do my bidding, and those girls are just gonna have to get used to it. I tell a boy to take me to a party, he's darn well gonna take me to a party. I tell one to drive me to the winery, he drives me to the winery."

Jessa was aware of the people in line listening to her sister, but Tootie didn't seem to care. "The mean girls have their panties in a bunch because all of the boys they're trying to talk to like me better. It's stupid."

"Dammit, Tulip." Dottie had clearly heard every word. "Then you might as well get up in here and help me. This line is halfway to North Carolina, and I already burned one batch of fries thanks to your sister."

Tulip passed by Jessa and climbed into the truck without

argument.

"I've gotta go," Jessa said. "Nelson's here."

"Wait." Tulip hopped back out. "Nelson is here? Y'all never tell me anything." She huffed out of the truck. "Is he inside?"

"No, he's pulling into the parking lot now."

"I've got a question for him."

"What is it?" Jessa scurried to keep up with her, taking time to smile and say a quick hello to the guests as they arrived.

They'd made it halfway to Nelson's car when Tootie suddenly stopped and faced her sister. "What do you think I'm going to ask him?"

"I don't know."

"I know y'all are hiding something. And I know he's your boyfriend now." She flipped around and began walking with a vengeance. "Since Mama won't tell me, you won't tell me, and Uncle Fred won't tell me, I'm gonna ask him if Mr. Warter is my daddy too."

"Toots. Mr. Warter is not your father."

She spun around. "Right. Of course. It's some random guy because Mama is a hussy."

"Mama's not a hussy."

"Y'all think I haven't heard you talking behind my back for days?" There was fire in Tootie's eyes. "I'm not stupid."

"Have you tried asking Mama?"

"Why would I want one of her made-up stories? *Mr.*

Warter has been your daddy all along. Aren't you mad about that? He's been right here in your face, and you didn't know it!"

"I was mad. But I'm working on it."

"I'm asking Nelson. Boys do whatever I say. He'll tell me."

"You can try, Toots, but he doesn't know."

"But you know?"

Jessa couldn't lie. "I know."

Tootie put her hands on her hips and flared her nose. "Then tell me." She was still shorter but had grown into her dark features and long hair. Teenaged Tulip was a beautiful little force to be reckoned with.

"We have to wait for Mama to finish up. Why don't you stay and help her? Later, you can collect the chicken eggs. June might need some milking too." It had historically been easy to persuade Tootie to do anything for the animals. If there was one thing she loved more than her hundreds of hobbies, it was creatures of all kinds.

"I see what you're doing."

"I'm sure you do."

"I'm still asking Nelson. If he doesn't tell me then you have to promise to tell me today. I mean it. It has to be today."

"I promise we will tell you today," Jessa said.

Chapter Thirty-Three

TOOTIE MADE A direct line to Nelson, who was stepping out of his vehicle. He looked over her head to Jessa questioningly, probably because Tootie was coming for him hot and fast.

"Hey, Tootie," he said, backing away slightly as she approached. "You good?"

"Ask her." She pointed aggressively at Jessa.

"We're experiencing a little conflict," Jessa said.

"What about?"

Tootie answered, "Who in the heck my father is."

"I promised we would tell her today, but she thinks she has an in with you."

"Tell me who he is," Tootie demanded.

Nelson shook his head. "I have no idea."

"I should've asked Gates." Tootie threw the words at them like a grenade and marched off.

"I know I promised you lunch," Jessa said to Nelson, "But the line is crazy long at the food truck and my lunch hour is getting shorter by the second. Uncle Fred's would be faster."

She hopped into Nelson's car, and he drove over the speed limit to Fred's. Ruby's little white bug was out front, and the island was hopping for a Wednesday. The line for homemade sandwiches and BBQ was out the door. Fred and Ruby were moving faster than usual, which was approximately the same pace as a normal person. Fred looked particularly stressed.

Jessa didn't hesitate. She hopped behind the counter and began taking orders at the register, then threw an apron at Nelson and gave him the job of filling little cups with whatever side dish was ordered—beans, potato salad, macaroni salad, or coleslaw.

"Looks like my little business went viral on social media," Fred said, piling roasted turkey onto a huge yeast roll.

"Is that what this line is all about? Mama's getting slammed at the winery too."

"Folks think this place is rustic. And someone out there started a rumor that I'm the real Santa Claus." He chuckled, and it sounded somewhat like a ho-ho-ho. "Guess I'll have to spray my beard white all the time."

Jessa handwrote an order and stuck it in the metal ticket holder above Fred and Ruby's workspace. She whispered, "Is Valerie still here?"

He paused for the tiniest second. "She'll be back tonight."

"I really like her."

He said nothing, but Jessa noticed his hands were shaking.

"Uncle Fred. Are you okay?"

"I'm not sick if that's what you're asking. I'm just feeling things."

"Is it about Valerie?"

"Guilt is not a productive emotion." He spread Duke's mayonnaise on both sides of fluffy white sandwich bread, then put two slices of tomato on top of that. "All these years I've been focusing on letting go. I was letting fate be the boss, letting things turn out however God meant them to." He handed a plate over the counter and yelled, "Andrew!" Then he put his attention back on both Jessa and the slip of paper telling him what to make next. "I have not allowed myself to feel this way for ages."

"That's why you never went after her, because you were letting fate decide?"

"I didn't presume I had the right to chase her." He put little tubs of side dishes next to three large pieces of fried chicken and called out, "Emily," before handing a trendily dressed twenty-something her food. "A smart person thinks about all of the possibilities and prepares for them. Right? But I wasn't prepared for this. I never thought she'd come back."

"Who are y'all talking about?" Ruby asked. Nelson said something to her quietly, so Jessa felt no need to explain.

They worked side by side for a few more minutes, and all the while Jessa thought about how lonely Fred must have been in his little houseboat out back. "I remember you saying something one time. *It's not the mistake that matters, it's what you do about it."*

Fred smiled widely. "I said that? I should've listened to my own advice years ago." His eyes sparkled like he had a plan.

Jessa used up her remaining lunch period making sandwiches and plating saucy mounds of shredded BBQ pork and chicken. She had to get back to work, so she filled a bag with side dishes and whatever meat they had the most of. Then she kissed Uncle Fred's whiskery face goodbye and waved to Ruby. As she left, she wondered if Uncle Fred would hold tight to his determination to let Dottie be the one to tell the truth about Tootie's father or if he would tell her himself.

On their ride back to the winery, poor Nelson got an earful about secrets and fathers and bad parental decisions. She should have told him about Gates, but she figured there was time. Once there, it was a *stuff-your-face-with-pork-and-coleslaw-while-working* scenario until they were finally satiated. The crowds grew as the day wore on, and by midafternoon, there was not an Adirondack chair or a picnic table or a swing or a tree root available to sit on. It was like an egg sack of spiderlings in the form of wine-drinkers had hatched and were crawling all over the island. Dottie had to shutter the truck early because she ran out of food. Jessa assumed that Fred would have to do the same thing with the store. It felt like a mild emergency.

One of the many nice things about Nelson showing up that day was he saw firsthand that as the manager, she was in charge of restoring order to the chaos. He, of course, was a part of that chaos, so she set up a spot in her office where he could get his own work done.

"Hey," he said when she ran past carrying a crate of clean wine glasses to the tasting room. "What was it you wanted to say to me?"

She was startled by a loud whooping sound. They both turned to the window and saw a drunken man pressing Skip on his forehead and trying to goad him into a headbutting competition. Jessa put down the crate and took off out the door. Skip was a nice goat, but if a person tried to establish dominance over him, he would fight back.

"Sir!" she yelled, running toward him. "Sir! Don't do that!"

At least five people surrounded the man, laughing, and she could quickly see that he was more interested in their attention than in her orders. Little black-and-white three-legged Skip was outmatched, and smaller white June stood to the side, watching. Jessa knew both of the goats well enough to see that they felt attacked.

Nelson got there first. He immediately took Skip by the collar and led him to safety. Jessa was going for June, but the goat managed to avoid her and lunged straight for the man, who had turned to watch Skip's exit. June rammed him in the back of his knees, causing him to crash into the ground like a felled tree.

Now there was damage control to be done. Jessa held her

breath as the man stood and dusted himself off.

All it took was one howl from the crowd and the rest of the group was in hysterics. "That's what you get!" seemed to be the overriding sentiment, and the man, thankfully, agreed.

"Good thing I wasn't trying to headbutt a gator," he said. "Critters around here hunt in teams."

Jessa made sure the man was okay as she held onto a loudly bleating June. Nelson came running back, having put Skip back into the fenced pasture. Together, they took June to join him.

How was she supposed to tell him about her feelings for Gates after he'd just helped her like that? Not just with the goats, but at Uncle Fred's place too. He really was a nice guy—not some big city bully. They walked back to the main building holding hands. It felt odd, his manicured hand in hers. He'd grown up on an earthworm farm, his hands should be calloused and rough like Gates's.

She looked up at him from the corner of her eye—Nelson Tucker with his perfectly gelled hair and crisply pressed suit still didn't feel known to her. He could be arrogant and showy, and he sometimes he made her feel like she wasn't educated enough for him. He was handsome and successful, but when she was with him, she felt about as safe as a crystal vase in an earthquake. How he reacted to her confession might very well tell her everything she needed to know about him.

The rest of the day was like working a surging crowd at the county fair. There was no time for any heart-to-heart talks as Jessa ran from one place to the next. When it was finally time to go home, she was in a hurry to get ready for her dinner at the Warters'. Who knew how long the discussion with Nelson would take? It could be hours; it could be minutes. She couldn't risk it. So, she said goodbye to him next to his Range Rover. She hadn't planned it, or even given it one thought ahead of time, but when he tried to kiss her, she turned her head.

Nelson drove off like a man who'd just been smacked in the face, and the people pleaser in her wanted to cry. He had taken the hint that whatever she had to say to him wasn't going to be good. Even though they'd only been boyfriend and girlfriend for somewhere near forty-eight hours, he was probably now recalibrating his plans for the future and spreading weedkiller over whatever growing feelings he had for her.

Jessa knew how difficult that was. Sometimes those feelings refused to die.

While she was at home getting ready, she called her mother. "Mama, I promised we would tell Toots about her daddy tonight."

"Now why would you go and promise a thing like that?"

"It's *Tootie*, Mama. You know how she is."

"I thought you were having dinner with Trigger and the witch."

"I am. So we're gonna have to meet up afterward."

"You know your sister has school tomorrow, right?"

"When is there ever going to be a good time, Mama? It's always going to be something, and right now Tootie is like a volcano about to blow. We've got to give her something or she's gonna burn us all."

"Fine," Dottie said. "Meet at Fred's when you're done with dinner." She paused. "And, Jess? You don't need the Warters, alright? You are just as you should be without those people in your life."

"I know that, Mama."

"Alright, then. Kick Cornelia under the table for me. Hard."

Chapter Thirty-Four

JESSA HAD BEEN coming to the Warters' house her entire life, yet it had never felt as intimidating as it did that evening. The dining room curtains were wide open, and the soft light inside highlighted the perfectly set table and fresh flower centerpiece. She could even see the condensation on the sterling water pitcher. The stage was set, and her first family dinner was about to happen. As she walked up the wide front steps past the thick white columns to the double front door, she held so tightly to the wine bottle in her hand that she thought the neck might crack.

Brooke answered the door before Jessa had a chance to knock. "Hey there, sister," she said with a huge smile.

Jessa recognized how generous it was of Brooke to be so accepting of the situation. From the beginning, Brooke had made it clear that any issue she had was with her father, not with Jessa. They were the same friends as always, just with an additional connection and a new title. As they'd grown and matured in their years since high school, Brooke's heart had become bigger and softer. Surely, Nate had something to do with that. He stood behind her, waiting for his turn at a hug.

Jessa heard voices coming from the kitchen and was glad to recognize Nana's. At least with Grace Warter around there would always be conversation.

Jessa knew the drill. She took off her shoes in the entry and followed Brooke and Nate to the kitchen, still holding tight to the bottle of wine she'd brought as a hostess gift. She was prepared to be on her best behavior with a stockpile of ma'ams and sirs, and even though her face didn't want to cooperate, she forced a smile onto it.

"There she is!" Nana declared as she danced forward in a colorful caftan and green velvet turban. "Oh, happy day. Just look at how much Jessa and Brooke look alike. Isn't it just the darnedest thing?"

Jessa and Brooke turned to each other and smiled. They had always favored each other, especially back in the day when Cornelia used to dye Brooke's hair blonde and insist it was natural.

Nana took the wine bottle from Jessa and set it on the counter, then took both of Jessa's hands and squeezed them tightly with a cold crooked strength. "We are so happy you're here." Then she pulled Jessa to the corner where Trigger and Cornelia Warter stood like reluctant children. "Trigger, hug your daughter."

"Hello, Mr. Warter," Jessa said.

Despite his stiffly starched white button-down, tie, and sport coat, his hug was remarkably warm and inviting. "You can, uh, call me Trig or ..." He took two steps backward and glanced at Cornelia for approval. "Whatever you want."

Jessa said, "Thank you." She had no idea what she wanted to call him.

Cornelia stepped forward and gave her a quick bony hug but made no effort to welcome her verbally. "The pork chops are ready. Anna Brooke, would you please set out the salad? Trigger, you may set out the sweet potato casserole." Her eyes squinted unnaturally as she turned to Jessa. "Thank you for the wine. We will add it to our collection. Now, all of our guests should please be seated." She took the serving platter of pork chops and led the way in her swooshing dress and high heels. After placing the meat dish at a spot nearest the window, she stood behind the chair opposite Trig's at the head of the table and waited for him to pull it out for her.

The curtain had been lifted, and the show was about to begin.

The pork chops Cornelia made were a little too salty, but of course Jessa raved about how delicious they were. Cornelia had always been gracious about accepting compliments. Nana carried the conversation for most of the meal, beginning with how Duke had a painful corn shaved from his big toe and didn't want to walk on it yet, therefore he was absent from dinner that night, bless his heart. Then she went on and on about the woodpecker that'd been pecking a hole in her eaves, followed up with a demand that Trigger do something about it before the critter built a nest inside. Then, speaking of doing handy-type things around the house, Nana turned the conversation to Jessa. "Fixing things is one of the many chores fathers are good for. Jessa, what do you need Trigger to do for you?"

"Nothing, really," Jessa said. She'd seen him build a treehouse once, and he'd been the one who lifted the log pile when it trapped her in the cellar, but she'd never considered him a man who enjoyed doing any sort of manual labor. "I think I have it all under control."

"Now, don't be all independent like your mother," Nana said. "You have a daddy now, and he is willing to help."

It struck her to hear her mother spoken about as if independence wasn't a good thing. Thankfully, Brooke took on that fight. "Shouldn't we all be independent, Nan?"

"Oh, right," Nana said. "We're living in modern times now. Is that what you're about to lecture me about?"

"No lecture," Brooke said calmly. "Just pointing out that independence is good."

"Well, so is manure but you won't find me rolling around in it."

The whole dinner, Jessa had avoided looking at Trigger yet was hyperaware of his presence. Everyone else was pretty much who they'd always been before, but not him. Fully half of his DNA was flowing through her veins. She was so nervous around him that her throat barely allowed for her to swallow, and she hoped no one noticed that she'd barely made a dent in the food on her plate. She jumped when his words were directed at her.

"Do you need some help getting things into your cellar?"

"That would be nice," she said.

"What time are you off work tomorrow?" he asked.

Tomorrow? That soon? She needed some time to prepare. She had a pile of laundry in her closet and a dishwasher to unload, and she hadn't dusted in weeks, and that ratty old couch was still on her back porch and, and … what she really needed was time to mentally prepare. The old Jessa would have simply agreed and put on a happy face, the changed Jessa would say no and then feel horrible about it, but the newest Jessa was beginning to realize that she could hold her boundaries and still be nice. "I think my plans for the weekend are about to change. Maybe, if you're not busy, you could come over then?"

"Saturday afternoon?" he asked.

She caught his eye that time and said the word "perfect" before quickly looking away. Something had occurred to her during that brief conversation. Something strange. Had she ever heard Trigger Warter say her name? Even when he'd yelled for her when she was trapped in the cellar, he hadn't used her name. She couldn't recall him ever calling her Jessa. Not once. Certainly, he'd never, ever said Carolina Jessamine. He had to have said it when she was young, right? All those times she was over at his house playing with Brooke—he had to have addressed her directly. Although she couldn't remember a single time.

"What else?" Nana demanded.

"Well, I have a wallpaper project I want to do, but I have to buy more first. And I was told I should nail my old milk door closed."

"Is it up off the ground? Can an animal get through it?" Trigger asked.

The moment he took an interest in her milk door, a violent surge of *what if* took hold of her. Had Mr. Warter been leaving the gifts? Her voice sounded small. "It's about four feet off the ground. It leads directly into my pantry."

"And it's just big enough for an old glass milk bottle?"

She nodded.

"It's probably not a problem, but I'll nail it up for you if you want me to."

"If y'all are going to be together anyway," Nana said, "you might as well come by for dinner Saturday night, Jessa."

"I believe we are going out," Cornelia spat. "Right, Trigger? We have our date night."

"We do," he agreed.

"Come to the Dogwood and hang with me and Nate," Brooke said.

It suddenly felt like everyone was taking pity on her, which was the last thing she wanted. "I'm fine, y'all. I have plenty of things I can do." Aside from going to Charleston with Nelson, of course.

"We are just trying to be gracious and accommodating," Cornelia said.

"Mother," Brooke said. "Don't get defensive."

"Anna Brooke, I am not getting defensive. This is my house, and I will do and say as I please."

"Yes, ma'am," Brooke said, then turned to Jessa. "Sorry about that."

"And now you are apologizing for me?" Cornelia began to stand, then noticed the big picture window and sat back down. She even smiled for the benefit of whoever might be walking or driving past. Which appeared to be absolutely no one.

"This is an awkward situation for all of us," Cornelia said sweetly. "And I'll have you know that this family is a close one. We are upstanding and have a strong reputation in this community. We do what's right. Always."

"Yes, ma'am," Jessa said, following Brooke's lead.

"Is everyone satisfied?" Cornelia stood and began taking plates, making it clear she was speaking of the amount of food they'd been given and not the content of the conversation.

"Yes, ma'am," Jessa and Brooke said together.

"Trigger and I will be taking our dessert in the den. You are welcome to have yours in the kitchen."

In other words, they'd better not try to eat it in the dining room. Everyone stood and took a few trips back and forth carrying dishes and glasses and silverware into the kitchen. "Don't mind her," Nana whispered while they were both at the sink. "She's just ornery."

Jessa wasn't sad at all to be sitting at the kitchen table with Nana, Brooke, and Nate. They each had a slice of chess pie with a side of ice cream, and Jessa's gullet finally loosened enough to allow her to swallow. The conversation was light and happy until Trig's voice was heard clearly from the other room. "I don't know how to do this."

Cornelia's answer was unintelligible.

"I'll tell you how to do it," Nana yelled in his direction. "You show up for her! That's it! Easy peasy! If you want to call yourself a man, Trigger Warter, then show up for your people." She ripped the turban from her head and threw it on the table. "Why do folks insist on making things so much more complicated than they need to be?" She didn't bother to smooth the matted spots and straight-up peaks of her white hair, she just reached out and put her hand on Jessa's shoulder. "You too, honey. I'll keep inviting you, and Brooke will keep inviting you, and if you want to have anything to do with this crazy imperfect family, then just keep showing up."

"Yes, ma'am," Jessa said with a genuine smile.

Nana might very well be the smartest person in the world.

Chapter Thirty-Five

WHAT A DAY it had been. Jessa just wanted to get home to her cozy bungalow and zone out in front of a good movie. There were at least ten texts from Nelson asking her to call him, but she couldn't deal with him right then. *A person can only put out one fire at a time*, she told herself. Once she left the Warters' driveway, she found that just the simple act of sitting in her car was glorious. She was finally alone. She'd survived the dinner. She gave herself a few seconds to enjoy the relief before driving away.

Jessa was so deep into her thoughts that she was caught off guard when the bright lights of Fred's gas station came into view. Not only was Dottie's food truck in the parking lot, but an old model Lexus sat next to Fred's pickup on the dirt beside the building. The sign on the front window had been flipped to CLOSED, so she parked and went around back.

Whiskey was at her feet before she got around the corner. He enthusiastically led the way to the houseboat. There, underneath the glow of Fred's nighttime fishing lamp, was a circle of folks seated on varying heights of beach chairs on the white marine plastic of the stern. Like a pretend adult, Tootie was there too. Laughter wafted toward Jessa and she figured they hadn't told Tootie about her father yet.

Whiskey barked Jessa's arrival, and Fred told her to climb on up. They'd saved her a spot on his fish cooler.

"We told her," Dottie said as soon as Jessa sat on the insulated plastic.

Jessa looked wide-eyed at her little sister, who appeared completely unbothered.

"It's cool," Tootie said.

She wanted to hug her, but the girl seemed genuinely fine. "Are you sure?"

"Yeah. No wonder I'm so smart. I've got a nice, wide gene pool."

"That you do," Valerie said with a smile as sanguine as Fred's personality.

Jessa had a question she knew she couldn't ask. She bore her eyes into Dottie's head, trying to get her to look. Dottie must have sensed that Jessa was dying to mouth the words, *Did you tell her about her mother?* because she never looked her way.

Surely, Tootie would not be okay if they'd explained that part. But if someone didn't tell her about her biological mother soon, Jessa would be complicit in the same kind of secret she'd been angry about for years. The words were there, but her mouth refused to speak them. She couldn't do it. She couldn't bring herself to devastate her little sister with the truth about her mother. So, she shut her mouth and said nothing.

"Isn't it weird how my Aunt Valerie isn't your Aunt Valerie?" Tootie asked.

"You wanna talk about weird?" Jessa said, "My best friend's dad is my dad."

"Yeah, the freaking Warters."

"Toots." Jessa leaned over as close to her as she could. "Are you sure you're okay with all of this? I know it's a lot."

Tootie shrugged. "Are you? I mean, what I heard at school is that the Warters are saying how much they have always loved you and have spent tons of money on your upbringing and crap like that."

"Always loved me?" Jessa was flabbergasted.

Dottie spat a mouthful of beer over the side of the boat. "Tons of money? *PUH*-lease."

"Cornelia's saying that too?" Jessa asked.

Tootie shrugged again. "That's what I heard."

"It's like the whole stage show," Fred said. "Publicly welcoming you into their family is the only way to redeem themselves at this point."

"Yeah," Tootie said, "like, you'll probably get an invitation to their family Christmas. You better not go, though. You belong to us."

"I would never leave my family at Christmas." She thought for a second about what was wrong with that statement. "I mean, my real family. My first family."

"The Warters suck," Tootie said.

Jessa felt like that was taking it a step too far. "Brooke is my best friend, and I really like Nana." She wasn't sure about Mr. Warter or Cornelia yet.

Tulip's normal buzzy personality stilled. "I don't like you talking about her."

"About who? Brooke? Toots, she's been my best friend my whole life."

"I've always been your only sister, and now she is too. I don't like it."

A pang of guilt hit Jessa square in the chest. Biologically, she and Tootie weren't sisters at all. But she absolutely could not tell her that. If Tootie was already feeling jealous, it would make things so much worse.

"Nothing has changed, Toots. She's still my friend and you'll always be my sister."

"And now you have the richest family on the island."

"Who cares? That's their money, not mine."

"You know Mama only has her house because of him."

"It doesn't matter where it came from. It's ours."

"Yeah, well, my dad is dead."

Jessa knew it. It wasn't so much the Warters that bothered Tootie, it was the fact that Jessa gained something when her secret was revealed, and in a sense, Tootie had lost something.

Valerie sat up straight when Tootie said that, a concerned look on her face.

"But did you know that he was meant to be smart?" Tootie asked. "If he hadn't gotten the brain damage when he was born, he would have had a better life. Right, Aunt Valerie?"

"Even with his hardships, he had a good job," Valerie said, clearly repeating something she'd said before Jessa arrived.

"He died in an accident at the dock right after I was born. But he did get to see me. And he got to hold me one time."

"That's good, Toots," Jessa said, heartbroken at the gratitude her sister had for such a small thing, and at the same time, filled with guilt that she'd just had dinner with her own biological father, no matter how imperfect he was.

"Have you seen a picture of him?"

Tootie nodded. "He looks just like Aunt Valerie, only his eyes are different. She said he was super funny and could make these drawings that he'd do upside down, and then when he flipped it over you could totally recognize that it was a person's face. Like, you could even tell who the person was. Right, Aunt Valerie?"

"That's right," she said in her rich, soothing voice.

It didn't go without notice that Tootie kept looking for Valerie's reassurance.

"Aunt Valerie showed me one he did of her, and it was like a professional did it."

"That's probably where you get your artistic talent

from," Jessa said.

"He liked shark teeth too. She's gonna give me his collection. Right, Aunt Valerie?"

"Absolutely. It's yours."

"He's got three megs."

"Are you serious? That's amazing!"

"It doesn't matter who he is, right? There are adopted people who never find out who their parents are and they're still happy and stuff." Tootie grinned and held up a bottle of beer. "Mama's letting me drink this."

"Mama!" Jessa said, turning on Dottie.

"Don't act all shocked, Jessa." Dottie made a face at her. "It's not whiskey."

Tootie took a large swallow and acted like she was about to fall out of her chair. "Uncle Fred, are y'all going to get married?" She slurred her words.

"Tulip, you're not drunk," Dottie said. "That was your second sip."

"I'd marry Valerie right now if I could," Fred said.

Valerie smiled. "It's been a long time coming."

"If you're gonna live here, Aunt Valerie, I'll show you all the best spots for finding shark teeth. I even found a musket ball down at the washout, and those come from before the Civil War."

"My little brother would be so proud of you." Valerie had a special way of saying things with an extra dash of heart.

"Did you love him, Mama?"

"Ummm," Dottie finished her beer in one long swallow. "I believe so, yes. I certainly love him for giving me you."

Once again, in order for Dottie to protect her daughter from a secret, she had to take a bullet.

Chapter Thirty-Six

It was Nelson who stopped reaching out to Jessa after that crazy intense Wednesday. She felt guilty about it, but not badly enough to take action. At the very least, she owed him a phone call, but the tiniest break from facing unpleasant emotions was so desperately needed, and the winery was still overrun with tourists and chaos. It was Saturday morning, and she was lounging in bed when she finally texted him an apology.

Hunger got her out from underneath her fluffy comforter. There was a golden roll of breakfast sausage in her freezer, and she had butter and whipping cream to make biscuits. She went to the pantry to get the good flour, the White Lily, and noticed a letter stuffed into the crack of the locked milk door. Her heart fell to her feet. Had Nelson been at her house again?

She pulled the rectangular white envelope free and opened it. Inside was a letter.

Carolina Jessamine,

Here's your first installment of bad poetry.

If I'm lucky and you show up tomorrow you

CAN HAVE AN ENDLESS SUPPLY OF IT.

Tomorrow? Show up where? She read through the poem so quickly, she had to go back and read it again.

You're the kind of girl
Who makes a man want to be better.
You are strong and delicate, fortitude and velvet.
Your optimism makes me hopeful.
Your ability to see the best in people
To forgive
To look past
To see into
Makes you extraordinary.
When I'm with you, I'm at peace.
Will you meet me on Sunday?
I'll be at the boneyard
When the tide is low
Waiting.

Who would know about the boneyard except Gates? Her breath caught in her throat. It was where they'd first hung out together back in the high school days of Camp Dogwood. It was where they'd shared her first kiss behind the big bleached-out log on that hot day when the pluff mud was baked solid. Had it been Gates leaving the gifts all along? The truth was, she hoped so. She really, really hoped so.

She tried to imagine a poem that Nelson might write. It would probably be something along the lines of *you need a man like me, and you're lucky I like you.* He was always trying to prove how much better he was than everyone else. Plus, he would never call his poetry bad.

Then again, Nelson had been to the Dogwood, and if he explored the grounds at all, he had seen the black-and-white painted signs Brooke put everywhere—the jumping rock, the swimming hole, the lighthouse, the boneyard. And he was probably the type to do anything to win—even pretend to be someone he wasn't—like a humble bad poet. The fact was, he and Gates had a competition going, and Jessa was the prize.

But only a man in love would be willing to write something so embarrassing. Was embarrassing the right word? Maybe it was tender and sensitive. In which case, it had to be Gates. Right?

Or maybe she was just getting suckered in with meaningless words.

Jessa put the letter in a drawer and got back to cooking. She used a pastry cutter to blend cold cubes of butter into her flour and added cream, salt, baking soda, and a few pinches of sugar. Then she transferred it to a wooden cutting board that she'd covered in flour, folded the dough in half, and pressed it down five times. Any more than that and the biscuits wouldn't be fluffy. She flattened it with her hands, knowing better than to use a rolling pin, and used Grandma

Boone's biscuit cutter to cut the dough into circles. Oh, wait. Was it even her grandmother's? Drunk old Grandma Boone probably didn't make biscuits. Dottie probably got the danged biscuit cutter at Walmart and passed it off as a family heirloom.

At least Jessa understood now. She wasn't mad about it anymore. Dottie did her best to create a family atmosphere for her daughters. And for her, that included made-up stories. Wasn't life about perspective anyway? Truths long held in families could be seen in very different ways depending on who you asked. What was the difference? Aside from knowingly telling lies, Dottie's intentions had been honorable. Still, Jessa wanted to know where the biscuit cutter came from. She made a mental note to ask about it.

The doorbell rang, and as always, Jessa jumped a foot and let out a little yelp.

She opened the door wide. "Hey, Toots. Want some breakfast?"

Tootie shot her a suspicious look.

"You can put your eyebrows back down where they belong, Tootie. I'm cooking for myself."

"Your boyfriend Nelson isn't here? What about your boyfriend Gates?"

"No boyfriends, Tootie. Get inside so I can close the door." Jessa led the way to the kitchen, which smelled like bread and sausage.

"Gawd, Jess. Don't you ever have any fun?"

"Don't start with me, Tootie." Jessa pulled out two plates from the cupboard and handed them to her sister. "Put these on the table and get us some forks. We need juice glasses too."

She'd finally been given a moment to tell Tootie the truth about her mother. She had to decide if she was going to be the honest sister who told her the harsh truth or the sister version of her mother who held onto secrets and lies.

"You're probably wondering what I'm doing here," Tootie said, stuffing a hot piece of breakfast sausage into her mouth straight from the pan.

"Not really," Jessa said.

As a matter of fact, she wished Tootie would drop by more often.

"Mama said she's gonna be a cat today." They both knew that meant Dottie was going to be in her pajamas all day taking turns eating and sleeping. "That means you've got to go into Charleston with me. I want to go to the docks and see where Vance used to work."

Vance. It felt healthier for Tootie to use his actual name rather than calling him father, or worse, Daddy.

"Aunt Valerie said he has a grave right outside of the city too."

"I wish I could take you, Toots, but Mr. Warter is coming over to help me with some fix-it things."

Tootie slumped into a chair at the kitchen table. Jessa put a plate of biscuits, gravy and sausage in front of her. "I don't want that," she said. "Not hungry."

Jessa felt the first twinge of panic. Maybe Tootie wasn't *cool* with who her father was after all. Maybe having different fathers was going to be a much bigger deal than she'd initially thought. She needed to be smart about how she handled her sister. These first days could be pivotal. "You can still hang out here today, though. I was thinking about making a wreath for the front door. We can gather up magnolia leaves."

"You got a glue gun?" Tootie asked.

Jessa nodded.

"Okay. I'll stay. I wonder what your daddy will think of me being here."

"He's not my *daddy*. He's Mr. Warter, and he just happens to be my biological father."

Tootie sighed loudly. "I'm done with all of this daddy stuff." She took a few big bites from her plate and washed them down with orange juice. "Tell me about Nelson. Is he a good kisser?"

Jessa hopped up and pulled the poem from her junk drawer. She placed it on the table next to Tootie's plate. "Someone has been leaving me gifts and notes through my milk door."

It was like throwing a match into a can of gasoline. Tootie came alive with color and excitement. She read over the page like it was a treasure map. "Is this from Nelson?"

"I don't know. Could be."

"Are you going?"

Jessa nodded.

"Well, you're not going alone. I'm going with you."

Tootie had a point. Why would a single female go alone to a secluded place if she didn't know who would be waiting there for her? It might be less romantic to bring along her little sister, but it was much, much smarter.

"Thanks, Toots."

"I'm just doing what a good sister would do."

"You're a very good sister, and I love you."

Chapter Thirty-Seven

TRIGGER WARTER SHOWED up at Jessa's house wearing jeans and carrying work gloves. Jessa and Tootie watched him from a crack in the curtains and Jessa was surprised to see him exhale and look up at her home like he was gathering the courage to walk up the front steps.

"I thought he didn't have any feelings," Tootie whispered.

Jessa didn't answer. Feelings or not, Trigger Warter had shown up. She ran to the door and opened it before he could knock. She was going to show up too—by being happy to see him. She met him with a smile on her face.

"Hey there, young lady," he said. She noted the absence of her name in his greeting.

"Tootie's here too," Jessa said as Tootie waved at him from behind her.

"Nice to see you, Tootie," he said.

"Would you like to come in?" Jessa moved aside to allow access to the foyer. "I have some freshly made sweet tea."

He looked torn, and she assumed it was because he'd never been one to talk much. He relied on his mother and

Cornelia for that. "I figure I'll just get straight to work," he said.

Tootie set out to gather magnolia leaves while Jessa and Mr. Warter took items from her garage and carried them to the cellar. There wasn't much conversation between them aside from comments about how her bicycle needed the tires blown up, or how a box was particularly heavy. Occasionally, one of them would crack a joke and the other one would laugh. But there was no steady stream of communication, no deep questions or uncomfortable dialogue. It was nice, actually, to work side by side with someone who didn't appear to have any other motive aside from helping. Once there was room in her little garage for her car, it was Mr. Warter who drove it in for her. He added grease to the hinges, rollers, bearing plates, and chain of her garage door until it was tuned and quiet. Then he took a broom to all of the corner spiderwebs. Over and over again, he asked her if there was anything else he could do. When she told him how much she appreciated all he'd already done, he made her put his number in her phone so she could call him directly if she ever needed anything. Emphasis on *anything*.

As he was leaving, he waved to Tootie, who was on the front porch gluing leaves to twigs she'd bent into a circle.

Then he waved to Jessa who was on the steps nearby. "Come on by this Sunday for supper," he said. "Both of you. And Dottie too. I'll smoke a brisket and get some sides made up. We'd love to have you."

Trigger Warter was going to cook? And Cornelia would allow them for dinner on the Lord's day? That was reserved for the best, most prestigious guests, or the closest family.

"Jessa's got a date on Sunday, only we don't know who it's with," Tootie said.

"We'll be there." Jessa tried to override what Tootie'd said by stepping on her words before she finished.

Trigger stopped, his car door half open. "You don't know who …" He cleared his throat. "I have to say, I am concerned for your safety."

Over the years, she'd heard him blatantly tell Brooke *no*. She'd seen him send her to her room and tell her to get her butt home before the sun went down. It felt like that was exactly what he wanted to do with Jessa now. He wanted to lay down the law, but he didn't have the right.

"Is this one of those internet dates?"

"No," Jessa said. "Someone has been leaving me gifts through my milk door." Clearly, it hadn't been Mr. Warter. That left Nelson, Gates, or the small possibility of someone else. "I'm pretty sure I know the person, though."

"It's Nelson, probably," Tootie said. "But I want it to be Gates."

Mr. Warter still looked concerned.

"Don't worry," Tootie said, "I'm going with her." She puffed up like she could take down a beefy criminal with her scrawny arms and skinny little legs.

"We'll be careful," Jessa said.

"Where are you meeting this person?"

"At the boneyard."

"The Dogwood's boneyard? When the tide's out?"

Jessa nodded.

He finished opening the car door, but before he climbed in, he said, "Plan to bring whoever it is to supper. Low tide is probably around five thirty, so we'll expect you around six thirty."

Tootie giggled and Jessa felt like she was supposed to say *yes sir* but didn't. "See you then," she said instead. "Thanks again for the help." She was careful not to agree to bring whoever it was to his house.

As soon as Mr. Warter left, Jessa was so jittery that she felt like she'd just had three cups of coffee and an entire box of sugary praline candies. She had to do something with her hands, something to keep her body moving and her head clear.

"I'm gonna go work at the front of the property," she told Tootie, and took off jogging down the long dirt and gravel path to her vine-covered mailbox.

It was hot work pulling deeply rooted creepers and kudzu vines out of the dirt around her mailbox and street sign. Those plants had spent years establishing their spot on her property, and they didn't part with it easily. For Jessa, the challenge felt good. She allowed herself to grunt loudly as she pulled with all her might and fell onto her backside when the stems gave way. Many of them required digging, and she used her bare hands—thankfully the earth was still loose and damp from recent rains. When she unstuck the last tendril from the wooden post of her rusty metal mailbox, she mentally added *new mailbox* to the list of things she needed for the house.

Tootie was no longer on the front porch when Jessa got back home. She wasn't in the kitchen either, but the rest of the biscuits had been eaten and all of the orange juice was gone. Jessa washed the dirt from her hands and underneath her fingernails. Her phone dinged just as she dried them.

"Back at Mama's," came a text from Tootie. Then, *"call her."*

Sure enough, there were several missed calls from Dottie, but no texts or phone calls from Nelson. Jessa had never ghosted anybody in her life, but she was well aware that avoiding Nelson amounted to the same thing. Maybe her choice had been made for her, and he would simply fade into her past. Unless, of course, he was waiting for her at the boneyard tomorrow.

She called her mother immediately.

"Well, it's about danged time," Dottie said. "There are tour buses stopping at Fred's place."

"What?" Had Jessa heard her right?

"Tour. Buses," Dottie repeated. "Two so far. Those folks are buying up all the food and then taking it up to the winery. Thank God Fred has Valerie there to help. Word has it that another one is coming and suppertime is approaching.

I've been cattin' around all day, so I've got no prep work done, but I've got to get the truck out there. I'm gonna need help from you and Tulip."

"Mama, I'm covered in dirt."

"Well, fix that and meet us there. Make it quick."

Jessa showered and left the house with wet hair and no makeup. Tour buses? On Goose Island? Duke was going to have to hire more people. Fred would too—one little Ruby wouldn't be enough help, especially if Valerie was only there occasionally.

Jessa was surprised when she pulled up to Fred's place that not only was Ruby's VW parked by the building, but Nelson's Range Rover was too. *Again?*

Dottie's truck wasn't there yet, which was annoying considering the woman had lit a fire under Jessa to get there fast. Jessa could've taken the time to dry her hair at the very least.

Once inside, the first people she saw were Nelson and Ruby laughing in the corner by the canned goods like they were best friends sharing secrets.

"You beat your mother here," Fred said from behind the counter.

Did Uncle Fred notice that Jessa's supposed boyfriend had not even acknowledged her arrival? Did he know that Nelson Tucker was actively flirting with his employee? And, wasn't Ruby supposed to be married? Jessa had to pick her jaw up off the floor before she answered. "I heard you've been overrun by tourists."

"Like locusts on a wheat field." He chuckled. "I suppose I should consider this a happy problem especially now that I'm about to be faced with building a house."

"Where's Valerie?"

"Out back giving some nibbles to Whiskey and Roscoe. They've been neglected all day."

Jessa walked behind the counter and pulled Fred near the oven where they were hidden by a refrigerated glass display filled with nearly empty bowls of side salads and picked-over pre-made sandwiches. "What's going on with Nelson and Ruby?"

Fred shook his head. "Nothing good, I fear."

"I thought she was married."

"Their second try lasted about a week."

"Has this been happening a lot?"

"I see him here from time to time, but he always bought something, so I figured they were just being friendly."

Jessa couldn't make sense of it. Ruby was a pretty girl, but she wasn't particularly educated. Plus, she was in the middle of a divorce. And she was even less savvy when it came to the finer things in life than Jessa was. Her accent was thicker, her clothes were cheaper, and she certainly wouldn't know what a fork and spoon at the top of the plate was for. "Should I talk to him, or just let him keep ignoring me?"

Fred shrugged. "I've always been a fan of letting sleeping dogs lie."

Jessa thought about that for a second. It felt like the easy way out, and she was braver now. "Isn't that why you and Valerie didn't talk for years? Because you let sleeping dogs lie?"

Fred's eyes crinkled in the corners like he was proud of her for learning from his mistakes. "Your generation is much better about talking. Don't let things fester and grow bigger than they are."

"I think I'd better say something," she said.

Chapter Thirty-Eight

RUBY MIGHT BE a grown woman, but she acted like a child. When Jessa walked up and asked Nelson if she could speak with him, Ruby flat-out said no for him.

Nelson didn't even flinch.

"Okay, then," Jessa said, keeping her cool. If Ruby was going to stay, she would just lay it all out in front of her. "I think some things need to be said."

"Ruby!" Fred called for her from behind the counter. "Breaks over. I need your help."

Ruby let out a curse word and an annoyed sigh before walking away.

"What is it?" Now it was Nelson who was acting like a child.

"Is something going on with you and Ruby?"

Nelson shrugged. "Is something going on with you and Gates?" He smirked. "Look, I don't care what you've got going on with that dude. And you need to know that I don't chase after women, okay? They chase after me."

"Good to know." Jessa kept her voice calm and steady. There was no reason to call him out.

"I'm not giving Gates my account, by the way," he said.

"I figured that was the case." She could walk away at this point; she had all the information she needed to know what kind of a man he was.

She should have trusted her instincts the first time they'd met.

"Nelson? I want you to know that I wish you well. I want only good things for you. I never meant for all of this to get messy." She sensed the belligerent energy drain from him as she spoke the words.

He stared at her before seeming to surprise himself with what came out of his mouth. "Gates actually tried to keep me away from you."

Always err on the side of kindness, she thought as he offered that piece of information. You catch more flies with honey. "Thank you for telling me that."

"Why do you think I told you to stay away from him? He's got it bad for you. Said he always has."

"Thank you so much, Nelson." The relief she felt threatened to bring on tears. "One last hug?"

He reached out and gently pulled her in. "Good luck, Jessa."

Jessa stole a glance at Ruby. "Good luck to you, too, Nelson."

★

Jessa untied the ropes from the cleats, yanked hard on the pull cord to start the engine of the little jon boat, and made her way across the water toward the Dogwood with a sense of anticipation that stole her breath with the wind and deposited it far, far away. Once there, she would have to hike across the narrow asphalt road over to the marsh where the old bleached-out trees of the boneyard lay. She hadn't bothered styling her hair when it was going to be ruined by the wind on the way over. But she was ready with color on her cheeks, mascara on her lashes, and with her little sister at the helm as she set out to solve the mystery that had been quietly taking over her hopes and dreams with each opening of the milk door. The tightness in her chest didn't loosen until she saw Brooke waiting for her by the dock at the resort. "Thank God!" Jessa said as she threw her the rope for the bow.

"I'm so glad you told me you were coming." Brooke tied the rope to the cleat—around twice, crisscross, crisscross, tuck under, and pull. Jessa did the same at the stern. Then Brooke extended her hand and helped Jessa and Tootie step onto the dock. Jessa finger-brushed her hair, then took the hair band from her wrist, and pulled it into a long ponytail. "This look okay?"

Brooke took a tendril floating around Jessa's face and tucked it behind her ear. "Beautiful, as always."

"Where's Nate?"

"He's in town today. I had a whole list of stuff for him to get."

Tootie jumped in between them and grabbed Brooke's left hand. The diamond of her engagement ring sparkled clear against the gold band. "He did good."

"He did." Brooke smiled so widely her eyes squinted shut.

"It's crazy how far we've come," Jessa said as the three of them walked up the hill.

Brooke laughed. "Wait until you see who had to be talked out of bringing his shotgun."

"Is your dad here?" Jessa guessed.

"*Our* dad is here to protect you from whoever is hiding out there in the mud. Hope you don't mind."

On one hand, it meant a lot to Jessa that Mr. Warter had shown up. On the other hand, she didn't want him there. "Hey, Brooke?" Jessa stopped. "What if it's Gates out there?"

"It's great with me, Jess. I mean it. And our dad would be thrilled. My family was going to find a way to keep him one way or another. You're coming to the house tonight for Sunday supper, right?" Brooke asked as she walked away. "And if it's Gates waiting out there, bring him too. Cornelia's got the table set for a crowd."

Brooke jogged away and Jessa was grateful that Tootie was still there with her. She pulled her shoulders back, ran a hand over her hair to ensure it was smooth and bump-free going into her ponytail, and took a deep breath. She'd accepted all the gifts and come all the way across the water—she might as well see who'd been leaving them. "You ready, Toots?"

At the top of the hill, Mr. Warter looked every bit the out-of-date dad with his long shorts and crew socks with tennis shoes. The striped collared polo shirt didn't help his ensemble. Cornelia must not have set out his clothes that day. Jessa tried to suppress a nervous laugh. Something about him waiting for her and looking so unlike his usual suited self made her heart swell.

The hike to the boneyard was short, but there was one problem. In the hot summer during camp, the pluff mud around the old trees dried as hard as concrete. But it was fall now, and the mud was shoe-stealing quicksand in its natural state. She would have to stay on the edge outside the ring of spartina and cordgrass. Gates would absolutely know that they couldn't walk out to the grouping of dead bleached-out trees this time of year. The realization made her freeze, and she was suddenly grateful that Tootie and Mr. Warter were with her. From where she stood, she could see the boneyard, but to get near it would require walking through a thicket of a maritime forest–live oaks, wax myrtles, saw palmettos, and all sorts of tangled up trees and shrubs blocked their way.

She squinted into the distance, looking for a human figure—praying for Gates. If she was honest, she'd been holding on to the romantic notion that the gifts were from him, and that he'd planned this elaborate meeting.

It was Tootie who spoke first. "You can't get out there, Jess. Why'd he make plans for this place? It's all wet and overgrown. He's dumb."

It was the first time that Jessa thought of the possibility that maybe no one was there. What if the whole thing had been a ruse? "He could have changed his mind," she said.

A few more yards forward and it was clear that there was no more path, no clear way to move forward. The boneyard was impossible to get to. "Should we go back?" she said it more to Mr. Warter than to Tootie.

"I think we should," he said, sounding sorry for her.

Jessa wanted to run back to the resort. She wanted to be alone to sort out her feelings. But they all had to be careful to watch their steps so they wouldn't twist an ankle on the rocky, weedy ground leading to the main road. She prayed none of them would end up with a tick attached to them at the end of their hike. They would have to check. The whole thing was brutally embarrassing.

A loud whistle came from behind them. All three of them turned to look.

"Jess!" Gates came running from the woods, his long legs easily navigating the rough terrain.

"Gates!" The vision of him running for her at full speed was such a relief, she thought her knees might buckle. She fell into his arms as soon as he arrived. "I knew it was you," she said into his pounding chest.

"I'm sorry," he said, shrinking his body around hers. "It's swampy this time of year, but I couldn't wait any longer."

"I don't care!"

They held each other out of breath, their bodies pressed together. When she finally lifted her head from his chest, Tootie and Mr. Warter were nowhere to be seen.

"Why, Gates? What are we doing here?"

He smiled sweetly at her. "You're like the sand I left for you," he said. "You're everything and you don't even know it."

"You left the gifts … they're perfect. Each one of them."

"You might be the only girl who appreciates that stuff. I knew you would. You deserve those things, Jess. You need to know how important you are."

"The flowers, the bear, the camellia bowl, the blanket, and the poem." She loved each one of them as she listed them off.

"Let's not talk about the poem. Unless you liked it, then you can have a million of them."

"I loved it."

"Then bad poetry it is." His voice dropped low, and she felt like they were simultaneously experiencing an invisible lightning storm. "I know I keep saying this, and there's no excuse," he said. "I'm sorry about Nelson. I never should have brought him here. I made a big mistake."

"It's over. It doesn't matter."

She leaned into him, and he held her tightly as the marsh hay swayed and the brackish water lapped the shore. He held her as a crow called out before landing on the tallest branch of a pine tree. A squadron of brown pelicans flew overhead and far-off in the distance, a fisherman cast his line, having no idea that Carolina Jessamine Boone had just been irrevocably and eternally caught by Gates Lancaster.

"Can I show you why I brought you out here?" he asked.

"There's more?"

"Brooke helped." He took her hand and led her to the edge of the forest where she noticed a small path cut through the brushy undergrowth.

Gates led her by the hand down the path she hadn't noticed before. It was narrow and went to a small clearing with a perfect view of twisted white trees spread across an area the size of her house. "I didn't want to chase you, Jessa. I didn't want to barge into your life after hurting you when I chose Brooke all those years ago." He put a hand gently to her cheek. "I wanted you to see yourself through my eyes. To win you over slowly. To earn you."

"I'm not like my Mama," Jessa said. "I can't always trust how I feel or what I think the universe is telling me, but I knew deep down that I wanted it to be you. I've always wanted it to be you."

"Wait until you see what I made you." He was suddenly like a giddy little boy, like the Gates she knew from camp years ago.

He took her hand and pulled her to the side of a thick oak. There was a handmade wooden bench. The pine backrest had been meticulously carved with a vine she immediately recognized. It was the South Carolina state flower, the Carolina Jessamine.

Jessa gasped. "You made this? It must have taken you forever."

"I wasn't going to give up, Jess. Not ever."

Chapter Thirty-Nine

MATERIAL THINGS DIDN'T matter. Not really. Everyone knew the old saying, *You can't take it with you.* But for a girl like Jessa, things held value beyond money. Objects were legacies and antiques were peeks into the past. Things sparked memories, and memories were to be cherished and passed along. The bench Gates made for her with a view of the trees where they'd had their first kiss instantly had a home in her heart. And it wasn't like Grandma Boone's meat sauce recipe—it was real. In that moment, Gates had not only created a bench, he had created a memory. One that they experienced together firsthand. Not something made-up and passed along, no matter how good the intentions.

Jessa and Gates sat on the bench snuggled together like they were part of the natural habitat. "I have something else to show you," he said, reaching underneath the bench. He pulled out a light-colored wooden box. "This is my memory box, made by my granddaddy from cypress wood."

When he lifted the lid, the first thing she saw was his name engraved on the inside of it: GATES WILLIAM LANCAS-

TER. Inside, there was a glass bottle with an orange NEHI PEACH label, and in black Sharpie in bubbly middle schooler's handwriting were the words FOR GATES, LOVE JESSA.

"You really did keep it," she said.

There were all sorts of photos and letters; many of them looked to be from his grandparents. There was a black-and-white photo of a huge black horse, and a carved wooden dolphin. The slipper shells she'd collected for Tootie—the ones he'd put in his pocket the day they'd kissed at the boneyard—were spread around the bottom of the box. She carefully sorted through his treasures until she came across a folded piece of yellow construction paper with the word HER written at the top in all caps. Below that was a list written in purple magic marker:

1. SWEET/NICE TO PEOPLE
2. BLONDE HAIR. I LIKE LONG BETTER.
3. MAKES ME FOOD
4. LIKES FOOTBALL AND BASKETBALL. DOESN'T HAVE TO LIKE BASEBALL. BUT CAN'T GET MAD AT ME FOR WATCHING IT.
5. PRETTY, BUT ISN'T ALL HAUGHTY ABOUT IT. AND LOYAL.
6. LIKES ANIMALS
7. LETS ME PLAY MY VIDEO GAMES
8. JESSA

"Gates!" She pointed to number eight. "What is this?" It was a vague recollection, but her mother had foreseen this. What was it that Dottie said? Something about a list.

"I wrote that my first year at camp. It was what I wanted in my future wife."

All of those years Gates was with Brooke, Jessa had given up on him. She'd worked so hard at letting go. She'd stuffed her emotions and forced herself to be happy for them. She believed she would be a horrible person if she didn't wish them well, and it had worked. She still loved them both.

"The way you handle things with such grace always amazes me." Gates looked straight into her eyes, and she felt his honesty like it was her own. "Who you are, the way you are, has impressed me since we were kids."

"Why now, Gates?"

"I wasn't ready before."

"Ready for what?"

"For you."

Jessa had spent a lifetime trying to avoid heartache too. And yet, she hadn't. It was everywhere—in her childhood, in her adulthood, and on the bench beside her. "I've always thought that if I allow myself to love someone, I'm also giving them the power to hurt me."

"Same for me," he said. "Back then I didn't have the maturity to risk it."

She cut her eyes to his face—the dark eyelashes, the shadow of a beard forming, the beads of sweat at his hairline.

"I made this list on a rainy day when a group of us boys were stuck together in a cabin," he said. "A camp counselor told us to write down what we wanted in our future wives. He said it was never too early to start praying for her. *Her* for me has always been you."

Jessa looked from him to the yellow paper, the three letters written in the scrawl of a young boy. *HER*. And the only name on that middle school paper was hers.

"I'm afraid I am in love with you," he said. "I always have been."

"It's always been you for me too." Instead of putting her head on his shoulder, she did what no good small-town Southern girl would ever dare do. She made the first move. "You can kiss me now," she whispered.

Their smiles met and he kissed her deeply. This time there was no shame, no regret, no secrets between them. This time, their kisses were real and confident and the beginning of a million more.

They talked and laughed, soaking in their togetherness until the constant buzzing of texts from the real world got to be too much. They both pulled out their phones to look.

There were several texts from Dottie:

"Do I really have to go to the danged Warters for Sunday supper?"

"You owe me for this. Big."

"You know that Cornelia's face gives me hives, right. You want me to be itchy all night?"

"Tootie's coming. I didn't think she would and I sure as heck wasn't going to make her".
"I hear you got a bench?"
"Gates Lancaster?"
"Answer me already."
"My girls get more action than I do."
"Stop kissing that boy and answer me."

There were texts from Brooke as well:
"Sorry to bother y'all."
"Cornelia would like me to remind everyone to be at the house by six thirty"

Jessa looked at the time. It was already six fifteen. "Oh, shoot!" She jumped up. The people pleaser in her couldn't stand to be late. "The Warters are having everybody over for supper tonight and we're supposed to be there in fifteen minutes."

"I'll handle it," Gates said. "Did Trig leave?" A second later, he had him on the phone. "She loved it," he answered. "Yeah, thanks for looking out for her. I told Brooke and Nate not to tell anybody. I guess they figured that meant you too." He winked at Jessa. "We're heading to your house now. Great, thanks."

He smiled down at Jessa. "It's handled. We don't have to hurry."

"Thank you." She could have handled the problem herself, but it sure was nice to have Gates do it for her. "So,

Brooke and Nate have known all along?"

He chuckled and nodded. "Just since I brought the bench a few days ago."

"And they didn't even tell Trig." She was glad they hadn't told him.

She would treasure the memory of him showing up to keep her safe for the rest of her life.

Jessa wasn't nervous at all on the ride to the Warters' house. She'd survived one showy family dinner; she could survive another. As a matter of fact, she giggled when Gates pulled up in from their Grecian-columned house with the window coverings wide open, the interior lights bright, and fresh flowers set among the fine china. Cornelia walked past in a long white dress and heels, her lipstick as red as a rose. For a woman like her to have to contend with a child out of wedlock, she was actually doing fairly well. She'd opted for the acceptance route rather than the *dig-in-her-heels-and-refuse-it* option. For that, she deserved some credit. After all, it was trendy these days to behave your way to success, or do it until you feel it, or fake it until you make it. Maybe eventually Cornelia would grow to care about Jessa. That would be nice. But Jessa didn't need it in order to be happy.

Everyone was gathered around Cornelia's granite kitchen island. Trig, Dottie, Tootie, Brooke, Nate, Nana, and Duke. Jessa wondered if Cornelia had enough seats at the table. They all had a glass of white wine in their hand, except Tootie, who held a can of Cheerwine. When the hellos died down and Cornelia joined them, Trig tapped his glass for their attention. "I would like to make a toast."

"You can make a toast," Dottie interrupted. "But I will tell you right now that we are not going to spend all night talking about things in the past. Everybody hear me? There will be no discussion of fathers and mothers and childhoods and all that baloney. Tonight, we are normal people. Got it?"

"To being in the moment," Trig said, "and enjoying each other's company."

As soon as they all took a sip, Trig added, "Gates, welcome back. The guest room is still yours if you want it."

Gates seemed touched by the acknowledgment, and Jessa's estimation of Trig Warter's value in her life grew once again.

Nana clinked her glass next. "A toast to the woman who decorated the table and cooked the dinner."

"To Cornelia," they all said.

"Thank you kindly," Cornelia said. "And now, if you will all gather in the dining room. The curtains are open and I believe we have a show to put on."

Jessa mouthed the words to Gates—*she knows*?

"It was an excellent idea to keep the conversation light, Dottie," Cornelia went on. "That way we don't have any sour faces for the neighbors to see. We are in the height of the judgment phase, you know. Everyone is looking at us to see what we're going to do."

"Are we going to eat?" Tootie asked earnestly.

"What am I supposed to call this one?" Cornelia pointed at Tootie. "Is she my niece?"

Tulip shrugged and looked just as confused as Cornelia.

"Yes, we are going to eat," Nana filled in. "And you better look like you're enjoying it, or Cornelia will thwap you on the head."

"That is a lie," Cornelia said. "I will thwap you under the table." She smiled, and the whole group relaxed a notch. "Carolina Jessamine, would you like to say grace?"

Jessa was seated between Gates and her mother, so she took both of their hands and bowed her head as the rest of the table did the same. *If you're going to make a mistake*, she thought, *err on the side of kindness.* "Thank you, Heavenly Father, for summer camps and family trees. Thank you for people who love you enough to keep secrets, and those who love you enough to tell them. Thank you for seeing all sides of everything, and for giving people grace when they can't. Thank you for Mama and Tootie, Trig and Cornelia, Nana and Duke. Please bless the upcoming marriage of Brooke and Nate. And, Lord, thank you for using the only boy I ever loved, the one I never got over, to remind me that I matter."

And the show began with an extra-large close-knit happy family, a few of whom were seated on folding chairs tucked underneath the dining room table.

"Amen," they all said.

Epilogue

It was a foggy day—the marine layer was thick and wasn't near burning off. A high-pressure system was moving in, and it seemed to be keeping the tourists out.

"Mama." Jessa leaned into the window of the truck as her mother worked in the winery parking lot.

"Carolina Jessamine, I am busy."

"I've got to ask you something."

"Well, ask later. I've got tater tots in the oil."

"That list you saw, Mama, a while back. I keep meaning to ask you, was it yellow?"

Dottie froze. "How do you know that?"

"Gates wrote a list on a piece of yellow construction paper when he was little."

"You saw it?" Dottie was now hanging halfway out the window. "What was the word? There was a single word, a short one, at the top. Was it *she*?"

"It was *her*."

"Well, heavens be. I was right." It only took a second for the further implications to sink in. "The fates have finally brought you two together."

Gates came up from behind and put his arms around Jessa's waist. "Hey, Dottie," he said.

"Did you hear that I was right?" Dottie asked.

"I heard."

Jessa leaned back into Gates, her head fitting perfectly beneath his chin. "I think I'm more like you than I realized, Mama."

"Hold up." Dottie rescued the tater tots, then came back to the window. "How so?"

"Remember when we had that oyster roast down at the beach?"

"Oh, yes," Dottie said. "The moon ceremony."

"I think maybe it worked," Jessa said. "My wish came true."

"I know mine did." Gates smiled.

"Well?" Dottie shouted. "Tell us already!"

"I asked for a sign," Jessa said. "I asked for clarity about whether I needed to change—if I needed to be stronger, and less, I don't know, accommodating."

"I keep telling her that her kindness is her superpower," Gates said. "It's a strength."

"Yup. I dipped her in sugar," Dottie said.

It wasn't lost on Jessa that the thing she wanted to change most about herself was exactly what Gates admired. Maybe that was why she felt confident with him, why she liked who she was with him. Strength came from taking risks and choosing to connect despite her fears. He was her moon-given sign that she was worthy—that she'd always been enough. She didn't have to know about seafood towers at golf course restaurants or names of top-shelf whiskeys. She didn't have to have a college degree. And her value wasn't determined by her looks. But even more, her journey back to Gates came with a new understanding that it was important to leave room to grow. If she kept poison away from her roots by holding on to her natural optimism and gratitude, and if she continued to stand up for herself and others, she would flourish and flower as the years went on.

"I asked the moon for a chance," Gates said. "I asked for a do-over."

Jessa turned to look at him and was surprised that his eyes were glassy, his face utterly serious. She'd never felt more connected to a person before. "We got our second chance."

"Well, if y'all ain't just the sweetest," Dottie said. "I believe you're giving me cavities."

Their attention was diverted by a lyrical soprano voice that broke through the fog so clearly, it was like the clouds themselves were singing a siren song. They all turned toward the long tree-lined entryway to the winery, where a figure appeared like a heavenly apparition. Dressed in a cerulean blue gown with a long blonde wig and a bundle of flowers, Grace "Nana" Sharon Beauregard Warter strolled along the road. A car drove slowly behind her—a Cadillac, carrying Trig, Cornelia, and Duke. Nana was an expert at dramatic entrances. The only question was, why? Why did she go through all of that effort on such a dreary, empty day? And why were Trig and Cornelia taking part in it?

Nana sang notes that only an angel, or a fictional redheaded mermaid, could hit. They were all mesmerized until she came to a stop at the food truck. Everybody clapped for her.

"Where'd you get the pipes, Grace?" Dottie asked.

She had climbed out of the food truck and was standing next to Jessa and Gates with the same look of wonder on her face that Jessa felt.

Nana didn't answer, she simply strode up to Jessa, took a small container from her beaded purse, twisted off the cap, stuck her fingers inside, and flicked water all over Jessa's face.

"Hey!" Gates jumped in between them.

"It's holy water!" Nana yelled as Jessa wiped her face dry with her shirt.

Trig and Cornelia had since parked and stood next to Nana looking apologetic.

"Come here, Jessa," Nana said.

Jessa stepped around Gates.

"Give me your arm."

Jessa stuck out her right arm and Nana tied a piece of white string around her wrist. Then she splashed more holy water all over her. As she did, she sang the same ethereal song, only this time, softly.

"What in tarnation," Dottie began.

"Shhhh," Cornelia said. "This is a ceremony."

"Are y'all in some sort of a cult?" Dottie didn't attempt to quiet her voice at all.

"It's a new baby ceremony," she whispered.

"A new … Have y'all lost your minds?"

Cornelia moved closer to Dottie and whispered loud enough for Jessa to hear. "Nana went to the internet and found stuff, figuring that we had to make up for never celebrating the birth of Miss Jessa."

Nana placed a lace doily on top of Jessa's head. "Now," she said, placing the flowers from her fake blonde hair into a line on the ground, "jump over this."

Jessa held tight to the doily on her head and jumped across the flowers.

"What else was there?" Nana asked Trig.

"The blood oath," Trig smiled slyly.

"Oh, shut up," Nana scoffed. "We would like to extend an invitation for all of you to attend a sip-n-see at our house. The date is yet to be determined."

"Hold up," Dottie said, looking like a traffic cop with her arm straight out. "Are you saying Carolina Jessamine is supposed to be the little baby that people are looking at while they're sipping on cocktails?"

"That is correct," Nana said. "If there is one thing I will do before I die, it is make sure this family is bound together tight." She pulled a large silver ring from her right hand and placed it on Jessa's finger. "This was my mother's. No matter what your name is on paper, you are a Warter. You hear me? Don't you ever question that." She waved Trigger over, and it appeared as though he was happy to join them.

"Mama," Jessa said, and from the look on Dottie's face, she knew they were on the same page.

Someday, when it was time to tell Tootie about her biological mother, they would have a ceremony too. They would remind her through gifts and rituals, even if they were kooky and strange, that she was important. Just like Nana had been going out of her way to show Jessa, they would make sure Tootie knew that families were held together by more than double helixes and hydrogen bonds—they were held together by choice. It was all about showing up.

"I present to you ..." Nana began, turning Jessa by the shoulders to face Mr. Warter. "Your daughter."

"I couldn't be prouder of you, Carolina Jessamine," he said, taking her into a hug.

It wasn't the ceremony, and it wasn't the hug that sent tears streaming down Jessa's face. It wasn't even the fact that Trigger Warter had shown up and played along. It was the way he said her name *Carolina Jessamine*, like she was indeed the sweetest, most precious flower in all of South Carolina.

The End

Acknowledgments

During my freshman year at Auburn University, I was introduced to the Lowcountry of South Carolina, and this magical place has firmly held my heart ever since. The more time I spend there, the more I am enamored with the people, the culture, and the uniquely beautiful setting. Both South Carolina and my home state of Alabama are responsible for my deep love of the South. I hope you felt some of this affection as you read about Carolina Jessamine.

I owe every person who has ever shared with me a story, a particular vulnerability, or simply their time and personality, an enormous thank-you for helping to bring to life my characters. A fun part of being a writer is mining the world for details. I have several folks I'd like to thank for their contributions to this book and to my career: Kiki Lebaron, who is a recent college graduate, an avid reader, and my go-to person when I need honest feedback fast. So many of my sisters and friends have held launch parties and come to signings—they display my books in their homes and give them out as gifts. You know who you are, and I love you deeply. My dad, Bill, stepmother, Maureen, and mother-in-law, Sharon, seem as tickled about my new career as I am.

One of my greatest joys is sharing each new book with them. My children (including present and future spouses) Drew Bixler, Emily Beers, Allison Reese, Mason Clark, Natalie Reese, and Brooke Reese have all encouraged me and made space for this intrusive writing career that steals my time from them. They are my hope for the future and the solid core of my happiness.

The team at Tule Publishing is top-notch and I will always be grateful that they made this new career of mine possible: founder Jane Porter, developmental editor Kelly Hunter, copyeditor Nan Reinhardt, proofreader Monti Shalosky, cover designer Erin Dameron-Hill, Julie Sturgeon, Cyndi Parent, Meghan Farrell, Mia Gleason, and others I have yet to meet that have had a hand in bringing this book to the public. Thank you!

It was the most glorious shock when my first book launched to find an enthusiastic support system among so many of my high school friends. Heartfelt appreciation to the residents of Huntsville, Alabama, who still claim me as their own. You've stuck with me a long time, and I am so grateful.

Anyone who knows me well knows that all of the heroes in my books are in some way fashioned after my husband, Bryan. He soothes my soul and holds the world at bay for me. He is the reason I first attempted writing a book.

Finally, it is you, the reader, who I think about with appreciation every day. It is a vulnerable thing to put a book into the world, and so many of you not only buy them and read them, but you also post reviews and send notes asking for more. It is a dream come true that you are in my life. I hope this book brings you some of the joy you have brought me.

If you enjoyed *Chasing Carolina Jessamine*, you'll love the other books in….

The Southern Isles series

Book 1: *A Saltwater Christmas*

Book 2: *The Dogwood Days of Summer*

Book 3: *Chasing Carolina Jessamine*

Available now at your favorite online retailer!

More Books by Laurie Beach

Book 1: *The Firefly Jar*

Book 2: *Blink Twice If You Love Me*

Book 3: *Christmas in Crickley Creek*

Available now at your favorite online retailer!

About the Author

Photographer: Stephanie Lynn Co

Laurie Beach writes about small southern beach towns, quirky friendships, and true love. When she's not holding down the couch and typing out words, she stays busy keeping track of her husband and four children. A graduate of Auburn University with a degree in Mass Communications and Psychology, she worked as a television news reporter, an advertising producer, and a political press secretary. She now writes full-time.

Thank you for reading

Chasing Carolina Jessamine

If you enjoyed this book, you can find more from all our great authors at TulePublishing.com, or from your favorite online retailer.

Made in the USA
Columbia, SC
23 September 2025